THE HELLBEAST KING SERIES

THE HELLBEAST KING

STEPHANIE HUDSON

THE HELLBEAST KING SERIES

THE HELLBEAST KING

The HellBeast King
The HellBeast King Series #1
Copyright © 2021 Stephanie Hudson
Published by Hudson Indie Ink
www.hudsonindieink.com

This book is licensed for your personal enjoyment only.
This book may not be re-sold or given away to other people. If you would like to share this book with another person, please purchase an additional copy for each recipient. If you're reading this book and did not purchase it, or it wasn't purchased for your use only, then please return to your favourite book retailer and purchase your own copy.
Thank you for respecting the hard work of this author.
All rights reserved.
This is a work of fiction. Names, characters, places, brands, media, and incidents are either the product of the authors imagination or are used fictitiously. The author acknowledges the trademark status and trademark owners of various products referred to in this work of fiction, which have been used without permission. The publication/use of these trademarks is not authorised, associated with, or sponsored by the trademark owners.

The HellBeast King/Stephanie Hudson – 1st ed.
ISBN-13 - 978-1-913904-80-7

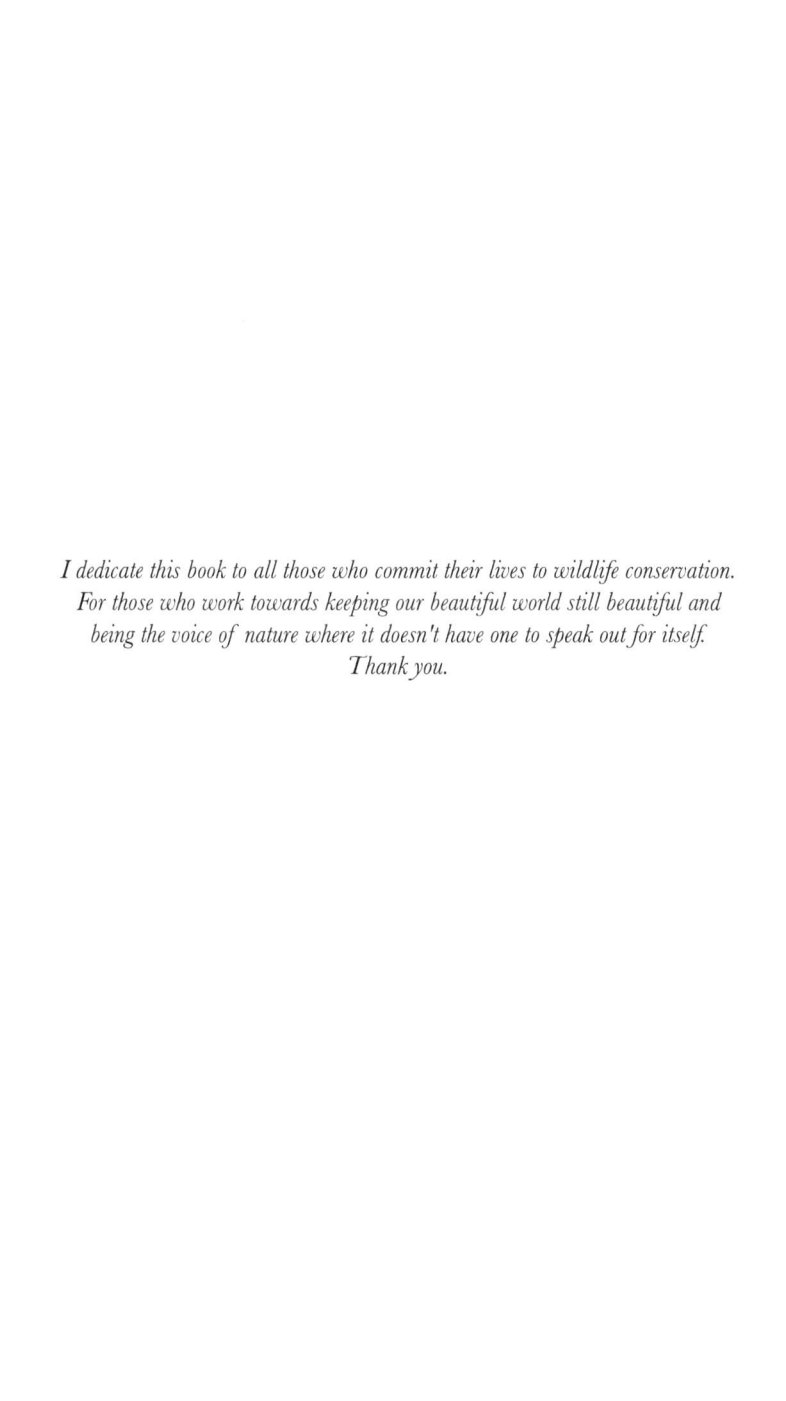

I dedicate this book to all those who commit their lives to wildlife conservation. For those who work towards keeping our beautiful world still beautiful and being the voice of nature where it doesn't have one to speak out for itself. Thank you.

STEPHANIE HUDSON

ONE

IT'S A SIGN

"*I can't believe I am doing this!*" I hissed, looking up and down the busy London Street. This before stepping foot down the ominous looking alleyway that God only knew where it led to.

"Bloody, Fae!" I hissed again, cursing my cousin, and using the only swear word my mom ever used. Which meant it always came out sounding native to where she grew up, in Liverpool, Northern England. As for myself, well, I was born and bred in the same house in Evergreen Falls that we lived in today, and I mean that in the literal sense as I was actually born in my family home… at the bottom of the staircase to be exact.

Evergreen Falls was about an hour away from Portland, in Maine, and was also where my father was from, which meant my accent was a mixture of US and Northern English twang.

Thanks Mom and Dad for that one.

But, as for right now, what I was doing was chasing my cousin around London. It all started with a school trip she had begged me to go on, seeing as it was my last year of high school. Seniors like me could choose the trip, one encouraged for those that were thinking about studying abroad or travelling around Europe after college. But the main aim of it was for the Sophomore's history class, and for us, it was a chance for two cousins to spend some time together before I went off to college. Although, my parents were hoping I would choose the one close by that my Aunty Kaz had gone to, who was Fae's mother.

It also had to be said that Fae was acting out of character. Fae was short for Faith and was my cousin's middle name, one we called her far more than her first, which was Amelia. She was a girl who was normally the epitome of good behaviour and as far as I knew, hadn't broken a rule in her life! Making me question what it was about this trip that had tipped her over the edge. Because it was when we were on the plane together and she had just woken me from a surprising new nightmare (something I suffered from on a nightly basis) that she confessed the truth.

She had snuck out of a window and forged the consent form, meaning that her parents had no idea she was even on this trip. Of course, I had freaked out, despite it being a bit late by that point. But she assured me that she would call them when we arrived, so they didn't worry further. To say I was shocked would be the understatement of the year, seeing as it was a case of good girl gone rogue. But part of me could understand it. As let's just say that her father was a little overprotective and well, a teenage girl who wanted a life outside of school and home was only going to be good for so long.

Meaning one Amelia Faith Draven had hit her limit.

But as for right now… well, I had no clue what she was planning. But I had a bad feeling that it had to do with a boy she liked and potentially had met over the internet or something. Of course, I had heard horror stories of catfishing, so naturally I feared for her safety. Because, despite her love of history, I had a feeling that meeting with someone here was the real reason behind this trip.

Which was why I had followed her from our hotel on the Strand and onto Fleet Street, having no clue of the time. I just knew it was dark and here I was, finding myself playing detective spy on the streets of London. And why was I doing this...? Because she was nearly sixteen, which made me the responsible eighteen-year-old and someone old enough to legally drink in this country. Hence, why it was the right thing to do when she told me she was sneaking out of the Savoy hotel.

But, after her confession to me on the flight over here, I wasn't exactly surprised to find her parents turn up shortly after, as naturally they had freaked out. Now, I know what you're thinking, that my cousin sounded bad news, right...? Wrong. She was actually what you would consider the geek of the family and basically the smartest person I knew. Plus, for the record, like I said, she never did crazy shit like this. Which was why, when she begged me to come along and sign myself up for the trip, I now understood the one condition she had, which was that I tell my parents last minute so my mom and her sister, my awesome Aunt and Amelia's mom, didn't have chance to 'chat' about it.

My cover story was simple. Someone dropped out last minute and they needed to make up numbers, so I got the trip as a reward for being on the honour role, which I was. And yeah, so Amelia wasn't the only smart one in the family, but she was definitely the smartest. But with her it was all about history and with me, it was all about nature. Well, that and at one time another passion… but hey, that seemed like a lifetime ago.

A happier one.

I shook off the melancholy thoughts and tried even harder to push the dream from my mind. Something I had to admit wasn't that easy. Ever since the first time I fell I'd had the same nightmare, but the one on the plane had been different, and every night since I had dreamt of…

Him.

He had called himself my Hell Beast King.

I shuddered at the memory of it and pulled my dark hood down over my red hair, one that would have been a beacon and dead giveaway in letting Fae know I was following her. But come on, what else was I supposed to do? She was like a sister to me. We didn't exactly have a big family and being that we were both only children, it made sense we became close, despite the age gap.

But as for what was happening right now, I knew some blame had to be directed at my aunt and uncle because like I said, it wasn't exactly surprising that at some point their daughter would push back. I mean, there were only so many times you could be told no when you asked to go out with your friends or to a party. Okay, so yeah, sneaking out and boarding a plane to Europe was a little excessive for a first-time act of defiance, as I was thinking something a little more low key... like the usual underage drinking with a friend or something. I mean, she did grow up in a nightclub for God's sake, so I would have had money on that one. But then, that was Amelia for you, when she committed to something, she didn't do it by halves.

God, and everyone had thought I had been the wild one.

That had always been my nickname growing up. Not because I was a juvenile or anything, but more the fact my parents could never seem to contain me. If I could have lived in a tent outside with nature, then I would have been the happiest kid in the world. In fact, my dad, Frank, loved it! I had been a tomboy through and through, and someone he could take camping and teach how to fish. I knew every knot there was and could have made them with my eyes closed. I could start a campfire with rubbing twigs together, and my dad joked that I could speak to the damn fish as I always caught more than him.

He used to joke that I used to whisper to them and could have just ask them politely to jump onto the boat and they would have. Of course, we always threw them back, because, hello, animal lover here. In fact, had I not grown up with a dad who loved steak so much and was a master at the BBQ, then I would most likely have turned out to be a Veggie.

Unfortunately, my will power only went so far and damn it, I loved a cheeseburger!

"Seriously, Fae, what the hell are you doing here?" I questioned on a whisper, feeling the comfort of my own voice as I glanced behind me for the millionth time, unable to shake the feeling that I was being followed. Then, I looked up at the building I had seen her slipping into, frowning when I read the antique illuminated sign overhead, one that flickered as though I had suddenly been sucked into some old-fashioned horror movie.

It read…

'Ye Olde Cheshire Cheese
Rebuilt 1667'

Wow, that was old. I mean, I was no history buff, but even I could appreciate something that old. I looked around the space, seeing that I was now stood in a mix of incredibly old and new rebuilt parts of modern London. The 'Wine Office Court' as it was called, started with a dark menacing alleyway, that looked more like some narrow tunnel that could have led to some drug cartel's secret hideout for all I knew. Let's just say, it didn't exactly look inviting!

But then it did get marginally better after this, as it opened up into a line of fancy looking townhouses that grouped together as one would have made up a mansion-sized house. A pathed street was sandwiched between the two different buildings before opening up into what looked like a courtyard. One that was surrounded by the backs of office buildings before a single lane road could be seen straight ahead.

"Again, what the hell are you doing here, Fae?" I questioned under my breath, not expecting an answer. But then the writing in the old-fashioned glass sign above me started to blur, and I found myself staring at it in shock. Yet no amount of rubbing my eyes would make sense of what was happening or would make it go away.

Of course, none of this helped my fragile state of

mind, as by the time my vision had refocused, it now read something entirely different…

'Cerberus
Devil's Elite
Fight Club
666'

"What the Hell?!" I hissed, questioning my damn sanity. I could have sworn blind that I just saw it read something different, unless I had read the name of the place off the sign on the wall and my mind had placed it there… if that was even a thing?

Did your mind do things like that?

I knew that it had the power to rationalise things that you thought you saw or heard. Like I would see a flash of something in the woods when hiking sometimes and tell myself it was just a deer or a buck. Not the man-sized wolf it had looked like at first. There was always an explanation for things. Like the shadows in my house, or old pipes groaning, things like that weren't ghosts, they were just physical elements that came with living in an old house.

I mean, just how many ghost stories did you hear from

people who lived in brand-new houses or apartments, and surely people died in all sorts of places. But you never heard of people seeing a ghost of a white lady lying on sun lounger by the pool, pretending she was sipping on a margarita whilst star gazing. And why did they only come out at night, huh, why weren't they seen much in the day? Why would they have to hide if they were ghosts? And if the reasons were to be believed, they were only there because they had unfinished business and didn't go into the light at the end of the tunnel like they should have. So, what if someone's unfinished business was missing out on that beach holiday they had been saving for before they died?

Okay, so yes, I was rambling in my mind but hey, that's what I usually did when I had cause to be scared shitless! Because according to that sign, my cousin had just disappeared into someone's bloody fight club! And what was with the name 'Devil's Elite'? Was that the name of some type of gang? And that name, Cerberus, where had I heard that from before?

Was it someone my Uncle Dominic knew, as I swear I remembered hearing it before?

But more importantly, wasn't it also the name of a

three headed dog?

Or more like…

"Oh shit, I muttered as my dream came back to me and I found myself then uttering,

"A Hell Beast that guarded the Gates of Hell."

TWO

INDIANA ELLA

"Jesus, Ella, where did that thought come from…? Definitely time to get a grip," I said before shaking these creepy thoughts from my head, knowing that my dreams were messing with me. I also needed to get my ass in there before I chickened out and left my cousin to her crazy mission. So, I approached the door and took one last look up at the building. It was one that was mostly built from dark brick, with the lower part faced with dark-brown wood panelling, that once I was inside, I saw matched that of the outside.

"Wow… homely," I muttered sarcastically, looking

round and already getting an even creepier vibe than I was from the outside. For starters, the pub looked empty, but the door was open. I mean, who did that in a city… unless it had been left open for Amelia?

Well, it wasn't exactly what I would have called a welcome if that were the case. I mean, I was older than her, but even I wanted to run from here screaming, it was that scary. Then again, the girl did grow up in what many would consider a bloody castle. The infamous Afterlife nightclub was one her father owned and a place she actually lived in.

Of course, it wasn't a nightclub in the conventional sense, as it was basically a really old building that had once been situated somewhere in Europe, but I forget where. All I knew was that someone in my uncle's family had been rich enough to have the building sent over to Evergreen and rebuilt there, brick by brick. Or should I say stone block by stone block as the place was incredible. It looked as though someone had cleared a space in the woods and dropped an old Manor house there. Not surprisingly then, the front of it was a Nightclub for Goths and the back part was where my aunty and uncle lived with Amelia. Oh, and a load more people that Amelia called 'family' but wasn't really. Well, other than the fact she had aunties and uncles on her father's side who lived with them. I mean, yes, it was a close family but then it wasn't exactly like the place wasn't big enough for them all.

Honestly, family gatherings were a Gothic riot as I had never seen so many beautifully eccentric people in all my life! But then again, I had kind of got used to it, seeing as I too had grown up with them around, and well naturally, I adored my Aunt Keira and Uncle Dominic. I used to call him Dom Dom, and my Aunt was always known as Kazzy or Aunty Kaz for short. But then as I grew up, I became very aware of how important and powerful a man my uncle was, seeing as he was mega rich and basically owned most of Evergreen.

Needless to say, this made me quite popular in school, as Afterlife was and always had been the talk of the town, along with the mysterious Dravens. I had also heard rumours and even stories from my parents of the day things started to change, and it all started with my mom's sister, Keira.

The story goes that before I was born, Keira arrived to live with my mom after something traumatic happened, a story I still don't know to this day. Anyway, before she arrived, Dominic Draven was like this Godlike figure that was worshipped by those who went to the club just in hopes of a glimpse of the mysterious man. But seeing as he kept mainly to the upstairs in the VIP area, one that no locals were ever allowed to enter, then not many knew anything about the handsome billionaire.

But then, one look at Keira one night in his club, and that's when it all changed. He fell in love, and being a man who always got what he wanted, he put his plans into motion of getting her. Which, according to my mom, first meant offering her a job at the club working for him in the very place he wouldn't allow locals inside…

Afterlife's VIP.

The rest was history, one I had always wondered about. But then even Amelia had always been tight lipped about it, making me question it even more. Because after Keira became his wife, the Dravens started living life less in the shadows like they had once spent many years doing. Of course, that didn't mean that my uncle didn't still make an impact whenever he was seen, as it was still like living with a celebrity in the town. In fact, whenever he was seen at the school for some reason to do with Amelia, my popularity would skyrocket for months after. Of course, even I knew that it was all just superficial, as they only wanted to be my friend because they thought I could get them into the VIP. So, the shiny coating of popularity didn't stay shiny for long as I never brought my friends to Afterlife. Besides, I wasn't blind as I became very savvy to all the bullshit early on, as did Amelia.

But even I had to admit, there had always been an air of mystery surrounding the Dravens, and one that you could never fully shake, no matter how much you tried to rationalise the things they did or the strange way they lived. Which made me wonder if there was some great secret to them, and being here now was the time I was going to discover what. Of course, I had asked Amelia about it, but she had always just laughed it off, as if I was being funny. Saying things like,

'What do you think? That we have a dungeon in the basement or temples where, as a family cult we worship the Devil?'

After this I would just end up feeling silly and laugh it off with her. But I admit, I would always go to bed wondering. Because if it wasn't dungeons and temples they kept in the lower levels of Afterlife, then what was it? It was true, I had only been in their home part of Afterlife a few times, but it certainly made an impact. So much so that

I would never forget all those castle-like walls filled with endless staircases and hallways, ones that I knew had to lead somewhere. And well, facing the facts, the immense building wasn't exactly being used as a hotel.

If I had to guess, then looking around this place now, it was something to do with her father, no doubt about it. Meaning that my catfish theory soon went out the window. This, even despite its lack of immense looking wealth and opulence I was used to seeing surround my uncle Dominic.

I mean, the guy had a car collection my dad would have wept over. In fact, whenever we got together for family days, it was one thing that my dad and my uncle would talk about as they were total gearheads. Which was why, for my dad's 40th birthday, my uncle had given him a rare Aston Martin known as a One-77. Meaning that there was only 77 of them ever made, and it was rumoured to have been worth well over a million when first bought.

Apparently, it had also been a car that my dad had fallen in love with the first time my uncle had used it to drive my Aunty Kaz home from a nightshift. Something he did after she injured herself at work or something like that, I can't remember all the details. Either way, I thought it was a cute story and that it would have made a good romance book.

Although, one look at Afterlife and it would have no doubt been turned into Paranormal Romance for sure!

And speaking of paranormal, well, I was just hoping that this one wasn't going to turn into a horror story, as this place was a big ten on the creepy o'meter! Of course, it wasn't just that it looked old and well used, but more the lack of life that gave it that sinister vibe. The small bar area on the right was only big enough for a few tables, making me wonder what the point was. Ten people, and this place would have felt packed full. Making me wonder if there were other rooms like this? Was it just like a honeycomb of small rooms that each held a bar? Well, the sign off to one side said as much, as it had arrows pointing both up the staircase and onwards telling me the names. Like the one named the 'Chop Shop' that was a sign held over a closed door to my left.

"Blood hell, are they serious?" I muttered, at both the name and the painting that hung above the door that was of an older woman in a black dress who looked to be in mourning. A string of three pearls at her neck and one of those faces that seemed to follow you as you walked. I mean, where was the fighting supposed to be, with the rest of the antiques and motheaten drapes over the dusty windows? Not exactly what I would have called threatening, but definitely more Hitchcock than Brad Pit Fight club and weird ass soap making.

I decided not to look at the woman again, as I swear I was seeing things as her eyes turned more white, as if some light was being reflected back off the glass... but wait, there wasn't any glass.

"Okay, time to move on now," I said nervously, and continued on to where the only light was, telling me that it must have been where Amelia had gone.

Downstairs.

"Please don't be a dungeon in the basement, please don't be a dungeon in the basement," I repeated like a useless mantra that would do shit at protecting me. Okay, so I was glad I wasn't tall, this staircase would have only been comfortable for children to walk down as it had both narrow steps and seriously lacked head height. Even the sign telling you to watch your step would have been close enough to lick, should the insane urge overtake me.

But then, when I reached the bottom, I actually found myself disappointed as it was a serious anticlimactic moment, being that it led to a pair of restrooms and what looked like a broom cupboard.

"Well, Fae, you couldn't have disappeared, so where are you?" I mused, before getting to the bottom and seeing a door to the left that looked as if it led to an old cellar that had now been converted into a place to put tables and chairs for customers. It was quite cool actually, and with its cream painted brick walls, it was definitely more welcoming than the upstairs.

The low ceilings were vaulted in sections and there seemed to be little nooks for a single table or two. Like a little labyrinth of steps up and down, with different levels so any space available was used to seat someone. Then, as I continued down to the very lowest point, I found another bar along the wall, and a space big enough this time to hold long tables and bench seats for bigger groups of people. That, or strangers would have to share a space together. Of course, there was a few smaller tables but nothing else in this room to suggest anyone had been here recently. For example, nothing like a fallen baseball cap I knew Amelia had been wearing to try and conceal her identity… now, if I could just figure out who she was trying to hide from then that might be a start.

Jesus, where was the Scooby Doo gang when you needed them? I decided to work my way back up, and the moment I felt something digging in the ball of my foot, I stopped and sat down in an arched brick alcove. One that only held a single small table with a stool either side. It felt as though I had something stuck in my sneaker, so I leaned over to take it off and give it a shake to get rid of whatever it was.

"That's strange," I said aloud, something I will admit to being something of a habit of mine as I was often found mumbling to myself. But there was no mistaking the single piece of silver confetti in the shape of a tiny skull with horns that had somehow got in my shoe.

It was the type you would have found scattered on some party table for Halloween or something. However, this didn't end up being the strangest part, as it was after I repositioned my shoe that I saw it. The same horned skull was burnt into the underside of the table. In fact, it looked embossed, as it was slightly raised from the rest of the wood and I didn't know what compelled me, but I found myself reaching out to touch it. The second I did, its snake like tongue flicked up as if it was made of metal and spiked my fingertip, making it bleed.

"Oww!" I shouted, snatching my hand back and instantly putting it in my mouth to suck. I hated needles, it went beyond a phobia but was more like a deep-rooted loathing and for good reason. But I wouldn't let my mind wander down that road now, not when I was currently living out these strange series of events.

That's when I heard it…

The sound of others above.

"Is anyone th… Ah!" I shouted after being cut off when suddenly the whole section I was sat on moved and quickly flipped around as if I had unknowingly triggered a rotating secret door. In fact, it reminded me of that movie that Amelia loved so much, one she would always make me sit through as she was a huge fan of the Indiana Jones films. I couldn't remember the name or all the lines like she could, but I was pretty sure I do remember him being tied back-to-back with his father at one point and a whole fireplace spun around.

Well, that was what was happening now and before I could do anything about it, because soon my cry for help was cut off with a resounding echo of stone hitting against stone. Meaning only one thing…

I Was Trapped.

THREE

ALICE HAD IT EASY

Okay… okay… just gotta calm down. *If there was a way in, that means there's a way out,* I told myself, only it wasn't as comforting as I had hoped. Not when I could hear my own fear when my voice shook like that.

I finally gave up on the door in front of me, as it was clearly locked, and after hopelessly looking for some panel or switch or anything that looked like a locking mechanism, I found nothing. I had to ask once again what I had got myself into, and this only led to more questions… *more like what had Amelia got herself into?*

It turned out that this question was going to be one I

would ask myself for the duration of the night, one that was only going to get creepier and creepier. Starting when I turned around and found myself staring at what could only be described as a hellish looking elevator. It reminded me of one of those that you would often see in some old lavish hotel or the first apartment buildings. An elevator you wouldn't dare use and was mainly only ever kept there for decorative purposes. Because really, just how many people would have trusted the old mechanisms used to power it. The damn thing looked more like a metal cage, and once inside you would feel trapped like a bird longing for the sky.

But after staring at it and getting over the horror of the thing, even I had to admit there was an eerie beauty to it. I had never seen one like this before, only knowing that they existed, making me wonder just how old it was? But why was it hidden in this old pub and more importantly, where did it lead to? Those were the questions I wanted an answer to above all, despite its hellish appearance. A cage of black, twisted wrought iron in a circular shape that was domed at the top, and decorated with what looked like a beast's clawed hand reaching for the top. The twisted iron was in an art nouveau style, a mixture of swirls of drooping lilies and vines intermixed with snarling heads like gargoyles. Like those you would have seen on the side of old medieval buildings, some of which I had seen in the few days I had been in London.

I looked around to see there wasn't much else in the space other than the long torches attached to the walls. These were topped with small, caged flickering bulbs but the style looked like someone had taken some thousand-year-old antique and modified it. As for the rest of it, there were no other doors leading anywhere else. Which meant there was no other way to go than the two double doors facing me that belonged to the elevator. I even looked up, and couldn't tell it went up to a floor above or not as nothing was obvious with this type of contraption.

So, what other choice did I have but to step closer to the elaborate doors that were both beautifully dark and also unwelcoming? It could not be denied the craftsmanship used to create such a mundane purpose, despite my discomfort at being forced to use it. Because we most definitely took elevators for granted these days, as looking at this one now and I couldn't help but feel as if we had lost some sort of historical craftmanship, as we certainly didn't make things like this today. No, something functional rarely had this much work dedicated to it. It was both terrifying and stunning all at the same time.

I looked up to see an old-fashioned arch with numbers painted on a strip of white, and underneath at the centre was a gold metal arrow mounted that was currently pointed at level 2. This half-moon shape was framed with curls of iron that were thorned and looked deadly. But then this wasn't the only creepy thing about it as the number counted, 1,2,3 and then jumped to 13 and last of all… *666.*

Hence why I wasn't exactly falling over myself to get in the bloody thing, but what other choice did I have? I turned around and tried one more time to find an opening or any way back inside the pub, but then I knew that I owed it to my cousin to make sure she was alright. and considering now it was clear there was only one place I would find her, then I felt I had little choice but to allow the elevator to take me where it wanted to.

And I had a bad feeling exactly which floor that would be.

Truth be told, if I had been given the chance, I would have gone back to the hotel and told my aunt and uncle where their daughter was, because I feared more for her safety than the trouble I knew she would get into by admitting she was here. Sure, she would be mad at me, but she'd be alive when she was doing it, and that was all that mattered to me right now.

However, that clearly wasn't an option, so I had no choice but to press the call button for the doors to open, jumping when they did with a resounding ding. Doors that were sectioned at the bottom with solid plates of black metal, decorated in a mass of thorns that reached up to the gated part that was twisted metal spindles. These were bent into arches that pointed up into a large deadly spike at the top, and in the centre was what looked like some family crest. Only I had to admit the symbol in the middle looked more demonic in nature than of the usual horses, flags and swords. This looked more like two curved blades facing each other, with a hollow circle in the middle. They both tapered down into thin lines that hooked back on themselves like half arrow heads. A thick black line slashed through the lengths, and under it was a thinner one. The whole symbol was encased in a triangular shield that had sides like a kite.

Of course, I only had a moment to see it as a whole piece, as now it had been cut in two, along with the thick metal strip either side of it that was made to look like an ancient scroll. On this were golden words that looked to be written in Greek, meaning I had no idea what it said. Only that if anyone knew, it would have been Fae.

She would have had no problem reading this...

'Cerberus ο προστάτης της κόλασης
χάντες καταναλώθηκαν.'

As for me, there was only one word I knew, and that was of course... *Cerberus.*

"Well, it was nice living while it lasted," I said aloud, before looking up as if speaking directly with God, making my goodbyes and crossing myself as if this would help. Okay, so I wasn't particularly religious but given times like this, then despite how hypercritical it seemed, I thought praying now was a good a time as any.

Which was my exact thoughts as I stepped across from stone floor to one of suspended metal, screaming when the doors slammed shut behind me with an echoing clang of iron. Of course, the fact that you could actually see through the grated floor down into the dark plunging depths below, wasn't exactly helping with nerves. Now I wasn't scared of heights, but this didn't mean I was ready to buy a daredevil suit and started jumping canyons on a dirt bike either.

At the very least, there were lights inside, even if the tear shaped lamps above didn't offer much. Each was surrounded by a rosette of metal vines that matched the theme, flickering ominously before the elevator started to move without needing me to press any buttons. Which was a good thing really as I had no clue what to press anyway. This was thanks to the old control panel that had switches you just wouldn't see today, like, slow speed, start, close, off, safety switch and open. Of course, it was the big red button in the centre that said *Emergency Out, Out*. I mean what did 'out, out' mean exactly? Did it need to be said twice just to get the point across, because I was at the point now where it was only fear of the unknown that stopped me from jabbing my finger at it like a mad woman! But then the flashing light above the keyhole was intriguing, making me wonder which floor that was supposed to lead to?

Hell... *definitely Hell, I decided.*

The only saving grace to this scary descent was that it didn't move as fast as modern elevators today and well, the curved velvet red seat was a nice touch at least. Even that had been handmade, and was all curved, carved wood that held the plush material in place with brass pins.

In the end, the only good part to having a grated floor was that I could see through it, which gave me opportunity to brace myself when I could see the end was coming. However, when the elevator rattled to a stop, I screamed as the light overhead cut out and plunged me into darkness.

"AH!" I shouted again when I heard the doors in front of me open and I was led only by sound for ten long, terrifying seconds, feeling my way out. But then the doors closed behind me, making me jump again before a light finally flickered on. This awarded me a slither of light, making it enough to show me an opening. I briefly questioned if this was the way Amelia had come, but then I knew I had only been minutes behind her so if not, then that meant there had been another way down here that I had missed. Unless she had gone up the stairs, ignoring the roped closed sign?

Jesus, I hoped I found her down here or this had all been for nothing, and God only knew what would happen to me if I was caught here. Because let's just say that the place had secret entrances and creepy elevators for a reason, and I doubted it was for shits and giggles. No, this was nothing short of a secret cult or illegal gang lair, I was sure of it.

One that held signs that said… *a fight club.*

"Jesus, Fae, what the hell are you doing here?" I said, then quickly muttering,

"What the hell am I doing here!" before pushing my way through the red metal door that was the only way there was to go. A sight that didn't exactly instil confidence in me when I saw the same crest on the door, this time, one that was decorated with a horned demonic skull over it. Oh, and not forgetting the words beneath it that said,

'Devil's Ring Fight Club'

"Oh yeah, I am totally screwed," I muttered before pushing open the creaky door, that most likely was announcing to everyone behind the doors that I had arrived, as let's just say the sound wasn't exactly subtle. Of course, the moment I popped my head around the small opening I had created, I soon released I couldn't have been more wrong.

Oh, so very fucking wrong!

"What the…" I let that curse trail off, as I was now faced with an entirely different sight than my mind had conjured up. Because the biker gang fight club or drug lord's secret lair I had been expecting, was as far from what reality I was now laying witness too.

A hellish fair ground, demonic freakshow…

Oh yeah, that was the rabbit hole I found myself in.

Which now meant only one thing…

"Just call me Alice."

FOUR

CAPTURED BY A CLOWN

I gasped in utter shock at whatever hellish spectacle I had just walked in on! It was as though I had just unknowingly lost months of my life and skipped straight to Halloween!

That was because everyone was dressed up as some kind of demonic freakshow character, and they were walking around a sort of fairground that had been created underground in some colossal cave! Of course, when I say fairground, that was without the fun rides and laughing children. But as for other stuff, well there was plenty around to give weight to the description, as dirty stalls were dotted around a large area closest to what looked like a curtained main entrance. One I had no doubt that anyone welcome here walked through first, as the way I entered looked more like a secret side door.

As for the stalls, they were grouped together like a market of street vendors selling their goods and offerings of fairground food with a twist. Like the one that sold 'Rotten Candy', that had the C crossed out with crude dripping red paint. Only I had to confess, it was the strangest cotton candy I had ever seen, as it looked like bundles of wound-up hair that had been fried and gave off that rancid smell of burnt hair.

Along with this, was the Poison toffee apple cart that made me want to vomit, as it looked like a small Chinese lady was having too much fun dunking what looked to be shrunken heads. Then she would use her knobbly walking stick to stir the big vat of black toffee. I watched then as she pushed up her wide sleeve of red silk and drip her long black pointed nails in there to grab one. Then with her talons, she hung it up to harden by pegging its stiff hair on the string above.

"Jesus," I muttered, making one person that walked past, laugh and say,

"Yeah, he can't help you down here, fleshy." Then he

continued on his way, making me wonder how he got that scaled effect on his body… was it paint, or had he actually tattooed it all over his skin? I mean it was horrifying but also sort of fascinating at the same time. All the effort put into a place like this, along with what must have been

props because this must have been all for show? Was that it, was this some kind of special themed party I had just walked into, and had Amelia somehow got herself invited? Because even I had to admit that the effects were amazing, as the costumes and makeup used to create the characters was incredible!

It looked so real! Real enough it would no doubt be giving me new nightmares for months! But then, as I looked around, it seemed that even the guests were also allowing themselves the chance to get into character, as there wasn't exactly anyone that looked normal walking around and discussing how cool the effects were or realistic the props were. Hell, but I would have been easily convinced I had just walked into a movie set had it not been for the distinct lack of cameras and people behind the scenes.

As for the rest of the place, the large circular room looked to have been carved right out of the rock before being whitewashed in a haphazard way. Although, it looked to have been done decades ago as it wasn't exactly clean looking. Patches of bare rock were dotted around, and other sections were swathed in aged striped material of yellows and reds. This making it look like part of a big top, giving it the creepy carnival vibe it was definitely going for.

Was that what the theme of this party was, some Circus in Hell?

I craned my neck the further inside I allowed myself to go, making sure to not draw any attention to myself by pulling the hood further down over my face. This whilst still trying to take in the rest of the room. Something that allowed me to see that there was a raised stage area at the far end that was surrounded by a fan shape of seats. A sea of faded burgundy that looked to have at one time belonged to an old theatre. But then they staggered down like steps towards the front of the centre stage, and those looked as if they had been carved from the rock just like the stage had. Of course, a crowd of the most unusual people started to fill them up quickly, as if getting ready for the show to begin or something.

I quite honestly didn't know where to look. One moment, I was watching a pair of girls walk past wearing the biggest striped black and white ball gowns, and the next minute, a guy walked past with what looked like a mechanical demonic monkey crawling out of his hat. These people must have spent crazy amounts of money on these costumes and props because I couldn't believe how realistic everything looked! Men wearing crazy monstrous masks that were made even more real thanks to the clever use of contact lenses.

Some people even had full sized folded wings and were dressed like gothic angels in black suits, complete with tailed jackets and top hats. A few women looked as if they had special effect makeup on. Like the one who made it look as though her face was melting with skin coloured wax pouring down her cheeks. However, one of the most disgusting sights I saw, was when one guy walked past me biting into what looked like a whole leg of goat held in his clawed hands. It was even bleeding on the floor from the end it looked to be torn from. Of course, I knew it couldn't be real because, eww! Surely there was only so far you were allowed to go… health and safety and all that. But it did make me wonder what it actually was made of. I suppose the blood could have been syrup and the legs made of chocolate, but as for the fur, now that was a tough one to explain.

The room was so big it was difficult to see it all from here but one part that was unmistakeable, was the raised area at the left side of the stage that held all the comfortable looking chairs. It was as if these had been reserved for VIPs. However, it wasn't just this area that held my attention, but it was one chair in particular that had my imagination running wild and that was…

Who sat on the throne?

Was it this Cerberus guy?

It would make sense seeing as his name was on the doors. Meaning he was obviously the one who owned the club, so wouldn't it be fitting for the guy to have the biggest and most imposing seat in the house? Well, one thing was for sure, with a chair like that, then he was the very last person I wanted to bump into whilst I was down here. It looked more like a throne fit for the Devil himself! The major details were lost on me from this far away, but it was huge, it was gothic and painted black.

Which was all the reminder I needed to find Fae and get the hell out of here, and fast! Which, unfortunately, also meant that I wasn't going to achieve this by waiting around here glued to one spot all night. So, with this in mind, I started to venture further inside, and doing so trying to stay closer to the walls. Because no matter whether these freaks were all just playing a part, they were still scaring the hell out of me and not the type of characters I wanted to bump into and say hello.

Like the guy on stilts who was wearing some patchwork jacket that looked as if it was made up of different types of skin… and Jesus, was that a tattoo I saw on one of the back panels? Well, whoever had been in charge of make-up and wardrobe needed to win an award! This stuff was far too real. Of course, the guy was currently juggling wine bottles and skilfully taking a swig from one every third catch, making me wonder how on earth he managed it without even spilling a single drop.

I passed him, and nearly bumped into a demonic clown that had a forked tongue and crumpled skin, like his clown face had been drawn first on tissue paper before it had been torn up. Then it had been pieced back together like a puzzle and glued to his face, giving it the appearance of painted flakes of skin.

He snarled down at me before licking his lips with a hissing sound.

"Out of my way, human flesh!"

"Oh jeez, sorry," I said, backing up into another guy, this time, one who looked like a horned demon in a pinstriped suit that looked like something a gangster would wear from an old movie. All he was missing was the tommy gun and a trilby hat. However, what he lacked in accessories, he made up for in hellish makeup as it looked like some latex had been used. And like the woman I had seen, it was done to create the effect as though his cheeks were melting, along with his chin that looked elongated into a horned point. Even his hands were demonic looking, with wrinkled reddish skin tipped with wicked looking nails at the ends of his fingers.

"Oh dear, sorry again… great makeup by the way." At this he snorted out a huffed breath before snarling his pointed yellow teeth at me. Even his flaming red contact lenses added to the frightening appearance, yet how he got them to glow like the way they did, I had no clue. Either way, it seemed the guy wouldn't break character for anything, so I decided, before he went too far, to get the hell out of his way.

However, when the devilled figure stomped past me from the right, I had to wonder just how far the staff in the party were willing to go, as I swear his whole body had been painted to create a stone effect. He even had sound effects added, making him sound as if his stone joints were grinding against each other. Where he hid the speaker, I had no clue and really, I didn't want to know either, seeing as the guy only wore a ripped, grey loin cloth.

Another 'eww' moment for sure.

"You shouldn't be here, human!" another voice said, and when I turned, it was a woman with striped black and red trousers, that were combined with a frilly white shirt and a line of little bowties down the front instead of buttons. She also had on a large, floppy top hat that matched her trousers. Black suspenders completed the outfit, along with a long black rope of hair that looked as if it had been plaited with a dead snake.

"Err, yeah okay," I said with a nervous giggle, knowing it was all just part of the show. But then she pulled a large sword from behind her back, making me stumble backwards in fear and into a clucking cage of what looked like black chickens.

"Lord Cerberus doesn't like your kind," she said, and then swished her blade up in the air as if she was about to strike me down before telling me,

"Although, watching him gut you will be fun, wanna

see?" Then as I covered myself to protect my body from the assault, she chuckled, and I braved opening my eyes when I didn't feel the pain of being maimed. However, I started to wish that I hadn't and instead run away blindly when I saw that she had plunged the blade down her own throat, swallowing it all the way to the handle. Then, with a wiggle and a wink at me, she pulled it back out, and at the end was what looked like her bloody stomach!

"Holy shit!" I screamed, before scrambling back and rattling the cages further before turning and seeing that they looked like zombie birds! Birds with more bone and bare bloody flesh than feathers!

"Jesus!" I screamed again, before gaining my feet and making a run for it, foolishly into the crowd, doing so to the sound of cackled laughter from the freak show knife girl!

Although, the problem with this was that I ended up running straight into another freak, and this time it was one that wasn't going to let me go without paying the price for sneaking into this Hellhole!

"Hey, flesh Cookie, now just what do you think you are doing in a jar like this?" I heard his confident voice before I had chance to face him and to do that, I had to first rip myself away from his hands that held me at the tops of my arms. Of course, the moment I did so I was faced with one of the most unusual characters yet.

A tall handsome jester that was a strange mix of both playful and mischievous as he was dangerous. He had this knowing aura about him that told you there was always a lot more going on behind those painted eyes of his than what his smirk let on. Intense eyes that narrowed at me now as if they were searching into my soul or hell, into my future! Well, whatever he was seeing, intrigued him… *greatly*. I knew this when he raised a single arched painted brow and with a knowing look, he commented cryptically,

"Now that is interesting… or at least it soon will be." I frowned in return and shook my head a little before muttering,

"Wh…what is this… place?" At this, his smirk turned into a full-blown grin as if he was feeding from my fear. Even his athletic build tensed a moment before he relaxed with a visible shudder. In fact, he reminded me of some jungle cat, sleek and at the ready to pounce when the time needed it. His entire being seemed to scream predator with a body made for speed and agility. This was despite his unusual face and his even more unusual costume. He looked like some handsome clown that had dressed as some dashing buccaneer, with his pirate sword hanging at the ready by his hip and an old-fashioned gun mirroring it on the other side. A pair of dark leather trousers clung to long muscular legs that held patches of armour-plating at the knees. These disappeared into leather boots that folded at the top just below the knee. One of which had a dagger's hilt poking out the top.

Wow, so the guy was definitely packing, as he even had weapons strapped to his back. In fact, the more I looked, the more I realised that none of this stuff looked like costume props at all! And speaking of which, I was seriously starting to wonder if I had been drugged as the things in this room were started to look less fake by the minute!

As for the rest of him, under the belt that held his arsenal, he had a fringed scarf tied around his slim waist that could be seen beneath his long, red leather jacket, one that was definitely battle worn. Tears and frayed rips looked as though they had been made from slashes from a knife fight. Which, given the guy's appearance, I wouldn't have been surprised as there must have been a reason the guy was packing so many blades.

The jacket also had stitched panels that split at the back to allow for more movement and was edged with piped black leather. This also matched the arrowhead shaped patches that surrounded each black button. A cravat of black silk was tied loosely at his neck, matching the overly long sleeves of a black shirt he wore underneath the cool jacket.

But then it also had to be said that his outfit definitely came second to his make-up, that was nothing short of sinister. A painted clown made regal, thanks to the handsome bone structure beneath it. Skin painted white with two thin diamond stripes running down through his startling dark blue eyes. Blood red paint that only stopped at his jaw line in thin points and above curling up like horns at his forehead. Another single red line was painted from his bottom lip all the way down his chin and the length of his neck. The high arch of his dark brows gave him a questioning arrogance that always seemed to be amused. This was made even more so when he grinned down at me, given his taller height. Of course, he also looked like a vampire with his fangs longer than the rest of his gleaming white teeth.

"This place? Oh Cookie, you have no idea where you

just sneaked into, do you?" he asked with a fake sense of sympathy, one I wished in that moment was real enough to trust. Because I just needed one person to help me, and I could then start putting this living nightmare behind me.

"I...I... don't," I stammered out, hoping there was still a possibility he would take pity on me. However, the moment he stepped closer and grinned that disturbing sinister smile, I knew that I was hoping for the impossible. Especially when he ducked his head and whispered in a menacing tone,

"Then let me enlighten you, doll face..." Then he raised up my face with a hold on my chin, until my hood fell back and his eyes started to morph into a shocking sight. This was as sapphire turned into blood red before glowing with demonic glee. And that's when I knew the truth. Because contact lenses didn't do that.

No fucking way!

"You entered an Alpha King's lair and for pretty human flesh, he is always hungry... *but just to be sure, let's make it official, eh?"* I sucked in a startled breath that turned into a little cry of terror when he grabbed me roughly by the arm, and this time there was no yanking free. Jesus, but the strength on him was enough to snap bones, which was why I knew it was useless fighting as I would only end up getting hurt.

"Good, sweet cookie. Fighting will only get you broken sooner," he said as if being able to read my thoughts. So, I had no choice but to let him drag me along with him and I had to admit, the moment we got closer to the stage was when I really started to freak out.

Oh my God, just what the hell did this crazy guy have planned for me? But more importantly…

Who was this Alpha King?

And what would he do to me?

FIVE

RED RIDING HOOD

"Are you freaking bat shit crazy? He will eat her alive if you send her out like that!" This was said by what seemed like the only rational mind I had met in this whole place, and that had been five seconds ago. And as it happened, I found myself agreeing with this statement and I didn't even know who the hell this Cerberus guy was!

No, all I had learned was nothing but insanity since that strange jester had dragged me into this part of the club. A place that seemed to be where all the acts were getting ready, like some tented dressing room that was situated next to the stage. One that was on a higher platform, so it put the opening at the same height, no doubt for ease for the performers.

It was also at this point that I felt as if there were only two possible explanations for the situation I found myself in. One was that I had unknowingly snuck into some secret cult whose only criteria for new members was, like my new friend had said, to be bat shit crazy. The second was a little more radical if that could be believed, as I could have been been sucked into another dimension where demons and other creepy shit was real.

Naturally, I was praying for the first option.

Although, thinking about it, I suppose there were other options, as though everyone here was sucking in some poisoned gas making them crazy. Or I had been drugged and was therefore the only crazy one seeing stuff that wasn't real in a very realistic costume party. So, there it was, my top four explanations, and all of them off the back of having ten minutes to think whilst I was forced into a costume that had been thrown at me. One I had no choice to put on as they gave me only two choices… I put it on myself, or they put it on me.

Needless to say, I stepped behind the curtain and

changed quicker than Superman in a damn phonebooth! Anything to save me from having their freakish hands on me. Painted girls with small horns that were red skinned, wearing little else leaving very little to the imagination. Dwarfs that looked ready for battle and demonic musicians that looked like they were waiting for the go ahead. Of course, after the strangely handsome jester had marched me up the steps and tossed me through the striped curtain, it didn't take long before he was barking an order. Now saying only one thing, and this was after taking one look at my flaming mass of curls that rained down my back.

"Red Riding Hood." Then, with a nod of his head, he was gone. Which was why I soon found myself wearing a ridiculous costume that made me feel as if I was being catapulted into some gothic fairy tale. An old child's fable I could only hope didn't end with me being eaten by the wolf like dear old granny. Although, one glance down at myself now, and I was more worried about being ravished by that wolf before being eaten! Jesus, but I had never worn something so provocative and sexual before, and that was all thanks to the corseted part of the dress. At the very least, I was thankful for the white shirt beneath it, even if the puffy little sleeves kept falling from my shoulders.

As for the skirt, it was flowing red silk that twirled around my legs like liquid. It was also decorated with black-velvet Fleur De Lis entwined in a thorny vine around the hem, and matched the torn black stockings I had been made to wear. This made it look as if the wolf had already had a go at trying to catch me and nearly come close. The only part of the outfit I admittedly had been excited about seeing, had been the red ballet shoes. Even sat putting them on again made me suck in a deep breath, as if just tying the ribbons around my ankles centred me somehow. As if this was just all another show I was to perform. Just another stage. Just another play.

I could do this.

But then, the moment I stepped back out and was handed the thick, red-velvet hooded cloak to put on, I couldn't help but lose some of the bravery I had got from the shoes. I swallowed hard, having no choice but to tie the thick black ribbon around the base of my neck, and purposely trying to contain all my hair in the hood to hide myself better. Something that didn't give me much confidence when a woman with unusual orange coloured hair stepped inside and, after taking one look at me, shook her head.

"Pencil dick has finally lost his mind," she said the moment she saw me, continuing to shake her cute head to herself. For the first time I was also faced with someone who had a kind smile for me, one that was painted orange like her bright hair and framed by a piercing on either side of her cheeks, like two metal dimples. She also had a bar running through the bridge of her nose, but surprisingly none at her ears. The choppy hair style suited her, even with the sharp cut of a fringe high up on her forehead, about an inch from the hairline.

She was short but full of big curves that she most definitely knew how to work, as she seemed to have this confidence and swagger about her. She also had makeup on that reminded me of some 50's pin up girl, with thick eyeliner over her hazel eyes that had flecks of amber in them. This matched her style, as she wore tight black capris, with a thick red belt high on her waist that her black and red striped top was tucked into. High-heel open-toe red shoes completed the look, along with a bandana she wore around her head.

"What's your name, chickadee?" she asked in a kind tone.

"Ella," I answered honestly without thinking, and also

hoping that she might appreciate my honesty.

"Alright, Ella, I am Smidge and I have to say, I have no idea how it is even possible for you to have made it this far, but you get that you ain't in Kansas anymore, right?" At this I almost choked out my answer,

"Erh, yeah... scrap that and make it a hell yeah." She scoffed at this and said,

"Well, you would be right with the hell part, sugar." In all honesty, I didn't think I had been called so many nicknames in my life and in such a small space of time too. Something that only continued when the jester walked back in and said,

"Oh yeah, Cookie, now that is what I am talking about... now this is going to be oh so perfect!" This was when the one called Smidge (which it had to be said, was a name I had never heard before) said,

"Oh, but of course, you're the dickhead to have thought of this!" He smirked down at her before winking, and then with a gothic looking staff in hand, he jerked it up before catching it again and used it to point to the dancing girls,

"Right, bitches, I have a new act for you. This delightfully scented human cookie is Little Red Riding Hood, and you tits are the wolves. Now, go and use the costumes from last week's performance of the wolf who cried demon granny and make it work… chop, chop," he said, clapping his hands together after swinging his cane under his arm. It was one that was carved out of dark red wood, with a twisted vine design that curled around the demon's skull at the top. Its curled horns made up the handle and with its mouth open, its fangs held a clear crystal ball in place.

It was at this point that the orange haired girl stomped her foot and asked if he was bat shit crazy.

"Oh, come on, Smidge, as if I could pass up an opportunity like this," he said with an evil grin.

"He will fucking kill you this time, idiot!" she argued, making me shudder. However, he didn't look worried, not in the slightest. In fact, he looked almost gleeful as if he couldn't wait for something… *like serving me up to the big bad wolf on a platter!*

"Oh, sweetheart, have I told you recently just how much I love it when you and that big, beautiful ass of yours worries for me." At this she rolled her eyes and shook her head, muttering something about him dreaming.

"You're a dead man walking, Marcus," she said trying again, and letting me know his name this time. At this he stepped closer to her, his gaze heating up before tapping her on her cute, pierced nose before saying,

"No, he won't… besides, you don't know what I know."

She cocked out her curvy behind and put a hand to her hip.

"Yeah, and what's that, asswipe?" she snapped, as it was clear these two didn't exactly see eye to eye but there was still something between them… something both were hiding. I could tell. Because there was something in the way his eyes would glow slightly whenever she challenged him. Something he liked… *a lot.* Well, that was if the mischievous glint in them said anything. This was when he got in close and took hold of her chin before whispering,

"He is going to like this human, and when I say like, I mean… to death… you and your delectable big ass, can trust me on that, peaches." I gulped, whereas Smidge dropped her sassy guard enough to lean in a little closer, making his intense blue gaze heat up in a way that once again turned his eyes crimson. Then, the sound of a bell could be heard, and it was enough of a distraction to remind him that he obviously had a job to do. Which was why he pinched her chin hard and yanked her to his lips before kissing her

quick and saying,

"That's my cue, Peach!" Then he let her go and she growled in annoyance as if he had just played her in some kind of way, making her mutter,

"Jerk!" Then she turned to me and said,

"Men can be such assholes, don't you think?!" I gave her a slight look of shock before nodding quickly. Because, well, he most definitely wasn't on my nice guy list. Not seeing as the creepy handsome guy was about to force me on stage as some punishment for being caught in here. Naturally, she wasn't going to get an argument from me.

"Of course, you do, I bet it was one of the jackasses that got you mixed up in all this, right?" I gave her wince and told her,

"Not really no, but if it helps, this Cerberus guy doesn't sound like he is going to like me much," I said being brave and hoping that it wouldn't backfire. At this she sighed and replied,

"You might be right about that, Ella girl. I don't know what Marcus was thinking."

"Marcus… that's the jester's name, right?" I asked, wondering why I was even bothering and not just trying to run away as fast as my eighteen-year-old legs could carry me.

"He's not really a jester, although he certainly acts the clown. No, he's a Seeker, and a cocky one at that seeing as he's one of the most powerful, hence assholeism to its fullest. Anyway, no reason you should get your pretty head bitten off because of that biggest bag of the douches... let me go and see what I can do about getting you out of here before Jared gets a glimpse of your forbidden candy," she replied, giving me a lot in all of that to think about, having only understood half of it!

Although, the part I focused on the most was what made me grab her hand and say,

"Oh my god, you're going to help me?!"

"Of course, I was human once too, you know," she said with a smile.

"Er, I don't want to offend but isn't this acting all a bit much... I mean, big kudos for everyone's commitment to being in character and all..." At this she burst out laughing, pulling me by the cap over towards the main way onto the stage and pulled back the curtain. Then she said,

"Does that look like acting to you, sugar?" she said, nodding to what was no longer a stage but in fact an electrified fight ring. One that now held dwarves all dressed in what I gathered was the seven deadly sins with a definite twist. Some were even wearing heels and feathers and would struct their stuff across the ring, holding out their weapons to the creature at the centre. At first I would have said it was nothing but make-believe, guys in costumes like the rest of this place but then this was when the impossible started to happen.

That cute long-haired creature with its big eyes and stretch of rounded teeth, who stood about as tall as the man that was no doubt inside him, started to open his mouth. At first, I thought the guy was going to pop out and start acting out the fight.

But no.

Actually, make that a big fucking no!

"Oh shit!" I shouted, as two demonic hands started to claw their way out of the now baggy skin of the creature, as if his skeleton was breaking free. Then, once nothing was left of the once fluffy white creature, it was discarded on the floor like a used fur rug, making me gasp,

"Hhhow… is this… possible?" I muttered the question, unable to take my eyes from the sight of the monster that had just crawled out of the body of a giant teddy bear.

"Time to light 'em up boys!" Marcus said, swinging a

different staff over his head this time and making it crash down like thunder on the floor. A massive switch was then flipped, one that wouldn't have looked out of place in Frankenstein's monster making lab!

The moment this was down, the whole ring turned into an electrified fence to keep the fighters inside, something I admittedly was thankful of considering this nightmare just turned deadly real!

The fight had begun, and I felt sick in seconds as the skeletal monster, still with bits of flesh hanging from its bones, started to roar down at the seven fighters. It now stood easily at seven feet high and when they started to charge at him, he ripped out two of his own rib bones, now using them as weapons. This was when I felt myself starting to sway, coving my mouth after uttering,

"Oh my God!"

I had just found my proof. It was all real. I knew that now, as I was forced to realise that my nightmare was true… this place… it wasn't just make believe. It wasn't some freakish party or some fantasy land where people could lose themselves for a night. *No, it was real…*

Very fucking real!

"Oh, trust me, sweetie, there is only one God in charge

here, and if he takes one look at you dressed like that, it won't be a heavenly ending, but one of a very different kind." I shot her fearful eyes and then grabbed her to me, and said in panic,

"Please help me. I didn't mean to come here! I followed someone… my… oh God, my cousin is out there somewhere!" I confessed, knowing that I had no choice because this girl might possibly be my only way of getting out of here alive, and if that was true, then I needed to try and get her to help me save Fae too.

Her eyes widened in shock and then narrowed in question, before she voiced it,

"I have a bad feeling I am going to regret asking this but, *who exactly is your cousin?"* I swallowed hard, looked back out at the fight of demons, and with a silent prayer added, I told her,

"Amelia Draven." This was when her reaction surprised me as now, it wasn't my eyes that had suddenly grown fearful. Then, she looked back out with me and said one thing that told me that my cousin was most definitely no stranger to this world like I'd hoped…

"Oh, fuck… A Draven."

SIX

WOLF IN THE SHADOWS

After this, Smidge told me to wait, as after naming who my cousin was it seemed as though I had dropped a Draven bomb and Smidge was now panicking. She ran off, saying something about desperately needing to find her boss, and I could only hope that she did and this whole nightmare would be over soon.

However, she must have anticipated the fight on stage to go on a lot longer than it did, because far too quickly the seven champions were lapping up the cheers from the crowd. This, as they all started dragging their spoils from the fight off towards the backstage, this being the dead carcass over their small shoulders.

"Ah!" I screamed as I was spun around, to find one of the dancers that was now dressed like a sexy wolf, laugh and tell me,

"Save the screams for the stage, fleshy, as the crowd with love 'em." Then she snapped a pair of shackles around my wrists and started to drag me towards the stage, only pausing long enough for who I now knew was named Marcus to introduce the next act.

Now the sides of the ring had lowered, and the electricity was turned off, it was once more back to looking like a stage rather than a fight ring, which did little to ease my nerves.

"Congrats you happy, stabby, little devils you! And as for Snow White, well we can all agree it looks better without a soul of bones… enjoy your new rug, boys, you earned it!" Marcus said, now lifting a bottle of beer to salute them before taking a large swig of the brown liquid.

"Spoils of war and all that, speaking of which, this brings me to our next act and boy Georgie, you are in for a corker tonight, I can tell ya!" he said, now smirking at me over his rising bottle as he downed the rest of it before tossing it to one side, making it erupt in an explosion of glass near the crowd. Although, why they cheered at this I had no clue but it was like this guy was some kind of celebrity in here or something!

Then he threw up his cane once more before catching it and spinning it under his arm, this looked to be his signature move whilst on stage. After this he nodded towards the opening in the curtain where I was pushed to, and as a spotlight illuminated my frightened face, he used his cane to point at me before addressing the crowd once more.

"We happened to come across Little Red here…" He paused for a dramatic purpose so he could whisper the rest behind his hand as though what he was about to say was shocking,

"…Who is human." I frowned at the crowd when they all gasped before an echo of boos and insults were being called out.

"But Little Red here obviously got lost in the woods without grandma in sight, and didn't she know…" Again, he took another dramatic pause to whisper to his audience who were lapping up the theatrics.

"Down here there is more than one Big Bad Wolf to play with human bones!" It was at this point that everyone joined in the sickening fun and started howling at the cave's ceiling like they were mimicking a pack of wolves. As for me, I'd had enough and chose this moment to try and break free, pulling all my weight backwards. But it was no use as the dancers started to crowd around me, pushing me from behind, laughing as they did.

As for the man behind it all, he grinned at me before continuing his game.

"So, for one night only, I give you the Devil's Ring dancers and their new human pet, their very own Red Riding Hood... shake things up, girls!" he shouted, before dropping to curtesy as the girls all started taking to the stage, dragging me with them. Each of them were now dressed like sexy wolves, covering all their female assets with real looking fur and, had it not been for the ears and tails, I would have said they looked more like cavewomen in ruffle skirts.

They snarled and growled like kittens at the crowd, making the males wolf whistle and shout cat calls of a sexual nature to them. Oh, and boy did they seem to enjoy this, making the most of being the centre of everyone's attention.

As for me, I was still focused on Marcus, begging him with my panicked gaze not to do this. But I knew it was pointless when he raised his head from where he was still bent at the waist and winked at me. Then he rose to his full height and nodded to someone I couldn't see. This was when two more people emerged, adding to the act with instruments in their hands. A man dressed as a wolf who was definitely a lot less sexy and a whole lot more sinister. This was because he was wearing what looked like a suit made from an actual wolf skin, and the head part was worn as a hat making me want to gag, as it was still bloody. He carried with him an ornate Spanish guitar and as for the girl, she carried with her a violin that she soon tucked under her chin as soon as they reached the raised podium where the band obviously usually played.

A quick and furious beat began to play out as the dancers started calling out in tune with the song, and at the same time they started dancing around me in a mocking way. This fast folk fusion flamenco style of music made for a really good beat to dance to, and had I not been terrified I would have joined in. They were all kicking their legs out and tugging on the length of rope between my shackled hands that were like ornate handcuffs. This meant that I was pulled one way and then yanked another, making me dizzy as they spun around me.

They started to create a story as they made me start trying to get away from them so they could act as wolves trying to get me. They would reach out to me with their paw covered hands as if trying to scratch me, and then growl before dancing away on a spin.

Needless to say, I was getting pretty pissed off by this point as they continued to humiliate me in front of the crowd, and I knew that given half the chance I could have danced rings around these women! But then what was I talking about…

I did have the opportunity.

I was on a bloody stage!

Fine, if these freaks wanted a show, then I would damn right give them one! So, I waited until I knew the song would pick up again to its fastest point and that's when I started to move, dancing in a way that I knew the others would never keep up with. It was a fast enough song that my feet started to move without even asking them to. I was tap dancing, combining it with other moves that had my legs kicking out and spinning around before sweeping low to the floor, barely gracing my toes with the stage. I felt as if I could fly I was moving so fast, taking great steps around the stage and jumping in the air on a whole-body spin. I knew it looked both graceful and fierce combined with the pace of the music. For the first time since my life changed, I felt at peace. I felt at one with the music and completely lost to it. A slave to the notes that were being played so beautifully.

I didn't notice the crowd, I didn't notice the other dancers, nothing around the room that had once been a nightmarish world of horrors. None of it mattered anymore. It was just me, the stage and the music.

And I danced like it was my last.

A combination of so many hard things I had learned over the years, ballet, modern and expressive dance, along with moves I had mastered where others in my class hadn't. But then suddenly the music was coming to an end and my last move was the finishing touch on what had been a heart wrenching experience.

Like one last goodbye.

I leapt across the stage, spinning and lowering to the ground before bending my body back, lifting my leg straight over and around, creating a perfect circle of motion before it swept under me, and I propelled myself up so I now had my hands in the air, with my head thrown back. My hood fell from my head, and I felt the mass of curls of my long red hair fall back from my face and cascade down my back.

But a few seconds was all it took for my reality to start seeping back into my subconscious, and my situation slapped me across the face the moment I saw that shadow. And just like the dream I'd had on the plane over here, that single shadow was rooted to the spot and staring at me like a hungry wolf.

Only this time I had a name to go with the dangerous sight, and this time it wasn't Puppet Master.

No, it was…

Cerberus.

SEVEN

HELL BEAST KING

"*Oh God, no,*" I muttered on a barely heard whisper but somehow…

He heard it.

I knew it the moment he cocked his head to the side, as if he had just picked up the sound on the non-existent breeze or something. Jesus, I would have asked who the hell was this guy, but I knew. Of course, I knew.

It was him.

The one they all seemed terrified of. The one they called the Alpha. The HellBeast King. That's what he had said in my dreams and now here I was, facing the threat in real life! And I couldn't breathe, I couldn't move. I could do nothing but take in his terrifying presence and mentally drown by the power he held over me.

The dangerous wolf who looked as though he wanted to eat me. To devour me whole and lick his lips and grin the whole time he feasted on me. I could quite easily say that I had never been so frightened in all my life, and that included the endless minutes I had been trapped in this place! But the entirety of the room, the gruesome and the terrifying, those that I now knew were all real… well, they had nothing on him.

Nothing.

I knew why they called him what they did because, simply put, he was a beast of a man! He was threatening and intimidating and controlling even without needing to move a muscle, something he certainly had an overabundance of.

Just like in my dream, the guy was huge!

He looked as though he could have crushed me with a bear hug, and he was still stood in front of his throne with enough space between us that I knew I could run. That I could try and might still have a chance. Which is precisely when my mind came unstuck, and it decided that I wanted to live. So, despite the silent warning he gave me the second he knew my foolish decision was made, I started backing away slowly. But then, still keeping him in my sights just in case he decided to pounce suddenly, I noticed his handsome face start to change. His scowl deepened into a hard narrow gaze as if trying to pin me in place with just a look.

I gasped in fright.

And then the silent spell that had me entranced in his wordless trap vanished with the sound of the crowd going crazy. A crowd that unbelievably were going crazy for me. A mighty eruption of applause echoed around the cave and all for my dance. I swear, if I hadn't currently been hunted by their King, I would have allowed myself a moment to relish in my triumph, despite how much my bones ached… it had been worth it. Especially when I had a bad feeling it might have been my last, as the intense look he gave me was both deadly and soul consuming.

However, the sound of their admiration didn't only break the spell for me but for him also, as he was shaken out of his silent claim. The invisible chains snapped and the hold he had on me was shattered. Meaning, I did what any sane person would have done…

I ran from the wolf.

However, after turning round to run, I only made it four steps before doing a foolish thing when I heard that demonic growl of anger that had the power to shake the whole place behind me.

I looked back.

This meant that I nearly fell forward in an uncoordinated attempt at trying to escape, as the sight of his supremacy was impossible to miss. This was because I'd just caught sight of him as he lowered enough in his stance before he launched into motion. I screamed as I saw him power all his body forward in a run like a wild beast would do. This before throwing his weight forward in an astonishing show of strength as he leapt from the VIP platform, clearing the space between his throne and the stage, so in mere seconds my life was flashing before my eyes.

My oh so foolish life.

A foolish life that continued down that path of idiocy as I insanely believed I still had a chance. Which was why I turned back to the direction I was headed and continued to run from him, this time doing so to save my life. But that was when I felt it. The immense hum of power behind me, one that nearly had the strength to bring me to my knees! It was like a wall of strength I knew was closing in, and a heartbeat was all I was left with as it rose to stand behind me.

This was before I felt my shackled hands shift as if the cord attached to them was being caught. Something that was proven when I felt myself being tugged violently back, not just stopping me in my tracks, but whipping me around so fast it could have caused whiplash.

Just like he had done in my dream.

But then, just before I fell from the force of it with the floor being the only place I was headed, I was tugged again. This time it counteracted his strong actions and made me spin straight into…

My captor's arms.

It was in that moment that my entire world came crashing to a standstill, as if this was the most profound moment I had ever experienced so far. This, casting what I had thought had been into the shadows as if there had been nothing before meeting him. As if nothing would ever be the same again, and as if my body and heart had never coexisted before this point. As if suddenly my weak respiratory system wasn't the reason I was trying to claw in breath.

No, it was all down to him.

All down to the beast who now had me held captive in his unyielding hold. Jesus, but I didn't think I had ever seen such powerful raw masculine beauty before and when I did, I never would have thought it would have had the strength to consume me! To render me numb to everything else around me but him. This menacing ruler that I knew commanded his people with an iron fist. The handsome, hard lines of his face said as much. Those molten silver depths that narrowed and seemed to glow at the sight of my fear told me everything. Eyes that would have had the power to hold me prisoner even without the immense strength of his hold.

But in that look, there was something more, something I could tell he was trying to hide. Was it surprise? Shock at finding a human intruder in his sick and twisted club or… *something else?* Because I knew he was holding himself back, and no doubt it was stopping him from attacking me out right in front of our audience. Because, let's face it, after all I had seen on this stage and around this room, it was clear they were all here for one thing… blood or naked flesh.

Which made me then question why he hadn't done it already. Why hadn't he just given his people what they wanted yet? My confusion was added to when they all started to chant for the wolf to claim his prize… to claim his Little Red Riding Hood.

Of course, my hood had fallen down and left me with a mass of red curls sticking out in every direction, as I could feel my untameable hair all around me like a halo, one he suddenly seemed fascinated with.

In fact, one calloused, rough hand reached up, and I held myself so still, like some frightened fawn ready for the sound of a bullet to come tearing through the trees. His silver-grey eyes looked down at me, watching my every move, my every reaction as if he was studying me, willing me to react to him and please him. He was so tall… so much taller than me, that I only came up to his chest, as he towered over a head height above me.

But he surprised me further when his movements slowed after I visibly flinched. Which was when he finally spoke, and it was a soft rumble of words that held a roughness to them no matter how softly they were intended. This fact again shocked me in itself, for they weren't the harsh words of a threat or intimidation, but instead ones of… *comfort.*

"Easy now, Red."

I swear he could hear the hard lump I swallowed down as if I had been dropping a pebble in a well of water. In fact, the moment I saw him smirk, I refused to look at his eyes any longer, knowing the power they held over me. So, I focused on the other elements of his face. Like the trimmed facial hair those full lips were the centre of, hair that tapered down into a full beard ending just past his chin. This matched the long, thick hair that was a strange charcoal grey colour and was currently tied back from his chiselled face. One made to look even more frightening by the wicked scar that started at his brow and made a jagged journey down the side of his face before snaking back into his hairline by his jaw.

But his face was actually the softest part about him if that could even be believed. Because the rest of him was all solid muscle, starting with his wide shoulders that managed to block out most of the world beyond him. Thick, muscled biceps that the leather jacket he wore didn't hide, and those long legs encased in dark denim, screaming out that biker was his choice of style. This was confirmed when he finally reached my hair and took possession of one of my curls, causing my shame to get the best of me. It made me lower my head, finding first his heavy skull and bones belt buckle, and then further down his heavy biker boots. A pair that looked well-worn and only half tied as if he just couldn't be bothered wasting the time doing them all the way up.

Of course, I couldn't help during this journey of discovery to notice the hard ridges of his stomach just barely seen beneath the thin material of his dark T shirt beneath the leather. Jesus, but did this man have a single place on him that was soft or did the guy just live in the gym? But then again, that idea of him didn't exactly fit either, as I could more likely put his incredible body down to chopping wood with an axe. Or maybe he too was a fighter and was a regular in the ring, pounding on demonic faces?

I couldn't help but shudder at the idea, and he took the reason for what it was… *fear.*

"Soft," he muttered to himself in regards to my hair, as if he was surprised or maybe it was confirmation he wanted. I just didn't know. I mean, I knew my hair was soft, as my hairdresser usually commented on it, as it wasn't as coarse as it looked and often surprised people because it was so thick as well. But then curls were often soft, weren't they? Oh God, and now I was here in front of

this gentle brute questioning my own damn hair!

I didn't know how long we were stood here for, as it felt as if we were trapped like this, and time had stopped because of it. But in reality, it couldn't have been more than a few minutes. Yet even that I knew was too long, as I could tell the crowd was becoming shocked that their king hadn't yet got on with the maiming and bloodletting part of claiming his human intruder.

"Young and oh so naïve," he said with that rumble to his tone that I could have quite easily become addicted to… that is if I had been suicidal of course.

"Please," I finally whispered, and the second I said this I knew I had done something wrong as suddenly his hand snaked in my curls and tightened before he yanked my head back, so I had no choice but to be forced to look into his eyes.

"Mmm… now I must admit, I do like the sound of that word coming from those tempting lips of yours… shame then, *that they come from a human."* He snarled this last part and I flinched back, or at least tried to, but he tightened his hold on me. His other hand was held at my waist and his fingers flexed hard enough to make me whimper. But that little moan couldn't be helped as I knew his hold would leave bruises. But this wasn't because of his intent to harm me but more an after effect of my defective body. I wasn't like most humans he would have known. I was one in a hundred thousand after all.

No, I would not think about it right now.

I would not think of the pain dancing would cause me. Because I knew nothing would be more painful than being forced to watch as the days went by and those bruises would fade, and the memory of his touch would leave my skin. As if this night never happened, and what a freak it made me to admit that I didn't want that.

Not now.

Not after… him.

But then I had to remember what the others had said. I had to remember all those warnings. This beast didn't like humans, and I swear I had never wished to be anything but human before that moment. Just anything that would have made this wolf want me. And yes, it was official… I was broken.

Insane.

Lost.

Which is what I decided to tell him.

"I… I am just lost… so please, just don't…" I paused

when a small growl vibrated from his chest, and I swear that I felt it in my toes!

"Don't what?!" he snapped, and I flinched again and closed my eyes before telling him,

"Dd... don't... eat me," I whispered, making him suddenly chuckle, and my eyes snapped open as he growled down with mirth,

"I make no such promise, my Lost Little Red." Then as my mouth dropped open in shock, he suddenly let me go and just as I was about to take a step back, thinking this was my true answer, I shrieked out in surprise. He wasn't letting me go at all... no, he was just making his next move. One that started with him ducking his large body and planting his wide shoulder in my belly before tossing me up over it like a fireman.

"Ah!" I shouted, as he stormed over to the edge of the stage and jumped from it like he had a feather pillow over his shoulder and not a five-foot two girl that was now utterly blinded by hair and leather.

At this the crowd went wild, cheering for their king, and I had no other choice but to hold on, gripping a fist full of his jacket and praying with every step he took it wouldn't be my last. That the very real threat of this handsome harsh beast wasn't about to end with the sight of my blood spilling over his skin under some full moon.

Of course, I had very little faith in this hope for my future that didn't include me taking my last breath. Especially when I suddenly found myself being dragged up and then down the length of his huge body. This was before I was walked backwards until a wall was felt at my back and I had nowhere else to go. I was trapped, even more so when with each step he took, he wrapped the length of rope in between my bound hands tighter and tighter around his fist. Then, when there was little left, he lifted it above my head, meaning that my hands had no choice but to move with it.

Soon enough I was trapped, not only with his large intimidating body against me, but also by having my hands pinned above my head like some virginal sacrifice.

"Wwhat are you… going to do with me?" I asked, with fear making my voice wobble, something he liked the sound of if the smirk was anything to go by. Which was when he leaned closer, dipping his head down so he could whisper in an amused tone,

"What do you think I am going to do with you, Red…? After all, you can hear the crowd, and I am what they say

I am."

"And what's that?" His eyes sparked with amusement before he told me,

"I am their HellBeast King and guardian of the gates of Hell… and unfortunately for you, little human…" he paused so his next words were said against my cheek…

"You just wandered into my own brand of Hell."

EIGHT

A CHILLING PROMISE

The second I heard this, was when I finally snapped out of these mental chains he had me wrapped up in. However, when I struggled, it was the very real chains that became my biggest problem. Well, the shackles and the beast who held them in his grasp.

"Let me go!" I shouted, now twisting my body and trying to use my weight as a way to pull free of his hold. But then I should have known this was pointless as his strength was far too great to fight against. Although, I had to say I was surprised, as instead of the threat I expected growled back, he simply stepped closer, pinning me with more than just his hand. This making me swallow hard as he now kept me restrained me with his body before he looked down at me.

"Easy, girl, I didn't say I was going to harm you," he said as softly as what I knew a man like him was capable of, the knowledge of which made me still instantly.

"Yyyour not going to… to hurt me?" I stammered out, making him grin down at me, and for once it seemed genuine and not one with the sole purpose of evil mocking. I knew that when, with his free hand, he skimmed the backs of his thick, strong fingers down my cheek, then as he watched their journey he told me,

"No, Red, I am not going to hurt you." I released a deep and relieved sigh but then he leaned in closer, so his molten silver eyes were all I saw. Then, this time bred from more lust than anger, he told me on a throaty growl,

"But not all punishments are physically painful, *Pet of mine.*"

Just as he was about to dip his head enough to cut out the inches that kept us apart, he turned his head and snarled. I froze in his hold at the threatening sound, one he had made as if he had heard something coming from behind that he didn't like. However, it was such a frightening sound that I started struggling in his hold once more, making him snap his gaze back at me. I flinched at its terrifying harshness, something that changed instantly when he took notice of my fear.

"Word to the wise, Red… *in my Hell, your fear is intoxicating to feed from.*" Then he lifted my chin up as if silently telling me not to be afraid, which was a contradiction to telling me it was intoxicating.

"Jared, no!" This time I heard the desperate cry coming from my cousin, something he must have heard before I had, the first time she shouted it. As now Amelia had reached us and was frantically trying to get him to stop what he was doing to me. Which, unbeknown to her, was sort of comforting me, as I didn't get the sense that he was going to go back on his word and suddenly lash out at me in anger. But then I had to be honest, I was utterly shocked at how brave my cousin was when she finally reached us and grabbed the beast's arm trying to get him to release me.

Was she crazy!

And what had she called him… *Jared.*

Was that his first name?

Jared.

Jared Cerberus.

It suited him.

"She's my cousin! Please, Jared, it was my fault! She didn't know... Gods... Jared, she... she didn't know," Amelia said, looking towards me with nothing but sorrow in her eyes and the guilt of it all was easy to see. Jared looked down at her, taking in all she had to say before the mention of who I was made his eyes snap back to me. It was as if he was seeing me for the first time all over again.

"She is... she is Dominic Draven's niece?" The way he said this was like some kind of spell being broken for him as the words were growled down at Amelia. She nodded telling him yes, before adding,

"She is my mum's sister's daughter and very much... *human.*" At this my eyes widened, knowing that this was the confirmation I needed... my aunt's life was a lie. The Dravens weren't who they said they were. My eyes must have said as much as Amelia looked to me and whispered,

"Ella... Gods, I am so sorry." I tore my face away and Jared growled again, but this time it was for a new reason as someone else had joined our little group. A person that I couldn't help now frown in question at, asking silently who he was.

I mean, there was no doubting it, he was utterly gorgeous and at a guess around my age, possibly younger. It was hard to tell as he was so tall for his age and already packing muscle, even if it was on a slim build. Nothing like the raw and powerful man that still held me as his prisoner. But even I knew that when he became an adult, that would be a different story. In fact, he reminded me a bit like my aunt, making me wonder if there was some connection. His hair was a similar blonde colour, if not a little darker. He also had that typical boy next door thing going on, making him cute one minute and then handsome the next. However, right now, there wasn't a soft line on him as he was tense and looked ready for a fight…

Ready to play the hero.

Well, it had to be said, he definitely had balls to go up against Jared, that was for damn sure! I mean, the guy didn't even flinch a muscle when Jared growled at the intrusion, making me jerk back. Jesus, but it was still one of the most frightening sounds I had ever heard, and one I doubted I would ever get used to without reacting in fear. But then Jared didn't seem to like this and shocked both my cousin and the mystery boy she stood next to when he turned back to me. Then, in that raspy gentle tone of his, he hummed down at me,

"Ssshh, calm for me, my Little Red." I quickly sucked in a shocked breath, surprised at how deeply it affected me.

"Please, Jared, she didn't know, she was just following me as she was worried about me… this is my fault, please don't hurt her," Amelia said, pleading for me now, as she was clearly worried that this beast who held me captive was planning on hurting me, no doubt just like he would do to other human trespassers found in his club. But then, just before he had chance to respond, the handsome teenager tensed his muscles and added a threat, telling me he was either crazy, had no fear or that he was more powerful than he looked.

"Do as she says and let her go!" This time Jared snarled down at him over his shoulder, and to give the teen his due yet again, he didn't even flinch, neither did he back down. But when the lad didn't make a threatening move towards him, Jared's snarl turned into a sinister grin, one that was turned on me the moment he heard me suck in another ragged breath.

However, the second he did, the handsome teen took a step forward, obviously fearing for my safety, when it was Amelia who stopped him. Doing so with a shake of her head and by slapping a hand over his chest, telling him quietly,

"Don't be a hero." The boy scowled down at her, being that he was taller than us both, and despite his boyish features, his size definitely said he was older.

Of course, I wasn't given long to ponder on his age as I was still in the beast's clutches and before either of them could act, his gaze snapped back to Jared's, because Jared, the HellBeast King, was obviously about to do something out of character. Now making both Amelia and her friend looked utterly astonished when my captor once again showed me what must have been an unusual sign of kindness. He raised his hand to my cheek and then, as he slowly pushed back what I knew was a riot of red curls back from my face, it looked how it felt… *like a gentle caress.*

"I will let her go…" he said to Amelia. But then, just as I released a premature sigh of relief, he suddenly gripped my chin. My fearful eyes snapped to both Amelia and her friend, silently asking them to help me… when it was clear Jared didn't like this. Which was why he forced my chin up so my eyes could only focus on him and no other. Then, once he had a hundred percent of my attention, he finished off his statement, and this time there was no way you could miss the threat that coated every word.

"...But be warned, Little Red, the next time I find you in my club... *this wolf may not be so quick to give you back.*" I sucked in a sharp breath, one that turned into a yelp of fright when he suddenly pulled down my arms. Then after taking my wrists in his large hands, he yanked hard enough that the chain between my shackles snapped. But the strangest thing of all was that even during this brutal action, it was almost like he did it in a way so he wouldn't hurt me.

But then, before I could even linger on this thought, he spun me away from him and pushed me into Amelia's arms, as if he was done with me. I had to say, I should have felt nothing but relieved, but then that would have been a lie. Because I foolishly felt something deeper. Something profoundly more painful. As it was like he said,

Punishments weren't always physically painful... and well, he was right. Because his dismissal of me was the most painful of all. So, when I hugged on to my cousin, I did so now less with the relief I knew I should feel, but more so out of needing the comfort from pain he inflicted on my heart.

I was after all… *a foolish girl.*

"Orthrus, take the girl back to where she came from!" Jared barked out the order, making me wince in Amelia's arms, hating how indifferent his tone now sounded. How just moments ago I could have believed I had meant something to him. Something more than just a little prisoner to have a bit of fun with. But like this, then what I was to him couldn't have been more clear.

Nothing.

I was nothing more than an intruder in his world. One that didn't belong. One that was inferior. I was the outsider and a human he loathed. So yeah, the pain he inflicted just kept coming, along with his harsh scowling gaze he directed at me before refusing me another glance.

Now, as for who he had been speaking to, this was a huge hulk of a black guy, one who looked as if he bench pressed other security guards in the gym! I mean, Jared was big, but this guy was definitely a contender for beating him in size. But like his king, he was also drop dead gorgeous and looked as if he should have been playing handsome villains in Bond movies!

But then this was when something curious happened. The man named Orthrus was just about to reach for me, when Jared got there first and stopped him. He did so by grabbing hold of his arm in his meaty grasp. Then with a stern look he spoke to him in another language, giving him another order, and one I didn't understand. However, when Amelia sucked in a surprised breath and looked at him as if asking who he was, I knew she had understood and was shocked by it.

As for the big black guy, he nodded once and now, instead of trying to reach for me, he just nodded his head in the direction he wanted me to go. Which had me wondering if his order had been not to touch me?

I looked back at Amelia who let me go, squeezing my hand before she nodded to the one named Orthrus and told me,

"It will be fine, Ella, you can trust them, I promise, they won't hurt you." But this was when I finally snapped, having enough of the untruths that she had allowed to stretch between us all her life. Because she wasn't just my cousin, she was also someone I considered a best friend. A friendship that went beyond being thrown together as family but a deeper connection.

But as for all of this… well, it simply felt as if I didn't know her at all. I didn't know anyone. Not my uncle or my aunt. And as for my mom and dad, did they even know? Had they too kept this part of the world from me? In fact, right now, the only one who had seemingly been truthful with me was Jared and his minions, and I very much doubted that had been done out of kindness!

Which was why I first cautiously looked back at Jared before allowing my anger to bite back.

"And you?! What about you, Fae?" Amelia released a heavy sigh before telling me,

"I know this all seems crazy, but I promise I will explain everything to you." I scoffed at her promise and narrowed my eyes at her pleading tone as if she was willing me to trust her. Which was why I warned,

"You'd better, Fae, or the next person I will be speaking to is your parents about this place because something tells me it's not just you that's been keeping secrets but in fact, your whole family!" I shouted, making her flinch as if I had physically struck her, and I guess it would have felt that way. Especially as she had often confessed to me that I was the only one she felt like she could really connect with sometimes. And well, if this world was true, then I now knew why.

I was the only bit of normality in her life.

Something that Jared had made sound like an insult…

'Mmm… now I must admit, I do like the sound of that word coming from those tempting lips of yours… shame then, that they come from a human.' That's what he had said. As if saying he would have found me tempting had I not been some lowly human. Hell, right here I wasn't just a little fish in a bigger pond, but I was the wrong damn species altogether!

Which was why, after one more glance at Jared, I let him see for just a spilt second the anger I let consume me as I narrowed my eyes at him, totally ignoring the frown it created on that handsome face of his, before tearing my eyes from both of them.

Then I left, following the guy called Orthrus and turning my back on this world. Turning my back on this madness.

But most of all,

Turning my back on a HellBeast King who…

Watched me leave.

NINE

SUPERNATURAL KINGS
11 YEARS LATER...

'*Shame then, that they come from a human.*'

"Ah!" I shouted as I bolted upright from my bed, and like many nights before, I woke with his face as the last I saw before reality took hold once more. Reality… ha! That safe place where I can try and pretend that fateful night never happened. One where Jared Cerberus was a name I didn't know, and one that didn't come with those perfect lips framed by rough skin and dark facial hair. A name that didn't come with biker clothes and large manly hands that shamefully had felt so good on my skin. A reality that didn't come with piercing molten silver eyes and an overabundance of hard muscles, that had unfortunately featured far too many times in dreams of a very different type.

Those were the worst and the hardest to pull back from.

The ones where he tells me I'm human and then tugs me closer to him before growling down at me how he doesn't care. How he can't stop himself from wanting me anyway. The ones where I melt into him and beg him to make me his.

To claim me.

Yes... *those were the worst.*

Those were the ones that clung to my brain like an infection that would take days to pass. Of course, they were less frequent these days. Not like before. No, for weeks, months, even years, if I were being honest, they would haunt me. Dreams of him and his world. Dreams of him saving me, and being the one in place of Marcus, it was him that I would first bump into. He would be the one that would make me dance for him. Watching, not just as a man in the shadows, but sat on that mighty throne of his as he watched me glide across the dance floor just for him. Eventually the rest of the club I had been running from would simply disappear with a click of his strong fingers and we would be completely alone.

Just the two of us.

Oh yes, that dream had haunted me the most.

But that had been back then. And even though now he still managed to sneak in there, it wasn't anywhere near as often as it had been before. And yet, with this still being said, I had to admit that even after over a decade had passed since that night and the one and only time I had seen him, his image still held power over me. Because with time, I would have thought his image would have faded. I would have thought it would have twisted into a mess of uncertain factors. Questions like, were his eyes really that same intense silver grey as I remembered? Were his hands as large as they had felt when they gripped my waist? Had the bruises he'd left really taken that long to disappear?

But I knew every answer meant it was pointless even asking them. And as for those bruises, the ones he most likely had no idea he would have given me, then I will never forget the day I woke and found they had finally gone. As if the very last trace of him and that night had vanished and never happened. I couldn't have helped it even if I tried, which I did and failed. Failed as I slumped down on the floor in the bathroom and cried.

I had cried so hard.

I had cried until I could barely breathe.

My failure of a body unable to cope. Like it wasn't strong enough for the pain. It wasn't strong enough for the heartache. Well, that had been yet another trip to the hospital and another handshake with a respirator. Not that Amelia knew, as after what had happened with her sneaking out and what came after, then not surprisingly she had been shipped off to Scotland for a while (for her own safety, she said). I couldn't help but feel sorry for her after that. Because she described it all to me as soon as she could, which was the next day in the hotel room.

Although, the moment I saw her looking less than perfect, I freaked out, thinking it had been because of me. But then the moment I saw her own bruises, my hands flew to my face, and I shook my head already making excuses for a man I didn't know,

"No, no… he wouldn't… tell me… he couldn't have…" This was when she had taken pity on me and told me it hadn't been Jared. I had nearly collapsed to the floor with relief, one that wasn't logical. Then she took me in her arms and cried with me. Hell, we both cried for a good hour, and did so until we somehow ended up sitting on the sofa in our hotel room whilst she spent most of the day explaining everything to me.

You see, my cousin may have kept some pretty big things from me, but she also always kept her promises, and that following day was when she kept the biggest one of all.

She explained her world.

But it was more than that… she also explained why it was she had never told me, and I had to be honest that by the time she was finished, I finally understood. I understood it all. I understood why.

This was because if I myself hadn't witnessed what must have been only a glimpse of it, then I wouldn't have believed a word she said. It had been so unbelievable; it was little wonder she had never told me before. Because as sad as it is to admit, I would have been more inclined to have believed her being crazy than to believe in the fantasy world it seemed she had just created in her mind. A hidden world where demons and angels walked the Earth under the guise of being 'mortal'. Just everyday regular humans who lived their mundane lives in blissful naivety, unaware of the supernatural power of Heaven and Hell that surrounded them.

I mean, I could understand why it was all kept secret to be honest. The human world would no doubt crumble into chaos if they knew their beliefs about God and other religions were not what they thought. That there were those out there that were so powerful they could literally destroy millions and take over the world with a simple thought, seeing as many of them held power over the minds of others. But then why didn't it happen…

Because my uncle didn't let it happen, that was why.

It was in this moment that I discovered why the name Dominic Draven had made such an impact with Jared. Because my uncle was the powerhouse that ruled it all. He was known as the King of Kings and ruled over every supernatural that resided in the Earth realm. He was the judge, jury and executioner to them all, and one of the biggest rules there was for others to follow, was no impacting mortal life.

For he was the keeper of order and balance.

He was the reason that his kind didn't become presidents, or world leaders. Of course, Amelia admitted this hadn't always been the case as her father had once been a Persian King over two thousand years ago, and he hadn't been the only supernatural in power over humans. Naturally she didn't go into details, as she also admitted that she shouldn't be telling me any of this either as it was kind of another rule they lived by.

But then, my biggest shock of all came from when I asked Fae what she was. I would never forget the look of sadness on her face, and I had to say that when she gave me her answer, after what Jared had said to me, I could honestly say that in that moment… *I felt her pain.*

"I am human, Ella… just a plain old human." And I knew she hadn't said it to hurt me, but more in a way that told me she needed me. That growing up in a world where your dad was one of the most powerful supernatural beings in the world and his daughter had not even a slither of it, was going to be difficult for her. This she admitted, along with the reasons why she had gone there that night.

Lucius.

Lucius had been his name and as unbelievable as it sounded, he was actually the King of all Vampires. God, but even now after all this time I still found this stuff hard to swallow. Hard to believe. Hard to… *accept.* To know that night I had been stood in a club full of demons and yes, crazy to think but even some angels too… it… Jesus, it was all too... *horrific*. The stuff of nightmares and Heaven and Hell being the very place they were born from. The very myths that had spread knowledge of these creatures throughout the ages I now knew had once been a very real seed planted. They were all true, just like realising that my uncle was one...

A demon king that was.

My uncle, the man who had changed my diapers, babysat me and fed me chocolate and candy with a secret pinkie swear pact not to tell my mom. My Aunty Kaz who I adored growing up and really, still did as she was awesome and funny. Oh, and who I now knew, according to Amelia, was totally kickass. But the hardest part, was that I knew this secret about them. I knew all about their world thanks to their daughter, yet I was unable to say anything. I just had to continue to play along with their human charade and ignore the truth.

That demons and angels were real.

That Vampires and HellBeasts were real.

And that was what he was... *Jared Cerberus.*

Fae had told me about him of course. He was another King and the strongest of his kind. A shifter of sorts she said. An Alpha that used to guard the gates of Hell for the

Devil… and oh yeah, that dude was real too. Jesus, it had all become too much at that point. At that moment I had held up my hand and begged her to stop, admitted I could take no more. Thankfully she could see it was the truth. She could see the weight of it all, like sand raining down, closing in, and a few secrets more was all it would have taken to bury me under.

And who was at the centre of it all but my obsession…

A HellBeast King.

TEN

DECKS AND SHADOWS

Of course, I hadn't admitted it at the time, but one look at my face whenever she mentioned him, and she knew. She knew because she felt it too. She felt it for her own King, and one who saved her from being taken by her father's enemies that same night. At least that was what she told me when I asked about what happened to her.

It was then that she told me why her father had been so strict on keeping her safe, and it all made perfect sense. Because his worst nightmare had happened the moment he let his guard down. Which was enough of a reason to keep my distance and keep my promise of silence. Because those

I told would only end up being put in danger. It was the reason we rarely got invited to Afterlife, because keeping us at arm's length was the only way to ensure our safety. A way to keep my aunty Keira's human family protected, and I knew that he was right to do so.

My uncle, a man of integrity. A man of honour. But he wasn't a man at all, was he? In truth, after that moment in my life, it was the reason I left. I never told Amelia that, as I didn't want her to feel anymore guilty than I knew she already did. But I would be lying if I said it didn't play a part in my decision to leave. My decision not to go to college in my hometown took everyone by surprise... *everyone but Fae.* But then it surprised people even more when I decided to look for my dream job away from Evergreen Falls after I graduated. Of course, I hadn't expected for it to be in, Nelson, British Columbia, a forty-four-hour drive or sixteen hours on a plane.

Needless to say, my parents were crushed, something I still felt the guilt of today. But then all my life there were only two dreams for me to follow, and with one being snatched from me at only sixteen, then there was only one love left.

Animal conservation.

I didn't know what it was, but for some reason I seemed to have some sort of kinship with animals. A silent way of communicating with them which always surprised people. Hell, even the other rangers called me the fur whisperer and joked that when a call came in about a wild animal in need of help, they would say,

"It's time to send in the big guns." Meaning me.

It was my gift, and it was my passion. Of course, I couldn't really speak to animals, but I felt a sort of infinity with them. As if I could almost feel their pain or know exactly what it was they were searching for. And stranger still, more often than not, even the most hostile of animals would calm for me, where they wouldn't for others.

So, because of this, it meant that I was good at my job, and others knew it too. Which was why I quickly gained the respect as a Senior Park Ranger, and boy did the job keep me busy. This being because there was a lot of ground to cover. There was West Arm Provincial Park in the Kootenays with its diverse range of habitats, from lakeshore to subalpine, high-elevation forests and alpine areas. The Park protected important First Nations archaeological sites, situated along the shore of Kootenay Lake, and there was a historic trail up Lasca Creek, that wasn't maintained.

As for me, that was where I lived, on a waterfront property located at the nine mile stretch of Kootenay Lake. A place that offered privacy and buffered the highway sound. A ten-acre property that had over a hundred feet of waterfront.

What was most usual about it was that I got to enjoy the beauty and serenity of the Kootenay lake despite its proximity to Nelson, which was less than a fifteen-minute drive away. Of course, this property wasn't mine, but I was blessed to get to live here all the same. You see, when I turned eighteen, my parents surprised me by buying me the truck I always wanted. A 1997 Ford F250 XLT Crew Cab 4x4 that was rusted and needed a ton of work doing to it. But I didn't care as I fell in love instantly. You see it wasn't only fishing and camping my dad and I enjoyed doing together. And much to my mom's despair, I too had inherited his love of cars and basically all things that came with an engine and four wheels, old trucks being at the very top of the list.

After that we spent the summer doing it up together, starting on the long list of things that needed fixing or replacing. Like the manual locking front hubs that had seized, which meant that when we got it, it was permanently stuck in 4-wheel drive. The sliding rear window also needed replacing as it was leaking and wasn't fun when it rained. But the biggest job, was the whole engine needed a rebuild, which certainly would have taken a hefty chunk out of my college fund had it not been for my Uncle Dom. Someone who made it his mission to pay for the parts needed and of course, they were the very best. Which meant that on the outside, my 1997 truck may have looked old, but under the hood was a whole other story.

She was a beast.

In fact, not that anyone knew, but I had even nicknamed her the HellBeast, giving into the fact that yes, I was reminded of Jared whenever I swung myself up inside her. In hindsight this was a mistake but being that I got the truck a few months before the whole London trip, well let's just say the obsession had already taken root by the time we started working on the rusty girl.

Now, as for the other love in my life that went along side it, was my home. A rare 1990 AVION 38M aluminium 5th wheel travel trailer, complete with blue stripes down the side. It was also a graduation present from my grandparents who had bought it brand new, and thankfully didn't mind me making a few changes to get away from the retro 90's décor. They had passed it on, making me squeal with delight as I had always loved playing in it as a kid. Of course, my dad also had fond memories of it as a kid when vacationing with his parents and younger brother, my uncle Justin. So naturally he was pleased it was staying in the family.

But this basically meant that wherever I went, I was set up in my own home and could work anywhere the road would take me, and that road had led me to where it was still parked to this day, eight years later. This was thanks to one of the first friends I made when I arrived for my new job, fresh faced and just out of college. It was when I met Rex, a retired Park Ranger who was the guy chosen to show me the ropes.

Rex Hoffman was about as loyal and generous as they came. which was why he took one look at my old 90's 5th wheel that was rusting at the wheel arches, and told me he knew a great place I could park it. That's when I discovered this prized gem. Then he shocked me further when he told me it was his and that I would be doing him a favour parking here so I could keep an eye on the place.

The story went that he inherited it years ago with the

intention of building a house for him and his wife, being somewhere they could retire in. Heartbreakingly, he was only a year away from that when his wife passed away from cancer, and since then he found himself caught between an emotional rock and a hard place. On one side he hated coming here as it was a reminder of what he could never have. And on the other hand, he didn't have the heart to sell it as his wife had instantly fallen in love with the place.

Of course, he didn't tell me all of this on the first day I met him. No, it took years and twelve beers to get this story from him… *twelve.* Rex was hardcore when it came to drinking. Not that he had a problem with drink, it was just that when he did, then, Jesus, he could have put bikers to shame!

Needless to say, I loved Rex. He was like family and would often come and spend an evening sat on my deck, one we built together after he said for the tenth time,

"So, girly, you planning on staying here or what, cause if you are, then shit me, you need a deck to go with these beers?" Those were his exact words, I shit you not, and I say this because that was Rex, he liked to say shit… *a lot.* Even the steaks I cooked the night we finished my new deck were classed as 'the shit'. But in my mind, they were no way as great as having a place to eat them and cook them, doing so on my new grill whilst we sat looking over the lake with a fresh beer in hand.

Now, it had taken a lot to get me to that point, nearly two years in fact before he actually accepted my invite of steak and beers. It was the first time that he finally gave in and agreed to let me thank him for the lakeside view I woke up to every morning.

Two years for me to give him my thank you.

Which was when he had been on his twelfth beer and told me the story about his wife.

I cried.

He finished his beer, and after complaining about me needing real outdoor furniture to sit on and calling my fold out chairs shit, he thanked me for the food and beer and opened the door to my 5th wheel and said,

"I am taking the couch." And he did. Which was something he now did any time he came over and drank beer. He was sound like that. Hated drinking and driving and swore off anyone who ever did. He'd say, they can put their own lives at risk any damn day of the week but others… Hell no!

I had to say, I agreed with him on that one, one hundred

percent.

And this was precisely what I was thinking about when I made my morning coffee as I looked out to my awesome view and my place of solitude. A place where one Jared Cerberus would never step foot in, and the only beasts I had to deal with were the ones who roamed too close to civilization.

Or at least, this was what I had blissfully thought for the last eight years I had been here. Of course, I had been home since then but mainly only for the holidays, and then my parents would come here, staying at the Ainsworth Hot Springs resort not far away.

I could honestly say I was living the good life.

A life I had built, and other than having to travel to Vancouver once every two weeks for a few hours of treatments, then life was normal. As normal as I had made it. As normal as I had forced it to be. I had turned my back on my cousin's terrifying world and spent years pushing it to the shadows of my mind. And for the most part, it worked. However, during the night hours was when it got complicated. Because I had to sleep, and it was in those moments that I was helpless to those shadows. Shadows that wanted to come out and play with me. To torture me on how it had once felt to be held captive by those rough hands and prisoner to that heated silver gaze.

To be consumed by the memory of him.

In my dreams I was powerless to stop them. Powerless against him, just like I had been that night. And what I didn't know that morning when blissfully looking out to my serene normal life, was that it would mark the last day it would be like this.

And history was about to repeat itself and throw me hurtling back into that world I had tried so hard to run from. And unfortunately for me, there was only one man I would have to beg to catch me, and it all started with just...

A phone call.

ELEVEN

COFFEE AND BEASTS

"And here she is, mud coffee girl," Jenny said the moment the bell rang above the door, making her look over her shoulder at me. Much Mocha Love was the name of the coffee shop that was owned by the only person I knew who didn't like coffee but would tolerate just a hint of it in a cup full of chocolate, hence the name. She served every type of mocha flavour you could think of but what she sold most of… was yep, you guessed it, *it was just coffee.*

Which meant that when I started coming in and ordering the strongest black coffee they had, I was named mud coffee girl. Even to this day she still would hand the cup over with a disgusted look that wrinkled her nose.

But then I also knew this was the way she would remember her regulars' names and what their orders usually were. Hence why I sat down at the small counter at the end of where Jenny made the coffees and grinned at another friend of mine. Actually, he had only been in town for the last three months, but he was who I was quickly considering one of my favourite people in Nelson, apart from Rex of course.

"Hey, Captain Cappuccino," I said, mocking Jenny's nickname for him, making him groan in that deep masculine way of his. Of course, his actual name was Orson Esben and the best way to describe Orson would be a cross between some sexy trucker and an even sexier lumberjack.

Eyes like brown sugar looked back at me, with that slight crinkle of lines at the corners near his hair line. There were sometimes three of them when he really smiled. Yes, I had counted. Okay, so it was safe to say that since he'd sat down to speak to me three months ago and asked me what was good, I had started to develop my crush. But trying to play it cool, I had swirled the remainder of my black 'mud' coffee at him and said,

"If you want rocket fuel and to be awake at three in the morning watching crap on tv, go with black." At this he grinned and said back to a near swooning Jenny,

"I will take a Cappuccino."

After that, I admittedly would nearly swoon myself when seeing him, and secretly emitted a sigh of lustful dreaming every encounter since. Of course, it was nowhere near the mind explosive experience I had been given at the tender age of eighteen by the first man that I ever wanted to throw my V card at, begging him to take it like some willing sacrificial virgin thrown at the beast to save the village from… okay, okay, so yes it also had to be said that my imagination could run away with me sometimes. And well, no wonder after that experience!

But back to Orson, and his sexy sideways glance, something he always did when sitting next to me. In fact, this had become our daily routine since that day, where we would both come in for our afternoon coffee break at the same time. Of course, I had also had him round my trailer for grilled steaks with Rex and me, as I knew they would get on like a house on fire.

In fact, I could also tell that Rex thought he would make a perfect match for me, as let's just say he hadn't been subtle with his hints, saying things like, I'd best be leaving early and leaving you two young kids to your evening. That night he'd had half a light beer and didn't sleep on my couch that folded into a bed. No, that night, it had known a new guest…

Orson.

But then, after a few nights like this and over the space of three months, I'd pretty much given up all hope of him being interested as anything other than a friend. Sure, we flirted, but it never went beyond that. A few fleeting touches here and there, once hinting I was a beautiful woman, and then there was what I had named 'the Thursday cheek caress' when we had been out by the lake and the sun was going down. He had told me that the sun shining through it made my hair look like the feathers of a phoenix. I blushed nearly the colour of my hair as he brushed back the curls to tuck behind my ear with his thick callused hands. And yes, I was quite aware of this little fact, as I now had a thing for large manly hands after a certain biker HellBeast had put his own on me.

But then, that was half the problem, everything always came back to him. Like Orson's square jaw, one not as defined as Jared's. Eyes softer and less piercing as Jared's.

A body that was big and burly but not quite as big or hard as Jared's. It was always the same thing. Every guy compared to who was becoming more like a myth or legend than someone who was physically real.

Although, this most likely wasn't true as Orson was a big guy, but then that wasn't surprising seeing as he was a lumberjack and literally hauled around trees for a living. I mean, he even wore a red and black snap button plaid shirt for God's sake. This was combined with the classic stonewash jeans and workman steel toe cap boots that looked capable of crushing skulls. If I wasn't mistaken, then I think the term was shitkicker boots.

But then, with the weather changing cooler, as fall was getting ready to change to winter, he combined this favoured look of his with a dark tan suede jacket that had a cream borg collar. This meant I had months ahead of me before I would be once more awarded the sight of those corded muscular forearms, as he usually rolled up his shirt sleeves.

"Hey, Mud Coffee girl," he replied with a warm smile and a wink, that would have half the town throwing their panties at him before they self-combusted into a cracking firework sparking under their skirts. Yes… he was literally, *that hot.*

As for me, well I wasn't exactly conventional looking but then a girl with my colour hair never was going to be. This was because it was a natural cherry red colour that was streaked darker auburn underneath with flecks of amber streaks on top. Meaning I literally looked like my head was on fire when in the sun, or like a phoenix as Orson had commented. And then there were the uncontrollable spiral curls that I usually kept contained back in a bun or ponytail. One that ended up big enough it looked like a head of curls was constantly following me. I mean, even my friend in college used to make me put my head down between my legs when pulling out of a junction to check nothing was coming, as my head of hair would block the view of traffic.

Hence why I grew it long as if I cut it, I would end up looking like a funky red microphone. As for the rest of me, I had large, light green eyes that had flecks of amber in them, that were framed with long, dark red lashes that naturally curled up and tickled my lids. I also had a roundish face with one dimple that appeared whenever I smiled, and a light speckling of freckles across my nose and cheeks that deepened when in the sun for too long. These features also meant that I had a youthful baby face which was nice when people thought you were a lot younger than you were. But then not so much when you wanted to be taken seriously, say when dealing with important matters and asserting your authority, something that with my job, I had to do on occasion. Of course, normally it was nothing too major, simply asking for camping permits and fishing licences, that sort of thing.

In fact, the worst incident I'd experienced so far had been only three months ago when I had come in contact with a bunch of guys camping and celebrating a birthday or something. They had got drunk, started fires in reckless ways and were basically asking to get themselves attacked by bears seeing as they had littered their entire campsite with food. But the moment they saw me, they decided I was to be their entertainment as their overly friendly nature was getting out of hand when they started to back me up against a tree. This meant that I was forced to pull my gun the same moment a deep and threatening growl from a predator was heard from the forest behind me. Then, with them now fearing two things, I was able to demand for them to back away, before getting out of there quickly, knowing I was way out of my depth to handle them alone. That, and whatever animal had been closing in on them was not a creature I wanted to face, no matter how much my colleagues joked about me being able to tame any beast. A thought that was only backed up when I had met the worst and most frightening of all and survived the experience where others may not have.

But as for this time, I had quickly made my way back to my truck and called for back-up. However, by the time that backup came, and we went in there ready to make arrests for their attempt to sexually attack me, all traces of the group was gone. In fact, all we found was a single bloody handprint on that same tree I had been held against as evidence anyone had been there at all. Of course, I questioned what had happened to them that night, especially after finding a few empty shell cases. I decided that whatever animal had been out there that night, they had fought it off before high tailing it out of there, as it wasn't as if there was a trail of blood to follow or a littering of human limbs to collect.

In all honesty, when one guy's hands had grabbed me with sexual assault on the mind, it took me straight back to that night in the Devil's Ring… that was what Amelia had called it. Of course, this wasn't for the same reasons but in actual fact, the very opposite. Because it made me realise the difference. As I knew that I would have been safer with a club full of demons in Jared's arms than with my own kind after having too much to drink and fuelling dark and devious natures.

So, what did that mean?

Demons and Humans, which were the worst ones? Did it mean that it wasn't what you were that defined you, but what kind of soul dictated your decisions and guided your moral compass? Were we just as bad as some creature born in Hell? I couldn't help but think back to my uncle, knowing that he was good man, despite what he was. Did that mean I had allowed myself to be fooled by a prejudice that wasn't warranted to be held against them?

My uncle had been nothing but warm and kind and sweet to me and was a loving member of my family. I thought back to the snow globe of a wolf howling at the snowy mountains that I always kept by my bed. He had given it to me one night after I had woke up after a nightmare. I had gone through this obsession with wild animals and wolves, especially when I was young. Hell, even my aunty Kaz used to call me Ella Bella after my obsession with Beauty and the Beast growing up. Of course, when Fae had come along, she had quickly changed that to Ella Belly as I used to blow raspberries on her belly when she was little.

But my point was that even after all I had heard from Fae about the supernatural world and how her family was sat dead centre of it all, I still never slept without that wolf by my bed. Because despite what he was, I could never see him as anything but my uncle. The man who wanted to protect my dreams, telling me that at night the wolf would keep me safe, but in the day it was my job to keep him safe.

And that was from the King of Demons.

Which was why, after that night, I started thinking differently. I started to really question every preconception I'd had of Jared's kind and the secret kingdom he ruled. Because humanity was known for its acts of kindness just as much as it was equally known for its acts brutality. A taste of which I would have experienced the worst of had that animal not scared the guys enough to back away long enough for me to reach for my gun.

Meaning that once again, it felt as if I had been…

Saved by a Beast.

TWELVE

THE FISTED HANDS OF A LUMBERJACK

I stepped out of Much Mocha Love and took in that addictive fresh air with a grin to myself whilst ducking my head to don my dark brown Stetson. It was one that had a strap of leather around its diameter and silver BC park ranger badge attached at the front. Then I zipped up my pale green jacket, one issued with the rest of my uniform that also held patches on the arms with the forest logo and my name badge over my breast.

I didn't know what it was exactly, but every time I put my uniform on, it was like I was taking on a different persona. Presenting a part of myself I was most proud of. I believed in my job and the good of protecting not only the public that enjoyed Earth's beauty but also the wildlife and nature I knew we could easily destroy given the chance.

"Hey, Ella, just wait up a sec." I heard that deep voice rumble out from behind me just as I approached my Ford F250 aka, my second pride and joy. Then I smiled at my first pride and joy, who like always was fast asleep in the passenger seat like I knew he would be, as was his ritual on afternoon coffee breaks. It also meant that my golden retriever knew what coming when I approached the truck and the second he heard the handle jiggle, his eyes popped open, and his tail started wagging.

Treat time for Duke.

Or shamefully what I called him in my trailer when alone and scratching behind his ears, my Dukie Pookie. A name that did nothing for his male dog image true, but it made his tail wag all the same. Of course, I hadn't picked him, he had picked me, and after showing up scratching at my trailer door one night, he adopted me. But without a collar and no microchip then I was only too happy to call the handsome boy family… or fur baby when he wanted a snuggle.

I loved my Dukie.

"What's up, Orson?" I asked, turning around as he approached and took note of his worried frown, questioning it but then, just like that, it was gone, and an easy grin took its place.

"Hey, girl, I just wanted to know if you were free for…" Just then my name was said over my radio, and I almost groaned out loud in frustration… *had he finally been about to ask me out?*

In the end, I allowed myself a little sigh before holding up a finger to tell him one second before turning my head, bending my arm up so I could answer, speaking into my shoulder.

"Go ahead, Jimmy."

"I'm sorry, I know you were planning on finishing early for…" I quickly cut him off as there wasn't many that knew why once every two weeks I had to leave my shift early and I liked Orson, but I wasn't ready to share that with him yet. Hence why I cut him off quickly,

"Jimmy, it's fine, what do you need?" Orson narrowed his eyes in question down at me, being that the guy was over six foot and could easily tower over me even in my hiking boots, which admittedly I liked the thick heels for the added height… not quite like Orson's shitkickers though.

"It's probably nothing but I've got a report of some missing hikers that should have come back a few hours ago and have one upset girlfriend here that is naturally worried." I released another sigh and asked,

"Does she know which trail they were headed?"

"Lasca creek," replied Jimmy, making me groan.

"Of course," I muttered dryly.

"I feel bad askin' but…"

"Like I said, Jimmy, it's fine, besides, I am closer to Lasca creek and therefore will be able to get to those missing hikers quicker," I agreed, knowing this was why he'd called. After all, I was kind of predictable and it was afternoon mud coffee fuel up time. And for Duke, it was beef and swiss bagel time. Half of course, as the other half was mine, along with the all-important cookie.

I was a sucker for a cookie. Which, thanks to Marcus, king of the creepy jesters, had the ability to remind me of that night with every first bite thanks to his nickname for me. Obviously, he had no idea I loved cookies but still, it made an impact all the same.

"Well, I have also radioed it in to the Sheriff's office, just in case." I felt like groaning again, though I managed to keep it back, but I knew what this could mean. For of course, he would be all over this like flies on shit. Any excuse to bring him out here.

"Deputy Daniel Dickerson by any chance?" I said, making Jimmy say,

"Yeah, how'd you guess?"

"Unlucky like that," I replied dryly, making Orson frown openly this time as he questioned my scathing tone when saying his name.

Because this was one jerk who liked to throw his weight around, oh, and he happened to be the one and only date that in a moment of weakness I had agreed to. However, one date was all it took as he was an arrogant jerk who was full of himself. So, basically, the date went as such where the guy asked me nothing about my life, but instead much preferred to spend an entire evening talking about how great he was.

Needless to say, I didn't arrange another date and after three days of ignoring him, he'd hit his limit. But hey, I wasn't a bitch and the ignoring tactic only commenced after the first polite text I sent him. One that said,

Thanks for dinner but it's made me realise I am not ready for dating anyone at the moment.

Basically, 'Run to the hills' by Iron Maiden was at was top of the playlist after a date like that. I mean, I could have told him the truth, something along the lines of, 'sorry but you're an ass and have officially put me off dating for life, thanks though.'

Although one look at Orson and I knew that wasn't true.

As for the Deputy, admittedly he wasn't bad looking and unbelievably, the man was considered a catch in this town, meaning that his sparkling self-absorbed personality was being overlooked by most of the single female population of Nelson. Well, that was before his beefy replacement arrived, someone who was far superior in every way. *Thank you, Orson, for not being an A class jerk with a handsome face,* I thought, supressing a grin.

But as for Deputy Daniel Dick, I mean Dickerson, because of this bachelor status it naturally meant in his mind that he was entitled to any girl of his choosing, and of course, he would fixate on it being the only one who didn't want him. In fact, going back to my old childhood obsession, the whole thing reminded me of Beauty and the Beast, with the deputy playing the role of Gaston. Of course, the beast part of this story was shamefully still reserved for a certain King of club Freak, which I had lovingly named the place. And when I say lovingly, I mean the same type of love someone would have for fire ants crawling up their ass and biting the shit out of them!

So, basically, more on the loathe side of that love scale.

But back to Deputy dick, it also meant that I avoided him at all costs, as he seemed to adore playing the creepy leech, touching me at any opportunity as if this would make me fall madly in love with him. No, there was only one person on the planet I knew that had the power to affect me like that with only a single touch… although I had never met Chris Hemsworth in person so who knew, maybe he was number two. Okay, so yes, dressed as Thor, he would most definitely be number two on that list. And well, there was obviously Orson, but seeing as he hadn't asked me out yet, then I was starting to think he just wasn't into me. Because it wasn't as if he hadn't had ample opportunity, seeing as we practically saw each other every day at the coffee shop. And of course, there were steak and beer nights, where he had more than enough opportunity to take things further than a date, seeing as he was sleeping on my couch and all.

Not that I was that type of girl, but then, with that type of temptation sleeping only feet away and after six beers, trust me, I would have sold my soul to be given the opportunity to be that type of girl! I didn't need a dinner or a movie ticket for him to buy my goods, not when my vibrator had been used so much it had started to make a grinding noise like its gears were ceasing up. Not that I was a sex toy engineer or anything, as I was pretty sure that vibrators didn't even have gears. But I am saying that if they did, my glitter 'bob's' gears were shot and one happy dance away from us parting ways. Oh, the good times we'd had, my Battery-Operated-Boyfriend and me…

I will forever miss you, Bob.

But then, each of those good times I felt like a hussy, cheating on him by secretly wishing for better times in the form of an actual boyfriend… *batteries not included.* Although, after the amount of time that Bob and I had spent together, then when he actually did die the sparkly cock would be due an actual burial, complete with tears, black clothes and a wreath of flowers! Although even I had to admit a burning funeral pyre over the lake might have been a bit much.

Jesus, Ella, get your head back in the game and off how much being around Orson wants to make you run home to Bob!

"Great, well let's hope I find them first. You know how it is, they probably wandered off the trail and didn't even realise it," I said, getting my mind back on my job and off my soon to be neglected female lady parts. And thinking back to my job, I knew that hikers had easily wandered too far. This had happened before as the Lasca Creek trail wasn't maintained like some of the others. Of course, it didn't help that this particular area leads through prime bear habitat, so caution was definitely needed.

It was at this moment I glanced at Orson and saw that narrowed gaze was back, and those strong looking hands that I knew would have run Bob right out of town (or clean snapped him in half) were fisted by his sides.

"I'm sure you will, Connor, and don't worry about getting to Vancouver, Trent said you can take an extra day to get back," Jimmy said, calling me by my last name, something most of my colleagues did. Oh, and the Terminator jokes had taken about six months after I first started before they got old. But what Jimmy said made me relax my shoulders, knowing that it would have been painful and tiring driving straight back after my treatment. Trent was my boss, and he knew of my condition, as I'd had no choice but to confide in him, making a point of getting the job first at the risk of losing it all. But he understood, as he knew this was my dream and that I might not have had the chance had they known first.

Of course, Trent also kept it secret and let the rest think that my reasons for going to Vancouver were to give blood every two weeks as it was rare. People never questioned it when it came from Trent. He was good like that. The only other person who knew was Rex, and that was because he helped me out once when I had foolishly skipped taking my medication and broke yet another bone because of it. And where had I been...

Lasca creek.

Yep, me and that place had history. It seemed to be my personal curse, seeing as it wasn't far from there that I also found the load of drunk assholes. Well, here was hoping that I could break the curse and make it out of there without another thing happening.

"Thanks, Jimmy, and tell Trent thanks too, I owe him a sixpack." After this I said over and out and was left with a pissed off looking Orson, who was looking up towards the road that would take me part the way to the Creek.

"Sorry, Orson, can we pick this up another time?" I said, jerking him out of whatever troubling thoughts had him captive and also hoping he got the hint. That hint of course being that I wanted him to finish asking me his question just in case it should be him asking me out. But then he turned his serious gaze to me, and that brown sugar warmth made it back to his eyes, giving me something comforting to look at.

Well, that was before he started to freak me out by saying,

"Don't go up there, Ella." I frowned in question before asking,

"Why not?"

"Because it's not safe." At this I laughed once, shrugging it off and telling him,

"No, you're right, it's not safe… especially for inexperienced hikers that can get lost easy." Then I turned and opened my truck, making Duke sit up at the ready for his bagel.

"Ella, I am serious, it's not safe… *it's not safe for you,*" he said, holding my arm and whispering this last part as if he was trying to get across something deeper. Warning me of something more than I was willing to see.

"It's my job, Orson, and besides, I know these mountains like the back of my hand and the trails even better. Trust me, I know how to stay safe." At this he raised a brow as if he didn't believe me and for a brief and worried second, I had a feeling that he knew what nearly happened up there. But then he didn't say anything, and I laughed again, in one of those 'I'm nervous but trying not to show it' gestures. Then I hit him on the top of his arm in a friendly, playful way before I stepped up in my truck and paused long enough to say,

"Don't worry, Captain, I will be back at Mocha's before you know it." I gave him a nod and started the engine, letting her rumble into life. Then I gave him a wave of my fingers over the steering wheel after manoeuvring out of the parking space, making him nod back in return.

However, one thing I noticed as I did…

Those strong hands stayed fisted.

THIRTEEN

PICTURE UNPERFECT

O rson.

I couldn't stop thinking about how tense he had looked. How worried. And now, as I make my way up to the last known spot the hikers had been heard from, I continued to ask myself why? But then my own concern for others quickly overtook all other thoughts as I knew instantly that something was wrong as soon as I got there.

"Now, that's not looking good," I muttered to Duke, who had led me over to the discovery of a smashed iPhone. But then, on crouching down to take a closer look, I knew why he had caught a whiff of the scent as my dog wasn't exactly a tech junkie. Although he had chewed a pair of my headphones once. But this time it had been thanks to those small specks of red that had already seeped into the cracks.

Blood.

That's when I knew the result of the break hadn't been what must have been the most common cause for a smashed screen. But that blood... well, that said something else to me, meaning it was less likely for it to have simply slipped out of someone's pocket and cracked as it fell on the rough terrain. But that's when I started to scan the rest of the area, and what I found didn't exactly give me any more comfort. Not when I found another phone or should I say, what little was left of it. Because this one looked totally obliterated and scattered into little technical pieces. Almost as if they were both taking pictures of the same thing but then something went terribly wrong. Could it have been a bear attack? Had it charged after them and made them go running even further off the trail?

Whatever it was, they must have been in a hurry as the cracked phone wouldn't have just been left like that. Not when replacing a screen was a lot cheaper than replacing a whole phone, especially one that expensive.

Which was why I decided to radio it in.

"Jimmy, that girlfriend still with you? Over," I asked, hearing the crackle before his answer came through.

"Yeah, why, you found anything? Over." I released a sigh and asked,

"Maybe, ask her what colour her boyfriend's phone case was. Over." A few seconds later, I was closing my eyes tight, knowing that it wasn't looking good.

"She said it's blue with a surfboard on the back. Over." Yep, that was the one. Damn it!

"You alone? Over," I asked, not wanting to say the next thing if he was stood next to the poor girl.

"I am now. Why, what's up, Connor? Over," he asked, making me rub the back of my neck in frustration before telling him,

"You'd better call it in to the Sheriff's office and let them know I have found what could be possible evidence, let them know I am at…" I paused a second to look at my navigation point and told him the coordinates before telling him,

"And, Jimmy, tell them it had blood all over it. Over." It was his turn to pause before a short reply came back.

"Roger that."

I hooked my radio back on my jacket by my shoulder

and continued to look around, seeing now that it looked like they might have sat down here for a bit, as that's when I noticed a half-eaten protein bar and a foot away from that was a water canteen.

"Duke, no! Leave it, boy," I said, making sure he didn't start helping himself to the half-eaten bar, just in case it was as I suspected, evidence of some kind. But that's when he went snuffling off until he found something else and when I saw him go at something with his nose, I was walking closer and saw this time it looked like an expensive camera. Which made sense as, after all, most people didn't come to a beautiful place like this and not want to capture it forever in a picture or make others jealous by snapping a few shots and posting them on Facebook or Instagram.

After all, I had been known to do it myself a few times, especially when I first moved here. But then something about living here and doing the job that I did made life somehow slow down. You found yourself appreciating the little things more and more, as when I first arrived everything was so overwhelming, I could barely take in all the details. I was too busy trying to memorise maps, terrain, stop points, trails and procedures. I had spent an ungodly amount of time researching the area, from the different wildlife, plants and how people can affect such things. Because coming out here, you had to realise that being in such a wilderness as this you were agreeing to play by its rules, not your own. You were the outsider and the life that made this place its home was more entitled to it than you were.

That we were all just visitors to nature and we had to respect that. My rule, as well as with most Park Rangers, was enjoy it just so long as you left no trace of yourself behind. It was the rule we lived by because you didn't do a job like this without respecting nature, which meant that as I looked down at the evidence of human life left littered here, I had to fist my fingers to stop myself from bending down and picking up each single piece. Then doing what I usually would do which was put them into one of my trusty zip lock bags that I always carried with me. They were great for masking the smell of any trash that I found.

But the reason I didn't pick any of it up, was that I had this sense that something had gone wrong. I felt it deep in my gut. Because as I looked around trying to find the distinct trail that might have given an answer to what it could be, I knew now that it wasn't a bear attack. Of course, it was a misconception that bears would take one look at you and automatically want to rip you to pieces.

In truth, they didn't want to come across us anymore than we wanted to come across them, unless of course your dream had always been to see a bear in the wild. Naturally, there were deterrents that you could carry with you, I myself had bear spray in my pack. And they had created these alarm bell things which were supposed to scare them off. But in truth, grabbing a big stick and waving your arms around trying to make yourself look as big as possible while shouting like a mad woman, pretty much did the trick too.

Now, if there was one protecting a cub or they felt threatened, like when being startled, that that would cause you a serious problem for sure. They were powerful creatures after all, despite them not being inherently vicious but like I said, this didn't feel like this.

I remember the first time I came across one. He had popped his head up from the berries he was snacking on and looked straight at me. Naturally, my heart pounded but I ignored the urge to panic and startle him further by running for my life, screaming for God to help me. Instead, I simply backed away slowly, keeping calm, and said in a firm steady tone,

"Now, now, Yogi, you just stay there and take no mind to me." Then I stepped aside to give him a clear, wide path to leave, which thankfully he did. Of course, I also had my hand on my bear spray the whole time but was thankful that I didn't need it.

But like I said, this was no bear attack, which was why I knew that what I was seeing now could be classed as important clues to finding them, and therefore I had to be careful of where I stood and what I had touched, because I knew how this worked. Hell, but I had watched every crime show and real-life investigations on TV to know not to jeopardise a potential crime scene.

However, I still had a job to do, as this could have been a simple case of a couple of guys having a disagreement, a swing of fists, a couple of broken phones and maybe a bloody nose to be the worst of it. It sounded far-fetched, especially considering how much iPhones are worth but then again, I don't suppose it was too bad if you had insurance.

Now, as for the camera, I would have left this too but when I saw the screen was still on, it was as if someone had been taking a video and it had paused. So, crouching low, and using the edge of my sleeve, I pressed gently on the play button so the last video they took started to play back.

"Hey, Jen, making this video for you to show you what you're missing!" The voice of the guy behind the camera said, making me wince knowing this could be the last message he would ever get to tell her. He continued to explain the route they came and the incredible views. He even said they thought they'd seen a bear at one point but in the end, it looked like a shadow of something moving away.

"We just stopped for a... hey, Toby, what's that in the trees?" Another guy's voice broke through his commentary, and that's when the camera swung round to his friend who could be seen stood with his back to the lens, his arm pointed out at the thickest part of the forest. I sucked in a startled breath the moment he started to zoom in on the two red lights in the distance that were low to the ground.

"Is it someone's camera equipment?" his friend said, frowning back at the camera for a moment. And that was the worst part about it. They had no idea what it was.

But I knew.

I knew after only seconds what they were. I knew well before the hikers did. And most of all, *I knew the horror it meant.* Because they weren't lights,

They were eyes.

"There's some more! Hey, is anyone out there!?" the man behind the camera shouted, making me tense again, because I had a feeling of what was coming. And no matter how much I prepared myself for the sound that would be heard next, I still flinched when a deep, rumbling growl travelled through the trees.

"Matt, I think we'd better get going now, as whatever it is, it doesn't sound friendly." The guy named Toby said to his friend in front, who I knew was too close to the sound for it to matter now. Because it wasn't just the sound of nature getting too close to mankind. That was the sound of Hell getting too close to human life.

"Run… just get out of there!" I shouted down at the camera in a pointless effort to get them moving. But it was too late. I knew that the moment the guy screamed before turning around and running for his life. After that, there was a tumble of sounds as the camera fell from his hands, and a blur of motion as it dropped to the floor.

The screams, however, continued, making Duke bark at the sound. But I couldn't move. I couldn't focus on anything else other than that tiny screen that possibly played out the last moment these guys lived. Then a dark shadow could be seen fall over the position the lens directed and just before the video stopped, there was a demonic growl and a blur of a wolf leaping.

But then deep down I knew that it wasn't a wolf at all.

Because suddenly I was plunged back into my own history and the night a HellBeast drove me back to safety. And that night he told me not only about the dangers of HellBeasts but mainly the dangers of blood thirsty…

HellHounds.

FOURTEEN

HELLHOUNDS AND THE HELLBEASTS THAT HATE THEM

11 YEARS EARLIER...

Naturally, walking out of the club with the mountain of a man at my side wasn't going to get me in nearly as much trouble as it had when first walking into it. In fact, anyone who even got close to being 'too close' was met with a deadly growl or a flash of snarling fangs, making me jump every time.

Then he led me out a different way, and up through a spiral staircase that seemed to go on forever and made my legs ache, meaning that I nearly fell very early on. The man I knew was named Orthrus released a deep sigh and in one of the deepest voices I had ever heard, said something I didn't yet understand as if he was speaking more to himself.

"I think J would kill me for letting you fall and break your pretty little neck more than he would for touching you." This was the only warning I got before my tired, sore legs were swept out from under me.

"Ah!" I shouted, making him scoff a laugh before continuing up the stairs with me in his meaty arms that felt solid as if they would never tire.

"You're weaker than most humans, although it can certainly be said that you can dance alright," he informed me, making me respond before I thought better of it,

"Jeez thanks, Colossus." Then I slapped a hand over my mouth, now fearful of his reaction to my sarcastic comment. However, he just rumbled out a laugh and said cryptically,

"Oh yeah, I see it now." I frowned in question before asking what he meant by that, no longer fearing him as much. Because it was kind of hard to be afraid of someone who was carrying you up the stairs to ensure you wouldn't fall down and hurt yourself.

"See what?" I asked.

"Time, Red. All in good time." Again, it wasn't what I would have called the most informative of answers, hence why I gave up with Mr Cryptic and tried to concentrate on the never-ending staircase. Soon he was flipping a switch and allowing the streetlight to poor in. I frowned to see we were in a different part of the city, and not near the pub. Then when he cleared the last of the steps, I looked back to see it was like a stone trap door that quickly slammed shut.

I jumped, making Orthrus scoff before putting me down on my feet and telling me,

"Just so you know, you won't be able to get back in this way." I narrowed my gaze up at him for a second before I said,

"What, you think I am going to try and sneak in there again?!" My incredulous tone wasn't one I tried to hide. To this he just folded his arms across his massive chest making me gulp.

"Looking bigger isn't an answer," I informed him, making his perfectly shaped lips twitch in amusement.

"It's Orthrus, right?" At this he nodded slightly, giving me the silent go ahead to continue.

"Okay, Orthrus, here it is…"

"Here what is?" he asked, interrupting me.

"My vow, one that promises you that I will never be setting foot inside that place ever again… EVER," I said, emphasising the 'ever' part so he got the message. At this he unfolded his arms and scoffed, doing so this time as a gesture that he didn't believe it for a second.

"I am serious!" I shouted when he turned his back on me before shocking me.

"Best intentions mean nothing, little girl, when you're not the one in charge of making those decisions." I frowned as I tried to process what he meant.

"Now come on, the car is waiting," he told me in a gruff tone that also told me that this conversation was over. Yet I was stubborn, and for some reason I wasn't scared to push things around this guy, as if I felt some kind of kindship with him.

"Wait, what is that supposed to mean?!" I said after catching up to him as he opened the door to a fancy blacked out Land Rover. He released a frustrated sigh and I watched as his large shoulders dropped an inch. Then he looked down at me and said,

"What do you think it means. A HellBeast King might

have let you go for now but trust me, I know J, if he decides to take you, then your vows and promises mean shit." My mouth dropped open in shock and I said in a whispered tone,

"But… but he let me go."

At this Orthrus dipped his head closer to mine.

"For now, he did… but like I said, I know J, and a King as powerful as him doesn't look at a girl like you that way and not start planning for the future. So yeah, that's how I know you will be back, vow or not… the Devil's Ring will see you dance again, Little Red… now get your tired ass in the car," he said, making me do as I was told, and I shifted to the far end to make room for him to follow. Then he said something to the driver, whilst I was left to process his words. Words that left me feeling even more scared than before. Of course, Orthrus might have been wrong or just trying to get some kick out of scaring me. But I didn't think so. Because like I said, I didn't feel the same around Orthrus as I did around Jared. I didn't feel that danger lurking in the shadows around him or that rage that lay beneath a veil of water ready to burst free at any moment.

"How do you know him so well, are you his friend?" I

asked after a short while of silence. At this Orthrus glanced sideways at me before shocking me further.

"No, I am his brother." My eyes widened in surprise before I blurted out,

"So, you're one of these HellHound thingies too?" At this he snorted before saying,

"Fuck no! I ain't no fucking HellHound and nor was anyone else in that club." I frowned in confusion before he shifted side on to face me and told me,

"I am a HellBeast."

"What's the difference?" I asked, making his eyes start to blaze, which was when I noticed that they were similar to Jared's. A silver grey, only his had a dark black ring that bled out around the pupil and one around the iris. But then, unlike Jared's, his eyes seeped back to a warm amber colour after taking a deep and calming breath. That's when I knew I had insulted him.

"I'm sorry, I don't mean to cause offence…" he cut me off when he raised a large hand before telling me,

"HellHounds are wild, frenzied creatures that let blood lust dictate their actions and consume their minds. They are like adolescent pups with little control and have no host," he said with a distasteful tone.

"Host?" I asked.

"A human body. Hence why you don't often get many HellHounds up top," he told me, making me frown again.

"Up top?"

"Fuck me, Red, you ask a lot of shit." I rolled my eyes and told him,

"And do you really blame me, a few hours ago I thought werewolves in London was just the basis for an old B movie!" I snapped, making him growl a little.

"Let's get one thing straight, little human, we are not fucking Werewolves. We are HellBeasts and it's not wise to piss us off by calling us by any other name." At this I held my hands up and said,

"Okay okay, sorry, human, remember?" At this he huffed and straightened in his seat so he could look straight ahead.

"So, I don't make the same mistake twice, can you at least tell me the difference between a HellHound and a HellBeast?" At this he again sighed and told me,

"We are bigger. We are meaner. We are far more deadly, and we don't fucking like each other… that's all you need to know." At this I swallowed hard and decided to leave it at that, knowing there was only so much I could push it with him. However, a few silent minutes more and then it was him that was asking the questions.

"How did you get inside?" His deep voice was one that sent shivers snaking down my spine even if I wasn't afraid of him. Because despite his colossal size and his deep voice, it had to be said that he was not as intimidating as his King… *a man I now knew was his brother.* But then I also knew I was in the car with the type of person that could have snapped my neck like a twig without even blinking an eye. So yes, Orthrus might have been nice to me so far, but he still looked like a man that had been born in battle and never left it.

"It was a mistake, one I can promise you will not happen again," I said, ignoring his earlier comment about me not having a choice. He cleared his throat and shook his head a little before telling me,

"That's not what I mean nor is it what I'm asking." At this I released a sigh and looked out of the window as we approached the hotel down its fancy driveway right off the main street. I knew then I was running out of time as there was one last question I wanted to ask, but first I knew he was waiting for my answer.

"I followed my cousin inside, but I didn't exactly see

where she went. So, when I didn't find her down in the cellar, I sat down to take something out of my shoe, and I must have triggered something because the next thing I knew, the wall was turning." He nodded his head once as if he understood this but then lowered it again when he wanted me to continue.

"The door to the elevator opened and I stepped inside, you know the rest," I said with a simple shrug of my shoulders, but then his eyes widened in shock, and it gave me pause.

"It opened for you, just like that?" he asked, now clearly getting to the part he wanted to know as he seemed more than a little surprised. I was smart enough then to realise that this shouldn't have happened the way it did.

"Well, it opened up and I stepped inside. After that it went down and the next thing I knew I was inside that club and again, like I said, you know the rest," I answered, looking down at my lap and pulling at the skirt as if I had the power to erase the memory by burying it all under the silk and velvet. Like pulling at the very fabric of time wondering if something like that was also possible. I couldn't doubt anything after tonight.

But this was also when I realised that my clothes were

still at the club and also my precious hooded Harvard sweater that my father had given me as a gift. I had talked about going and it was an ongoing debate in my family as my mom wanted me to stay closer to home. But after this night, then quite honestly, I didn't know anything anymore. I was unsure about the future, replaying Orthrus' words and knowing I may not get a choice.

Little did I know at the time that I would also always wonder about that sweater, the first time being in that car. Knowing it was the only evidence left of me ever being in that club and how I would plague myself with the question, 'what happened to it?' Did someone pick it up, try it on and think 'Oh yeah, I'll play human for a day', putting aside the hellish Tutu and corset. Or did it just get chucked out with the rest of the trash at the end of the night. I didn't know why this last thought bothered me the most. Maybe it was the feeling of being considered as expendable, just some trash that needed to be swept away quickly. Like my drive back to where I belonged… my own world.

I would always wince at the memory of it.

As the car stopped, the bellboy looked our way, as if he didn't know whether to come and open my door or not. I think this was because he had received some kind of gesture from the driver to tell him that I wasn't yet ready. I didn't know whether this was true or not because as much as I wanted my answers, I also wanted to bolt from this car as if I knew it was about to explode in five seconds.

But Orthrus knew as well as I did that I still had one more question to ask. A burning question that would have consumed me had I not had the guts to ask it whilst I could. So, after knowing this was the last time I would see him, I turned and braved discovering what the answer could be.

"What was it that Jared said to you before we left?" He raised a dark brow, and I couldn't tell whether it was out of curiosity at where my question had come from or amusement that I had asked it at all. Either one, I was just thankful that he answered me,

"He told me to make sure that no one touches you or no one else frightens you… *myself included.*" After that I sucked in a startled breath, one that was added to the moment I heard the car doors unlock. This was my cue to get out and, in the end, it was something I did pretty quickly. But as I watched that car turn around and leave, I knew that after his answer I would end up spending a long time fixating on that piece of information. A long time questioning why he would have done that, why he would care enough... *why he didn't like the idea of me being frightened?*

In reality I knew that I would never get my answers because I very much doubted we'd...

Ever meet again.

Present Day...

I jerked out of my thoughts of that night and tried to focus on what I had learned during that car journey. I had been forever grateful to Orthrus and his willingness to answer my questions. And despite how much some of those answers of his had plagued me over the years, I knew now exactly what I was dealing with. Which was why the second I heard screams coming from behind me, my gut instincts kicked in and I went running.

Although, admittedly, I would come to regret that as I was running in the wrong direction. I was heading towards trouble instead of away from it. But then, as Duke went barrelling off towards the sounds, now barking and growling, all I could hope for was that they wouldn't chance getting caught. That the sounds of people coming would scare them off and in doing so I might have a chance at saving some lives.

This was the plan.

The plan that quickly failed.

I knew that the moment I turned a corner and was soon faced with an almost mirror image of the past. In fact, the truth of that night hit me like a sledgehammer as I was flooded with images of what really happened. Like someone had just flipped a switch in my brain and took away the lies. Back when those men had been moments away from violating me in the worst way.

Only now there was something vastly different about these guys. For one, they were a lot younger, barely out of high school was my guess. Secondly, there weren't exactly dressed for hiking being as they looked like punks off some street corner.

Oh, and as for the most blaringly obvious difference between that night and now. These guys were currently eating the remains of the bloody hikers and they most certainly weren't…

HellHounds!

FIFTEEN

DEAD WOMAN WALKING

Holy Hell!

My hands slapped over my mouth to try and stop my own screams. Because the moment I saw what looked like a group of bloody vampires in the middle of what could only be described as a feeding frenzy, I began to slowly back away. Doing so now as if I would have should I be facing a bear. But then, after managing only three steps back, Duke barked and suddenly one of their heads snapped up, pinning me with a demonic gaze. It was like two burning white hot coals singeing my flesh. I felt frozen to the spot, locked to the earth by his deadly gaze alone.

Then he opened his mouth and snarled at me, suddenly transforming that image of a vampire into something else… something entirely lost to a creature that looked far more terrifying. A flash, a movement like a flicker of an image over his skin, showing me seconds of horror as I saw the truth of what he was.

"HellHound," I whispered, unsure of how I could know this after never laying witness to such creatures. But as the guy started to change, now dropping to all fours and pawing at the earth with his hands, my gut was telling me not what they were exactly but more like, *what they weren't.*

HellBeasts.

Again, I didn't know how I could be so sure but as the changes in him were transforming quicker, that belief only strengthened. Because surely Jared wouldn't have allowed his own people to do this. But then again, I remembered what Orthrus had said, about HellHounds not having human bodies. They were without a host. So then why was I stood frozen to the spot watching as its skin started to split, starting from the centre of his lips. I swallowed down the bile that churned in my stomach and threatened to burn its way up my throat as a different head started to emerge. It started to break through underneath the skin of its once human face as it started to peel back either side, stretching as if someone were behind him with a fist full of his flesh. Tugging and pulling his features from muscle and bone, before soon all that was left was a black snarling head of a wild furless dog!

Its jaw seemed to dislocate itself from the rest of its skull before it grew forwards, now forming a more canine snout. The popping and snapping of bone was a sickening echo as its hands gripped handfuls of the earth, before these too started to change. Fingers cracked by an invisible force, breaking them at the knuckles and forcing them back on themselves before its wrists followed. Breaking before splitting the skin to allow a hound's paw to claw its way out. You could see the bulging under the skin as if some magical hellish force was making something grow under the skin until it could be contained no more.

Then it threw its head back up, emitting one last agonising roar before its yellow fangs started to push out its human teeth so pointed ones could take its place. Bleeding gums surrounded the base of each deadly fang, making crimson saliva drool down between the gaps in its teeth and land on the forest floor.

It was in this moment that I screamed, finally free of my mental chains as I turned around and ran. But as I did, I ran straight into someone's large, muscular frame,

"Orson?!" He looked down at me with an expression I couldn't decipher but I knew one thing, it wasn't one it should have been. Not when I knew what was happening behind my back, something he could see. But then, before I had chance to act, like screaming at him to run, he banded an arm around me, holding me tight against him. Then he looked down at me and narrowed his brown eyes.

"Listen to my words now, as I tell you it is not as it first appears, Ella." Just then, Duke started barking and Orson looked down at him and snarled, which seemed was all he had to do to get him to stop.

"Now go from this place!" he told my dog, and I would have said something to that but then when it worked, I realised it was for the best as I wanted Duke far away from the evil at my back.

Speaking of which…

"We have to run, we have to…" I paused when he shook his head and told me,

"When you turn around you will see something else."

Then, before I could ask what the hell he was talking about, he looked over my head and straight at the creatures I had tried to run from.

"Shouldn't you kids be elsewhere?" was his stern reply, and I frowned in confusion thinking that was the very last thing I expected to hear. Now, 'oh my god!' or 'what the fuck is that?!' would have made sense. But shouldn't you kids be elsewhere?! Seriously...*What the fuck?!*

They weren't kids, they were fucking animals!

Orson felt my entire body tense and I started struggling to get out of his hold, making him growl down at me... yes, *he actually growled!*

"Calm down, Ella." My eyes grew wider in shock at how insane that demand was, almost as insane as when Jared had asked me to do the same thing! Damn him and every fucking thing that took me back to the pain of him!

In fact, I was so angry I almost forgot about the threat behind us, and this time wrenched myself out of his arm before shouting up at him with my arm pointed out,

"Calm down! Are you fucking kiddin' me?!" Then he frowned, crossed his arms over his large chest and said,

"They're just a bunch of teenagers that got stupid with a rifle and took down a buck."

"What!?" I shouted before turning around to face them again, and I sucked in a startled breath.

"That's... that's not possible," I whispered through my shock. Because what faced me now couldn't be. It just couldn't. As Orson was right, it was now just four young guys that couldn't be over eighteen all crouched around a dead deer. One they were trying to gut and were making a piss poor job of it. I shook my head, trying to will my mind to understand what I had seen and now with the pain in my bones setting in, as it usually did when I pushed it too hard, I started to feel funny.

"No... no... no, this... they... that's not what I saw, Orson," I finally said as I stepped back, making one of the teens who I had seen start to change now go back to standing to his full height. Orson growled low at this and the next words that came out of his mouth were a different language, one I couldn't even tell you what type it was.

"Wasabu ana simtim alaku." (Meaning, 'Sit or go to one's fate and die.' In ancient Sumerian.) Amazingly the guy backed off, making me curious to know what he'd said. Or a more important question would be how Orson knew they would speak the same language. The whole thing seemed bizarre but not nearly as bizarre as what I had seen moments ago.

What the hell was wrong with me!?

"Hey, it's okay, Ella… wait… Ella, what's wrong?" he said after first gripping the tops of my arms and turning me back to face him. That's when I felt it, the moment it started to happen. The light headedness, the weak feeling in my legs, the way I could almost feel the blood draining from my face, one he now had gripped in his hold at my chin and was forcing back so he could look at me.

This was when I opened my mouth to say something, only it never came out. No, instead the only thing I managed was one last glance at the teens. and this time, there was no mistaking what I saw, as all four of them now stood up. Each one blood soaked and growling as if a pack of wolves had been disturbed from their kill and now felt threatened of losing it.

But wait… it wasn't just that. And as I felt myself being lowered to the ground, it was the look of something else.

It was… *eyeing up their next kill.*

After this, the last thing I heard before darkness overtook me was the unmistakeable sound of a furious bear. One that sounded twice as big as any other and ten times as ferocious. A true beast angry at anything living that crossed its path. And it was in that moment that I realised it was the exact same sound I had heard that time in the woods with the men who wanted to violate me.

Only this time I had no power to reach for my gun or more importantly,

I didn't have the power to run.

Meaning only one thing…

I was a dead woman.

SIXTEEN

TRUTH REVEALED

Strangely, the very last thing on my mind before I lost consciousness was a single face… *Jared.*

I didn't know why considering I had spent years and years working hard each day to push that face from my mind. But then, maybe my mind thought, what the hell, if it's the last thought I will ever have, why not make it a good one!

Only that was just the thing, I didn't know if it was a good one or not. Like seeing the Devil before starting your punishment, do you focus on him because he's hot and dangerously good looking or do you focus on the one that in the end you know has impacted the end of your life the most? Because after all, surely the Devil would have a big say on where you ended up?

Was that why I focused on Jared now, because he had been the one to impact my life the most up to this point? After all, I was running as far from him as I could get, and by doing so running from my cousin's world. I hadn't seen my aunt and uncle for years and on those rare occasions I made it home, I would make excuses. Because seeing them and knowing what they were and not saying anything was difficult to say the least.

I also had no idea if they knew I was aware of their secret world or not, as I honestly never asked Amelia and they certainly gave nothing away. In fact, the only thing my uncle had insisted on helping with was pulling strings on me becoming a Canadian citizen sooner than it would have taken. Of course, they never forgot a birthday or occasion to send a card or something, and I usually kept in touch with my aunt via email as that was safer than by phone.

I honestly felt bad as I really did love them, but after that night in Jared's club and the things he said to me, well… I knew that there was and always would be, a clear line drawn in the sand. One where I was firmly stood on the human side of things.

'Shame then that you're human.'

That was what he had said to me.

But then suddenly I was no longer focusing on the past but instead on the present, as my mind snapped back to what had just happened. Those last words lingering in my mind, reminding me not only of what I was but more importantly, what those guys had been in the forest. Because that hadn't been a trick of my own mind. It had been real.

Just like that night had been real.

The night someone had tried to make me forget.

I don't know how or even why, but the very second I saw them hunched over the bodies like that, I knew this wasn't the first time I had seen horror like that before. The truth of my past hit me like a slap across the face, one hard enough to rattle my brain and loosen the lies from my memories. At first, I thought that roar I'd heard had been the same one from that night when I had been forced to pull my gun. But now, well I wasn't so sure as my mind now scrambled for the truth, clawing desperately at the right scenes to play out once more.

Now leaving me with what really happened that night.

What really happened,

THREE MONTHS AGO...

I sighed when settling down the pan with noodles that would have to wait. Because once again it wasn't my shift but when Jimmy had called telling me had received complaints off locals about a rowdy group, I knew what was coming. It was Friday night after all. So, like always, I agreed to check it out, deciding to let those who had families and dates continue to enjoy their night. So, I found out the place they had been headed, groaning when I realised it was Lasca Creek trail.

"But of course," I muttered as I got myself back in my uniform and tied up my heavy boots, the ones that gave me a little extra height thanks to their thick soles. I glanced at the empty dog bed and sighed, knowing this time I would have to make it a solo mission seeing as Duke had gotten into my stash of chocolate covered cookies and made himself sick as... well, *as a dog.* I swear that dog was getting better at opening the cupboards and that at this rate I was going to have to baby proof my tiny kitchen! This also meant that my day off was going to be dedicated to rearranging my kitchen cupboards... *joy.*

Well, having to spend the night at the vets should

teach him, I thought with another sigh and a shake of my head. Becky, the vet, had told me he would be fine, but they had to keep him on fluids for twenty-four hours. I was just happy he was alright and thinking that at least this call gave me something to do. Besides, it was most likely nothing but a couple of campers having a few too many, so I got in my truck, and I went on my way.

My main concern of course was that they were being irresponsible by building fires or not keeping their food contained so as not to attract the bears. However, after parking my truck and making the trek up to Lasca Creek, I knew I had made a mistake by assuming this.

It was worse.

Because it turned out that the guys weren't just drunk, they were also snorting drugs, and this made for a bad combination. Especially now there was a woman around for devious minds to turn their attention to. I knew the mistake I made in coming here alone the second I walked into their shambles of a campsite.

I knew the moment all eyes swung around to me as I approached, and every face held the same expression after their initial surprise… *hunger.* It was in that moment that I twisted my body slightly, thankful I was still kept in shadows whilst I unclipped my gun from its holster. Then I tucked it into my belt at the back so they couldn't see I was armed and pulled my empty holster from my belt, throwing it to the forest floor.

I decided to say my piece and get the hell out of there. I warned them about the food, fires and whatever else before backing away and saying,

"Right, now, I will be on my way." Then I purposely reached for my radio, telling them all that I was expected back but drunk hands grabbed me, making it fall from my grasp. That's when things turned from bad to worse.

"Where do you think you are going, you sweet little bitch?" one with sour breath said, making me want to gag.

"Yeah, you are the fun we have been missing out on!" another guy said, spinning me around and pushing me back against a tree, making me wheeze out from the impact as my gun pressed painfully into my back.

"Fuck, you're pretty, not had a taste of pretty in a long fucking time," he added, making his friends agree.

"No, not with your wife!" another guy joked, making the asshole in front of me grin, showing me a row of yellow, crooked teeth. He must have been in his late 50's, in fact other than two of them who must have been someone's sons, they were all around the same age.

However, it was the guy with the big beer gut that pushed his way through the rest, being six in total who were all getting closer. Beer gut guy downed the rest of his can and threw it off to the side, making me scowl at him. He was wearing a baseball cap advertising engine oil and his grin was almost as bad as the guy who still had me held against the tree.

"It's my birthday, assholes, so that means I get to dip my dick in her first… my old lady hasn't opened up shop for me in too long and I want to get my cock wet in a cunt that ain't baggy!"

"Jesus," I muttered, turning my head away in revulsion, knowing exactly why Mr Dickhead's wife had closed up shop, this guy was a real charmer!

"Oh, sugar, God isn't here to help you with this one, no, the best you can hope for is making us happy by spreading those nice legs of yours or even better, opening that pretty mouth." This was when I let him get closer by acting compliant before I whispered,

"Come near my mouth with your dick and I will bite the fucker off!" Then I kneed him in the balls, making him bend over with a cry of pain.

"You bitch!" he shouted, before standing back up so he could slap me hard across the face. Then hands grabbed me roughly and pushed me back, before they started to try and take my clothes off, making me fight against them.

"GET OFF ME!" I screamed, and this was when something happened. Something that thankfully stopped them from getting too far, even if I did receive a few punches to the stomach and slaps to the face. But by the time the unexpected happened, I had managed to keep on at least some of my clothes, like my trousers and black bra. As for my tank top I wore under my shirt, well now that lay on the ground in pieces. I was just glad that in their drunken minds they had been more interested in my breasts than what was still tucked into my waistband at my back. Something I was planning on using the first chance I got.

"What the fuck was that?!" one of the younger guys said, now looking fearful at the trees. I hadn't heard anything over the sounds of my own screams but then when one covered my mouth with his sweaty hand, I had chance to listen for myself.

A deep, rumbling growl travelled to us before it started getting louder and louder. Then, when it turned into a full bellowing roar, it was enough to scare them into thinking a bear or something was close to attacking. They started backing away, which was when I could finally reach for my gun. I held it out in front of me with a shaky hand, the adrenaline coursing through me, mixing with the fear and realisation I had been just seconds away from being raped.

However, their own fearful gazes weren't on me…

No, they were on the Beast behind me!

"What the fuck is that thing?!" one said in a terrified whisper, when another replied,

"I don't know, but I am not waiting around to fucking find out!" He pretty much near tripped up over himself to run away, and this was when I finally decided I needed to find out for myself. So, I turned around, and that's when I saw exactly what it was they were seeing. There, in the trees was a beast so big, it looked easily five times that of the biggest wolf. A black shadow with two silver-white glowing eyes staring back at the clearing, with only the whites of its teeth reflecting off the moonlight whenever it breached the treetops.

"It's fucking huge!" one shouted, as he too scrambled to move whilst the others reached for their guns, making me realise that pulling my own on them would have been useless in the end. But something in me wanted to stop them from shooting at it, so I raised my own gun in warning.

"Don't you dare shoot it!" I shouted and then, just as he was swinging his gun in my direction, two things happened simultaneously. The first was that his gun went off before mine did. But whereas his bullet hit something, mine fired wide when I was tackled to the ground by a dark figure dressed in black. I barely had time to make out what had happened before I heard the screams of a man being attacked by the giant wolf.

No, not a wolf.

A HellBeast.

That's when I knew that Orthrus had been right. They were big. They were mean. And they were beyond fucking deadly! I started to scream, squirming under the large, heavy body that practically lay on top of me. But I barely cried out before a hand suddenly covered my mouth, and a voice I would have known anywhere growled down at me.

A voice from my past.

A voice from my dreams.

A voice I had heard say this very same thing once before…

"Easy now, Red."

SEVENTEEN

THE SCENT OF A KING

I looked up into those stunning eyes of his and could barely believe that what I was seeing was real. Oh yeah, so the enormous, crazed beast that was currently eating someone I could believe, but Jared Cerberus lying on top of me... no, he was the dream, the nightmare and myth all rolled up into one. He was the legend that was here now, the make-believe tale I had tried to convince myself wasn't even real.

Wasn't real beyond my dreams of him.

So many dreams.

So many nights spent with this man and not a single

moment had existed in reality other than the first. And now here he was, making me question my sanity because of it. I could see he was speaking to me, asking me something, but I was struck dumb and unable to hear the words. Which was why his gaze narrowed and that soft look of concern morphed into hard features as he gave me a gentle shake.

"Answer me, Red!" I shook my head a little before blinking back the daze.

"What… what happened?" I asked, thinking this was a sensible question to ask, making him release a sigh before ignoring my question and asking one of his own.

"Are you alright? Did they touch…" He took pause and clenched his jaw when he looked down at my body, seeing me now half naked with only my bra on. A low growl rose up, making me flinch beneath him where he still lay on top of me. But if he noticed my fear of him, he didn't show it. No, instead he swung his head towards two others, that I could now see as large shadows circling the clearing as if waiting for their King's orders. I would have liked to have raised my head a little more to see what these HellBeasts looked like. But with his bulk blocking near everything else from view, I was forced to remain still.

"Spread out. No one survives this night. But I want

the one who struck her… *His blood is mine and mine alone… Now go!*" The order rumbled up from his chest in a demonic tone that had me sucking in a quick breath and flinching in his hold.

Holy fuck, he was frightening!

Seconds later, and the growls and howls of excited beasts beginning the hunt died down, making the beast above me take a breath as if to try and calm himself. Then his intense gaze switched back to my frightened one.

"Did they do…" he swallowed hard at the question, and to save him the hardship of forcing out the rest of the words needed, I shook my head, telling him all he needed to know. I hadn't been violated. His jaw was set hard, and he hissed,

"Fuckers will die for this." He looked so torn. Half of him I knew wanted to be with his people, experiencing for himself the revenge his blood was pumping for. But then, as he looked down at me, his gaze softened enough to tell me that he wouldn't leave me. And all the while I was questioning why. Why he was here? Why did he care? Why did he seem so affected by the idea of what could have happened to me?

About what did happen.

I didn't understand.

"Are you hurt?" he asked in that grumbly deep voice of his, making me shake my head again. But it was as if he could see in the dark as he ran the backs of his fingers over my heated cheek, seeing for himself that they had marked me. Something I knew for sure as the burning on my skin hadn't yet left me.

"Is this all they did?" he asked, and I nodded, not wanting to tell him about the pain in my back or stomach. I would have the bruises from it tomorrow and I doubt he would still be around by then. But that wasn't my biggest concern. It was why he was here now, that was.

"Come on, let's get you home," he said before lifting his weight off me, and the moment he offered me a hand to take, I paused as I heard screams of men being hunted. A terrifying sound that seemed to vibrate through the mountains. I saw his jaw harden again before he told me,

"I won't let anything hurt you, I swear it. Now take my hand, girl." This was finished on a stern command that I dared not disobey. So, I did as I was told and put my hand in his much larger one. I gulped, just watching the way it was swallowed whole by his long, thick fingers, knowing what those hands were capable of in my dreams. Hands that as soon as I was standing, now swept me off my feet making me cry out in surprise.

"What are you…?"

"You're a smart girl, what does it look like?" he rumbled in return as he started walking away from the now bloody campsite, and I got the impression he wanted to get me as far away from it as soon as possible. Did he not want me to see what one of his HellBeasts had done? This was confirmed when he told me in a hard tone,

"Don't look back, Red." I swallowed hard before doing as he advised, and instead looked forward. However, it was after a few minutes of silence that I asked,

"Do you need me to direct you on where to go?"

"I know the way," was his blunt reply, making me frown in question.

"You've been here before?" I asked, unable to help myself.

"No, I can scent the way you came," he told me, making me realise just how different we were. *'Shame then that you're human'*. His words played back painfully, and I tried to push them down into the pit of my painful reality.

"Is that how you found me?" I asked in a small voice, making him glance down at me before tightening his hold for a split second as he rumbled out a one worded answer,

"Yes."

After this I didn't know what to think. There were just too many questions I had, and most of which I was too scared to ask. It had been eleven years, so why now? Why was he here after all this time? I mean he didn't strike me as the type of person to take a hiking vacation. Which was when I was finally brave enough to ask,

"Amelia, is she alright?" At this he frowned down at me, obviously wondering where this question had come from. Unless he forgot who she was to me?

"My cousin, I just wondered if this had anything to do with her, you being here I mean and if she was in trouble?" I asked, knowing that it came out in a tumble of nervous words. He chuckled once and told me,

"Oh, she is trouble alright but as for being fine, I will say so seeing as the last time I saw her, she was kicking demonic ass in Hell and saving the realm, so basic stuff for your family, it would seem." At this, my mouth dropped open and I muttered,

"You must be joking."

"Do I look like I am joking, Red?" He pointed out the obvious as no, it didn't look like he was joking. Not in the slightest, now making me wonder what the Hell had I missed in the month it had been since I last spoke with my cousin. Last I knew she had gone a little AWOL by taking a sabbatical from her job and going to Jerusalem. I also got the impression that she was running from something or more like someone. Especially when she begged me not to tell anyone where she was. And well, when she asked for the number of the coffeeshop to call, fearing my phone was being monitored, pretty much confirmed it. But then she admitted to me that she was fine but had in fact gone into hiding. She wouldn't tell me the details, only that she could look after herself and swore to me that she wasn't in any danger.

So, I kept her secret, only relaxing when my mom confirmed she was back in touch with her family a few days ago. But since I was still waiting for a call for her to explain what had been going on, I was still left in the dark as to what had happened to her. Which was why I wondered if Jared being here now had something to do with it.

"I will take that look of confusion as my answer that you have no clue," Jared said, making me shake my head telling him he was right, I had no clue. But then again, why would I…

I wasn't part of their world.

This was when I started shaking.

"Fuck!" he hissed suddenly, before he stopped and let my legs go, making sure my feet found the floor before taking a step back. I was about to ask what he was doing when he started taking off his leather jacket. This left him just wearing a dark T shirt, one that was moulded to his muscular body like it *wanted* to be close to him. As if the material was attracted to his skin, especially on the shoulders and biceps where it was at its tightest.

But that's not all I noticed. He also had a full sleeve tattoo, only with it being dark, I couldn't make out the details of it, despite wishing that I could. Just like the numerous bands of leather he wore, that all together created a thick band around his wrist. The details were unfortunately lost on me, just like most of the handsome features of his face.

His scent, however, was all hot-blooded male that I remembered from that night. Leather, cedarwood, a slight hint of smoke, and the distinct smell of someone who rode a motorbike. The hot oil, fuel and rubber mixing together with hints of exhaust fumes that would cling to your clothes. But all these combined and it made for a heady combination that was admittedly playing havoc on my lady parts.

Jesus, I needed to get laid by someone other than Bob!

"You're shaking like a leaf," he commented, drawing me out of my secret appreciation of how good he smelled but making me look down at myself in the process. It was as if I was now only realising that he had been carrying me in nothing but a bra, making me react stupidly by covering myself with my arms. This made him chuckle before he told me,

"It's a bit late for that, Red, I have a damn good memory." I opened my mouth in shock and he looked amused by my stunned expression, tapping on my chin twice for me to close my lips.

"As tempting as that look is on you, Kitten, I am only interested in getting your ass home before it freezes in my arms." At this I felt shame rise, making my face hot with embarrassment and again he looked to be enjoying my reactions to his words. Then, as he put his jacket around me, I sucked in a quick, startled breath when he jerked the two sides of the zipper towards him. This brought me only inches from him, and again my wide eyes of surprise looked up at him slowly. Then with his tone soft and gentle, he told me with a grin,

"Relax, pet, *I am teasing you.*" Then he zipped up the jacket, the sound of which jerked me out of this sexual daze he had me under. As for the jacket, it was so big on me that I had room to slip my arms through the sleeves even with it zipped up. I also had to stop myself from moaning aloud at how warm it felt against my shivering skin. I wanted to bury myself into it and stay there forever. Although, I think it had something to do with being completely surrounded by that incredibly erotic scent of his. Again, I resisted the urge to release a sexual dreamy sigh.

"There we go, temptation hidden," he said, making me wonder why he would say that. *Unless was teasing me again?* In the end, this question was overshadowed by another when he picked me up again and started walking once more.

"You know I am fine to walk," I said, making him scoff and tell me in a gruff tone I was getting used to,

"You are also fine to be carried."

"Yeah, but you must be getting tired, plus it's a long way to my truck," I argued, making him lift me higher as if proving a point before asking,

"Do I sound like I'm complaining?"

"Erh no, but I'm not exactly light," I said, knowing how hard it could be with a full load on your back when hiking. But then again, not only was this guy built like a brick shit house full of muscles, he also wasn't human.

"You're not exactly heavy either. Now, if I had to carry you across Canada, I might have something to say about it," he commented dryly, making me scoff this time.

"But…"

"Red, do me a favour and shut up about it, yeah?" he interrupted, making me suck in a breath as my only answer.

"Wow, will you look at that, you do know how to do as you're told after all… are you sure you're a natural redhead?" he asked in an amused tone, making me huff and snap,

"I am a natural redhead!" At this he chuckled again, which was annoyingly a sound I was quickly coming to adore, before he commented to himself,

"Ah, there's my kitten's claws." Again, I was stunned at him calling me his and making it sound like he had already claimed me.

After this we let the silence surround us whilst my heart was continuing to beat a million miles an hour. I had just snapped at him and more shocking than that, he seemed to enjoy it! Oh, hell yeah, I was questioning just about everything by this point, and near bursting by the time I realised we had reached the clearing where my truck was packed.

"Nice ride. Do all Park Rangers get one?" he asked, setting me down near the passenger side.

"You know I'm a Ranger?" I asked stupidly, making him raise his scarred brow before cocking his head as if looking down to the bottom part of my uniform. I was just thankful I had left my hat at home on this occasion as they were harder to replace.

"Of course, you do, otherwise what else would I have been doing up there?" I muttered to my boots, making him take hold of my chin and force it back up to look at him.

"Get in the truck, Red," he said with his voice sounding more gruff this time, as if it was thickened by some hidden emotion he was feeling. *A secret part of me wished it was called lust.*

"Okay," I said in a small voice before I moved to walk around to the driver's side, fishing my keys out of my trouser pocket, glad I hadn't lost them like I had with my gun, radio and everything else I had dropped. But then suddenly a hand shot out and grabbed me by the jacket, gripping the leather hard enough for it to groan in his fist. Then he used it to pull me back to him slowly. So, with me having no other choice, I walked backwards to him before he stepped into me so my back was soon pressed into the passenger door.

"Whatcha doin', Red?" he said, making me frown in question.

"I'm… I'm driving home," I said, stuttering a little.

"No, you're not," he stated firmly.

"But you just said…" I stopped speaking when he cut me off with nothing more than a single hard look. One that was powerful enough to me make fearful of what would happen should I be foolish enough to ignore it. Because with that scarred brow now arched for a different reason this time, I knew exactly what he wanted.

He wanted to be obeyed.

Jesus, but why did that single look alone make me want to beg him to fuck me! I swear I even stopped breathing and would have done anything he asked of me. Like letting go of my keys when he took my fisted hand into his and started to peel back my fingers.

I was oh so compliant when he simply plucked them from my palm, and told me,

"Now, time to get your ass in the truck." He then pressed the button to unlock it whilst shifting me to one side so he could open the door. I didn't even have time to turn around before he grabbed my waist, spanning his hands around my belly before lifting me up into the seat.

"Oh." I gasped in surprise before he gave my legs a bit of a push so I was fully inside and before he slammed my door, he told me firmly…

"I always drive, Red."

EIGHTEEN

RIDING THE BEAST

For ages it seemed as if I didn't know what to say as we travelled back to town, only when he took a familiar road off, I couldn't help but ask,

"How do you know where I live?" He glanced my way, and I couldn't help but notice how his fists clenched on the wheel of my truck when he answered cryptically,

"I know a lot of things, Red."

"Like where I would be and what truck I drive?" I commented, remembering back to the way he hadn't asked me which ride had been mine and my Ford F250 wasn't the only truck parked at the clearing.

"Leave it be, Red," he said, and before I could stop myself, I snapped,

"I have a name you know, or is that something *you don't know?*" I asked in a tone that told him that I was sick of not getting any answers.

"Oh, I know it, Kitten," he said, purposely not using it and making me want to growl in frustration. Then I watched as his fingers relaxed and flexed on the wheel before he told me,

"I have to say for her age, she drives smooth."

"Well, she should considering all the new parts I put into her," I commented on a sigh, but he shot me a look as if he was shocked.

"You?" He didn't even try to keep the astonishment out of his tone.

"Yeah, my dad and I practically had to rebuild the engine and we welded the shit out of her, she looked like swiss cheese when I first got her," I said, forgetting for a time who I was talking to because the conversation started flowing about something I was passionate about. Again, he looked shocked and now, a little impressed.

"So, you're a gearhead, is that what you're trying to tell me, Red?" he asked in an amused tone, that I was trying gauge if it was mocking or not.

"No, I am the only child of a gearhead who wanted his daughter to know how to change a tyre and do an oil change without getting ripped off by some asshole who thinks his female customers don't know shit. What happened next was just taking it to the next level so I didn't need a mechanic after all," I told him, saying more in that one sentence to him than I ever had or ever thought I would. But like this, in my space, my pride and joy, I didn't know why but it was just easier to talk to him and be myself whilst doing it.

"Sounds like a smart man," he commented with a nod of his head, making me grin and think of my dad.

"That he is," I agreed with a grin.

"So, I'm curious…"

"Not as much as me, I can imagine," I interrupted, making him scoff in agreement,

"No, I can imagine not."

"You're going to ask why I didn't become a mechanic, aren't you?" I said, beating him to it. He grinned and replied,

"You have to admit, a dancing mechanic sounds like a fucking Broadway show." At this I laughed once before feeling my cheeks heat at the memory. But then I released a sigh knowing it was time to cut this conversation short before he started asking more difficult questions.

"I don't dance anymore and fixing up cars is only enjoyable when I do it with my dad. The wilderness is my passion and keeps me busy enough," I told him, making him frown as if that wasn't a good enough reason for him, but when I looked out the window and saw my trailer, I sighed in relief.

"Well, at least it's petrol and not a dirty diesel," he said steering the conversation back to my car, and I had a feeling he did this for my benefit.

"Of course, it sounds better and it's more powerful," I agreed, again making him look slightly impressed, and the knowledge of that made my heart pound quicker.

"You ever been on the back of someone's bike?" he asked, shocking me with the question and making me wonder what he was really asking.

"No, why?"

"Good to know," he said to himself, not answering my question and before I could press for one, he pulled up close to my trailer. I had no option but to open my door as he had cut the engine and started getting out his side. Oh

and of course, doing so far easier than I did due to my lack of height.

But then, as I slipped from the cab, he clenched his jaw to see I was already out and slamming the door. Was it because he wanted to help me out? So far, he had manhandled me into doing what he wanted but he had strangely combined this with being a gentleman. Not something I would have ever thought to call him. But then secretly I also hoped it was because he had wanted the excuse to put his hands on me again.

A fantasy I would no doubt have fun dreaming about once this was all over. Something I knew was about thirty seconds away from happening seeing as we were nearly at my door.

"Well, I guess this is another goodbye, thank you for… uh, what are you…?" This was cut off when he unlocked my door and repeated what he had said earlier,

"Like I said, you look like a smart girl, Red, what does it look like I am doing?"

"But… but you can't just invite yourself in!" I argued, now looking around my small space and internally freaking out about what mess there was! Which was why I hurried to the small sink and started putting what I had left to dry into shelves. Then I turned around and grabbed the pile of washing I hadn't folded yet and stuffed it into a small closest space, all the while he watched me with a smirk playing at his lips.

"Don't clean up on account of me... although this looks a little dry for my taste," he commented with a knowing grin whilst nodding down at the hard noodles in the pan, making me blush.

"I was cooking my dinner when I got the call out," I mumbled, slipping between him and the hob, now grabbing the pan and dumping its contents in the trash.

"If that's what you call dinner then you haven't been doing it right all these years," he commented as dryly as the noodles. Damn him for being funny and giving me yet another thing to like about him.

"I am sorry but why are you still here again?" I asked in a snippy tone, that again looked as if it amused him no end. But then he started walking me backwards, and in such a small space it wasn't surprising that I soon had my back to something with nowhere else to go. Then he extended an arm over my head, doing so easily, making me look up at it and gulp before he leaned in closer and ordered,

"Eyes on me, little Red." They snapped to his as though

I wasn't even in charge of them anymore. As soon as he had them under his control and my gaze had nothing else but him in view, he told me,

"I am here to make sure that when you come crashing down from that adrenaline rush and realise what might have happened, *you don't do so alone.*" At this he then let his gaze lower, lingering a while on the sight of me wearing his jacket before a little smile played at the corner of his lips, and now that I had the light, I could see their perfect shape now framed by his dark trimmed beard, making me wonder what it would feel like when kissing him.

"It's fucking huge on you," he said with a shake of his head, and doing so more to himself which I was starting to discover seemed like a habit of his. And I don't know why but I would have smiled at the thought of knowing something intimate about his personality. Because up until now he had been nothing more than an enigma to me. Like crushing on a celebrity after watching them on screen and fooling yourself into thinking you know them.

Once again, the sound of a zip on the move was enough to draw me from my thoughts and I froze when I realised what he was doing. But his eyes turned heated before they sought my own unsure gaze, and it was as if he was now feeding from my emotions. Then, as the zip continued down, he lowered it so slowly as if at any moment he was expecting me to ask him to stop. As if almost daring me to when I knew I wouldn't.

I never would.

However, as soon as the last of the metal teeth were drawn through the zipper, he stepped closer, meaning my half naked body was hidden even from his own view. Then he leaned his head down and whispered in my ear,

"You're allowed to breathe, Kitten."

I sucked in a breath that was quickly followed by another, and a last shuddered one for good measure when he told me,

"Now, go shower before I mark this pretty skin of yours," he said, making my mouth drop and whisper a question,

"Mark me?" At this he lowered his hands to my shoulders and started to peel his jacket from me, doing so slowly enough to have me shamefully close my eyes against how good it felt to have him taking off my clothes. But then the second he growled, my eyes snapped open, and he told me with a rumble of words,

"The scent of others on you is riding my Beast hard."

I sucked in a breath, wondering if his words meant what I hoped they did or was it my hope that made them mean more?

"What… what does that mean?" I braved asking on a whisper. He closed his eyes for a moment before lowering his forehead to mine, and this time he stole my breath as I held it captive.

"Don't ask me that," he told me, holding himself so still over me, and again I was left feeling even more confused.

"But I…" I tried to say, until he bit out,

"No. No more questions, Red." I swallowed hard, and when I opened my mouth to say something more, he straightened and barked out his next order.

"Now go!" I snapped out of my haze the second he suddenly spun me around and pushed me towards the small door that was my bathroom. In fact, it was only when the door closed behind me that I realised I was now standing in there in only my bra and trousers, shivering.

Something that had nothing to do with being cold.

But everything to do with his cold dismissal.

NINETEEN

LIMONCELLO AND COOKIES

I don't know how it happened, but what Jared had said would happen… well, it did, and it did this when I was in the shower trying to get clean. It hit me all at once, the memory of all those hands grabbing me, squeezing my breasts, and the sound of my shirt ripping. The grunts and dirty promises of the vile things they wanted to do to me. The sound of my own screams drowning out the growls of anger as Jared found me close to being gang raped.

He had been right.

I was crashing.

I knew that the moment I ended up panting hard when

trying to scrub my skin clean, but nothing I did would wash the memory of them from my flesh. It was little wonder then that by the time I had managed to get myself under control, the water was freezing, and my skin looked red raw. I also wiped the steam from the mirror and cringed before tears sprang to my eyes when I saw the bruise already quick to form on my cheek.

I hated how weak my body was. Asking myself why, for once, it couldn't just show the strength of my soul. The strength of my will. I shook my head and drew an angry hand across my face in the mirror, smearing it from view with the condensation dripping down. Then, after wrapping my largest towel around myself, I walked out, quickly slipping to the only bedroom at the back. I briefly heard Jared speaking in that deep voice of his, assuming he was on the phone to someone as I couldn't hear any reply.

I quickly towel dried my hair as much as I could, before dragging a brush through it and letting it spring back up. It looked darker wet, and a lot longer, but it was easier to plait to one side, which was what I did. Then I grabbed the first pair of clean PJs that was a matching set, and didn't even realise what was on them until I was fully dressed.

"But of course," I muttered with a sigh, seeing the little

howling cartoon wolves pattern over the black cotton, and the white tank top that had a large wolf with words arched over the top. I also thought a white bra was wise to wear, even though I was obviously getting ready for bed. But hey, what else was I supposed to do, dress in sexy lingerie and give him a 'come hither look'? Erm no, I didn't think so.

But then I knew getting dressed in my normal casual clothes also wouldn't seem right, seeing as it must be past midnight by now. I also grabbed a large tartan wrap that I often used to ward off the chill when my little heater wasn't enough. This meant that by the time I walked out of my bedroom and didn't see him, I released a deep sigh, asking myself if I was disappointed or relieved. Of course, my heart knew the truth. Proving this when I heard his voice out on my deck, making my heart rate shoot up once more. And I swear he heard it as he looked straight at me through the window, finishing the call by issuing a stern order,

"Just get here." Then he ended the call and I pretended not to look as he walked back inside, instead focusing on how good the sight of his leather jacket looked over one of my dining chairs. *If only it could stay there forever,* my lonely heart thought.

"Howling for coffee?" he asked, making me grant him a questioning look wondering why he looked so amused. But then when he nodded to my top, I remembered.

"I like wolves and coffee," I told him as an explanation, making his smirk deepen to a full-blown grin.

"Not sure they agree with the combination but what do I know, I am not a wolf and nor do I like coffee," he told me, making me grant him a look of shock.

"You don't like coffee? What's wrong with you?" I asked, making him chuckle.

"I tell you I'm not a wolf and it's the coffee part you get stuck on," he commented with a shake of his head, and doing so didn't manage to displace the knot of hair at the back of his neck, not even once. Whereas with me, all I had to do was sneeze and my hair would fling out in all directions. Even now I could feel the shorter curls escaping my braid as they dried.

"I don't have much else to offer you," I said, wondering why saying that made me feel shy, as I brushed back the curls behind my ears.

"I'm sure that's not true, Red," he said in a way that my gaze snapped to his as I could swear, I heard the sexual intent lingering there. But then, after stepping closer to my kitchen he doused that thought in ice.

"You have this crap," he said, opening my fridge and pulling out a tall yellow bottle. I laughed nervously before he told me,

"Come and sit down before you fall down."

"I am fine…"

"Now, Red!" he ordered, this time making me release a defeated sigh before muttering,

"Are you always this bossy?"

"Yes, especially when faced with stubborn *natural* redheads that are shaking, now sit your ass down," he said, making a point of purring out the word 'natural' after what I had snapped at him earlier. And speaking of natural, I *naturally* sat down where he wanted me, which was on my sofa. Then I watched as his large presence made itself comfortable in my tiny kitchenette. He found a hand towel and lay it out on the counter, making me wonder what he was doing. Well, this was until he grabbed an ice tray out of the small freezer compartment, and slapped it down on the counter, hard enough to make everything rattle around him. He didn't seem to care, making me now wonder if there would be a crack there from the force of his heavy hands.

I also wondered how on earth those same hands had been so gentle with me?

He gathered the edges making an ice pack, causing me to comment,

"Looks like you have done this a few times," at which he told me,

"I own a fight club for demons, Red, what do you think I do there? I frowned, not understanding what he meant but watched him as he opened cupboards until he found what he was looking for. Then with nothing but two fingers he hooked a glass, and the bottle in the other fingers, and held the ice pack in another hand. After this he lowered to one knee before me and I couldn't help but answer,

"Enjoy watching demons beat the crap out of each other and frightened human girls dance in between?" At this he smirked, and his eyes flashed at the memory as if it was one he enjoyed thinking back to.

"No, that's just on the good nights." He winked at me, making my heart nearly stop before he placed the ice on my sore cheek, doing so gently. Something that still surprised me given his size and obvious strength. To be honest, I was still in shock he was here and making his mission to take care of me. Once again, another 'why' question to add to the ever-growing list of whys.

"Here, now hold this," he said, raising my own hand to take over his own by keeping the ice to my cheek. Then I watched as he poured me a large shot of Limoncello and handed it to me, soon issuing his next bossy order.

"Drink this, you're still shaking," he commented with a frown. I took it and swirled the yellow liquid around the glass, which was when he asked me in a seductive tone,

"Tell me Red, why do you shake?" I wondered if he knew what that voice of his did to me. I swallowed hard before being brave enough to look back up at him, as even kneeling down he was still taller than me.

"You make my home look small," I said, not giving him a reason but giving him something, regardless.

"That's because it is fucking small and so are you… now drink," he stated as simple as that, making me want to say that my dad always told me good things come in small packages. But somehow, I didn't think he would agree. Because I often tortured myself wondering what type of women Jared went for. What type of woman would he pick from the endless amount no doubt throwing themselves at him on a nightly basis? But of course they would, he was utterly gorgeous and had that obvious rugged charm going for him, especially when he flirted or offered out one of those sexy half grins. Those smirks, and flashes of his silver eyes, as if some beast deep within him was trying to communicate through his host.

I bet he had the most beautiful women in the world offering themselves to him on a blood covered platter, all tall legs and perfectly styled hair, and every single one of them just like him… *a supernatural being.*

Something I would never have.

Something I would never be.

"Not sure Limoncello is going to cut it," I said, faking a laugh and trying to push past the irrational jealously I felt.

"Your bar was lacking, Kitten, so it was this or coffee… oh and I should probably tell you that I think you have a problem," he added, making me grant him a questioning look.

"What's that?" I said, hoping he didn't now say that 'I know you're falling madly in love with me and have been obsessing over me for the last eleven years but you can never have me, so it's pointless and sad'. Of course, what he actually did say was also the last thing I expected him to say.

"You have a serious biscuit addiction." At this my mouth dropped before I corrected,

"You mean cookies?" His lips twitched with amusement before he told me,

"No, I mean biscuit."

"A biscuit is bread that you eat with your meal." He gave me a condescending look before he told me,

"That's a roll, bap, bun, cob or even a fucking barm cake, my point is a cookie is a biscuit," he said, and I could tell he was playing with me but by this point, I couldn't help but play along.

"And what makes you right and me wrong if they are the same thing exactly?" Again, this received another lip twitch before he answered,

"Well, seeing as England as a nation is a fuck load of years older than where we are currently sat, then I would say I win. Now drink." Okay, so I let him have that one and instead, looked down at my drink and said,

"I think I would prefer coffee."

"And I would prefer a beer, but you have none, so this shit was all I could find," he said, making me laugh once before telling him,

"It was a gift from my parents when they went to Italy… erm… not that you needed to know that." He gave me a small smile, and after sniffing at the end of the bottle, he told me,

"Yeah, well it smells like a lemon took a piss." At this I burst out laughing and I had to say, it really helped to relieve the tension of what just happened. Of course, when his eyes widened, I knew it was because he was surprised. I had a bit of a funny laugh, as I had been told many times before. Because it would start off normal and then I would hiccup before making a series of 'hee he, hee he,' sounds after it. So, by the time I had finished, he was actually biting his bottom lip as if trying to stop himself from laughing at me.

In fact, it was how handsome he looked doing so that ended up sobering me up. So, after swallowing hard, I took a sip of my drink and told him,

"That was funny." To which he granted me a soft look in return, and said something that made my heart flip over…

"Finish your drink…"

…My Pretty Girl.

TWENTY

HIS WILD ONE

"*Finish your drink, my pretty girl,*" he said, before standing and telling me, "I won't be long." Then he walked towards the door, and just so I could concentrate on something other than the fact he had just called me pretty, I downed it in one. This meant that I ended up scrunching up my face before sticking out my tongue in a 'blah disgusting' motion, hoping this would help with the god-awful taste! But then I looked up, and embarrassment flooded my cheeks as unfortunately it was something he hadn't missed. Needless to say, he left, chuckling to himself and shaking his head as if he didn't know what to make of me.

Well, I knew what to make of him, as I was starting to fall even harder than before. And how could I not, when he was making me smile, laugh and feel safe after what had happened. Even despite his bossy ways, I was falling hard. And well, I wasn't even going to get into how he made me feel as a woman, as I don't think I had ever been so attracted to a guy before!

Sorry, Thor.

I released a deep sigh and asked myself aloud,

"What are you doing, Ella?" After this I got up and put my empty glass on the sink, along with the ice that I could no longer be bothered to hold to my cheek. The damage had already been done. I would bruise regardless, so what was the point? Not that he knew that.

I pulled my wrap closer around my shoulders, stopping mid action when I heard his voice and this time, there was a reply.

"I want it all gone," Jared said, making me frown, wondering what he was referring to. I ducked my head, trying to see who it was he was talking to, but they remained out of view. Their voice, however, was one I knew I had heard somewhere before, and I tried to remember who it belonged to.

"Then what will happen when she sees six deaths in the paper, it might trigger something, J." I knew then that they were talking about me and the assholes that had tried to sexually attack me. Jared released a frustrated growl and snapped,

"I don't want a single memory left."

"It won't work like that, and you know it. Something will trigger it if I take too much," the unknown man argued.

"Fine, then take it back to the gun but nothing more," Jared replied, clearly not happy with this. But I couldn't help but wonder what they meant about taking it back to my gun… taking what back, surely they couldn't tamper with my memories… was something like that even possible?

"Nothing of you?" the man asked, and a harder reply was heard this time.

"I said nothing more, and I meant it!"

"Fine, but for the record, I think you are making a mistake," the voice argued in a defeated tone.

"Noted. Now give me ten more minutes with the girl," Jared snapped again before a cocky response was ignored.

"Sure thing, boss man," the guy said.

I looked towards the door to watch as Jared reappeared,

making me ask quickly,

"Who else is out there?" He looked surprised for a minute before looking back to the closed door and muttering to himself,

"Idiot forgot to mask himself."

"Who is..." I started to ask again when he began to stalk towards me, the sight of which cut off my questions quickly.

"Don't worry about it, Red, now it's time for you to lie down." The sound of that authoritative tone made me want to fight against it, and at the same time do as I was told... and quickly. In the end, I didn't get the choice or the time to make a decision before he was using his intimidating size to walk me backwards, this time placing a hand at my hip and steering me to the very back of my trailer.

"What are you...?"

"Bed!" He growled out the one word and when the back of my knees hit the edge of my bed, I had nowhere else to go but down, but with my legs still dangling off the sides. This was when he decided to take matters into his own hands... *literally.* Something that started when he lowered himself down over me, and I felt as if my lungs had seized! Only my ragged breathing was stopping me

from passing out as all my dreams of him had started to become a reality!

How long had I waited?

How long had I dreamed?

He scooped an arm underneath my back and started to pull me up with him as he crawled us both further up the bed, before lowering me down when my head was at the pillow. I couldn't believe he was here. He was here in my tiny room, on a bed that was barely big enough for him, let alone the both of us. But I didn't care. I didn't care that the setting wasn't perfect. I didn't care that I wasn't wearing something as sexy as I'd hoped, as I'd dreamed I would. I didn't care that I hadn't had time to shave my legs or other parts that weren't as smooth as I hoped they would be. I just didn't care for the perfection I would have spent hours trying to create for this moment.

He was all the perfection it needed.

"You shouldn't look at me like that, Red," he warned with a rasp, making me gasp, before braving the question,

"Like what?"

"Like you're waiting for a hungry wolf to ravish you," he whispered, making me squirm beneath him. This was when he rolled from me and with a groan of frustration,

sat on the edge of the bed pushing both his hands up over his head. I swallowed hard with the disappointment, that was near big enough to choke on. I also moved, and sat up, putting my back to the headboard that was fixed against the wall. I watched as he released a sigh, making his tensed back muscles relax. As for me, I was so confused. It seemed like he wanted me but if that was true, then why did he hold himself back?

Was it… *because I was human?*

I was so lost in my turmoil and disillusionment, a hope I had foolishly allowed myself to believe in that I nearly jumped out of my skin when I felt him touch me.

"Easy, Red."

"You say that a lot," I commented, making him scoff,

"That's because you flinch a lot when I touch you," he replied, and I guess it was true, if only he knew the reasons behind it. After a few seconds of my silence, I felt his touch once more, this time running the backs of his fingers down my bare shoulder, making me realise that I had lost my wrap along the way.

"Damn, Red, you scrubbed yourself too hard," he said in a gentle tone, and I couldn't look at him when I answered on a pained whisper,

"Not enough." This was when he hooked a crooked finger under my chin and forced my head back towards him. Then he applied enough pressure to force my head up, so I had no choice but to see the concern in his beautiful light grey eyes. Then he ran those same fingers down my cheek and said,

"You bruise like a fucking peach." I knew it was true, but only one of us knew why, which was when I tensed as his eyes travelled down the length of me and stopped when he saw the inside of my arm.

"But wait, what is this?" he asked when finding the bruise on the inside of my elbow, and there was no mistaking what it could be from. He growled low and angry before lifting up my arm and taking a sniff at the skin, as if trying to figure out what drug I had shot into my vein. I was, of course, insulted and grabbed it back from him, telling him firmly,

"It's not any of that! Jeez, I give blood at the hospital, alright!" He frowned down at me, but wisely didn't comment… *it also looked as if he didn't believe me.* But instead of admitting this and pressing matters that clearly didn't concern him, he looked back at my trailer. Then he homed in on the empty dog bed and, as if needing to change the subject, asked,

"Should I be expecting an angry overprotective mutt to come barrelling at me from outside for pissing off its owner?" I released a sigh and told him,

"No, he's at the vet." He cocked his head and raised a sexy brow, as if needing more information, so I told him,

"He ate my cookies."

"So, you had to teach him a lesson?" he said with a serious nod of his head as if he agreed with this.

"What no, of course not! I would never hurt… wait, you're teasing me?" I asked in shock, and for the first time I received a different type of smile. One that wasn't mocking, or even teasing. No, this time it was one created from a purely happy emotion. And it was breath taking! A smile that transformed his face into something so beautiful it almost hurt to look at, creating an actual ache in my chest.

Then he told me,

"Yes, Red, *I am teasing you.*"

After this I could no longer stop the most important question on my mind from being asked.

"Why are you here, Jared?" At this he raised his eyes, as if hearing his name for the first time on my lips affected him. They even glowed for a moment before turning darker and I gasped at the intensity of them. Then he warned in a serious tone,

"Don't go there, Red."

"But I don't understand…" I started to say but he quickly interrupted me.

"And trust me when I say that it's for the best that you don't."

"But…" I pushed, as I needed to know and pretty soon I knew he would leave, and I would miss my chance at trying to understand.

"Leave it, Red…" he said again, this time in a firmer tone that I was still trying to ignore.

"But I don't…" This was when he released a sigh and gave me something for the first time that I had only seconds ago given him.

"I said leave it, Ella." His warning was said softly this time, speaking my name and making me suck in a quick breath of surprise.

"Am I interrupting, only you did say ten minutes," a voice said from the doorway and the second I saw that familiar face, I shouted,

"Oh, hell no! Not you again!" At this Jared looked

shocked and turned his head slowly toward Marcus who was now looking as smug as ever, leaning against the door frame as though he was thrilled with my reaction. He looked just as I remembered him, although maybe a little toned down and less flamboyant. Though, with that being said, he still wasn't dressed like a guy that was trying to blend in with human society.

Not when his suit was lacking the usual attire that complements a businessman. For starters, his jacket was longer and flared out a little at the back, with a thick wide collar of black velvet. This matched the red velvet cuffs that were folded back against the ends of the sleeves. Underneath, he wore a loose white shirt that was pulled tight to his slim frame by the red waistcoat he wore, also known as a vest in my house by my dad who was American. My mom, however, insisted it was called a waistcoat, so I often used both terms to appease both parents. This thought took me back to the earlier cookie-biscuit incident, and despite what Jared said, they will always be cookies in my opinion. Although now I wasn't sure I would ever look at them the same as before.

Just another thing to remind me of him, I thought with a sigh.

As for Marcus, he had traded the conventional tie for a long, red silk scarf, that was loosely wrapped around his neck and half hung down his chest. Fingerless gloves, his usual jester makeup and a pair of dark round sunglass resting low on his straight, regal nose completed the arrogant look.

"Ah, nice to know I make an impression. Nice to see you again, Cookie." At this Jared snarled at him and snapped,

"Don't make this harder, dipshit, just get on with it!" This was when I felt a tremor of fear roll back down my spine as I turned my accusing eyes back to Jared.

"Get on with what?" I asked, making him release a frustrated sigh before running a hand back over his contained hair.

"You still want me to do this, J?" Marcus asked as if waiting for the go ahead, and I asked again,

"Do what?!" Jared didn't look at me but instead nodded his head to Marcus, telling him yes. I sucked in a frightened breath the second Marcus took his first steps towards me, answering for him,

"Very well… don't worry, it's just time to sleep, Cookie." This was when I started to panic, telling him,

"I can fall asleep by myself… I… I don't need his help!" I shouted, now getting off the bed and trying to barge past him, ready to try and demand they both leave. But then I don't know what I had been thinking, as this was when Jared took the matter in hand or should I say, both of them! Something he did by banding one muscular arm across my torso and the other around my waist and pulling me hard against him. I started struggling in his arms and every time I twisted, I winced when feeling the pain of it pull at my back and stomach. But he held on, knowing nothing of my pain, one that was both physical and mental, thanks to him and his betrayal.

A pain against my heart.

"I am sorry, Red, but it's better this way," Jared told me in a gentle tone, one that went against the way he forced me to stay as his prisoner in his arms. Something that was useless to fight against as he was just so strong.

Too damn strong.

So, after a moment more of trying to get free, he must have felt the fight go out of me as I relaxed in his hold, crying out a sob and unable to hold it back anymore. I felt him smooth back my hair from my face now he had me trapped with one arm, holding my wrist to my shoulder that was forced across my chest under the heavy weight of his own.

"Ssshh now, it will be alright, Ella, my little Red, my little dancer," he cooed as Marcus came closer, now with the grin completely wiped off his normally cocky features and with something else replacing it entirely. Something that worried me more as he now looked concerned.

"J, are you…"

"Just fucking do it!" he barked back, making me flinch in his hold and I turned my head, not wanting to watch whatever it was they were about to do to me. My heart and my breathing were close to breaking. My lungs, not what they once were, started to fail me as I could feel the panic building.

"Fuck! Okay, okay… Ella, listen to my voice. Can you hear it, how soft it sounds, how comforting… *tell me you can,*" Marcus said, and after his initial curse, his voice sounded completely different. It had now taken on a gentle, soothing tone of the likes I had never known. In fact, it made me instantly relax, as if my limbs were no longer my own. Then I allowed my eyes to close after hearing a silent wish for me to do so in my mind.

"There she is… good girl, Ella, good girl. You're doing

so well, now take a breath for me… that's it, and now another," he said, making me do as he asked, now with a contented smile on my face, no longer scared of him or anything he had to tell me. It was also at this point that I felt myself being lowered to the bed and soon that strong, unyielding hold left me.

"She will be safe with me, go on, this won't take long," Marcus said, making me wonder who would be safe. I hoped it would be me because I never wanted him to stop talking to me. I felt drunk from it, so light… the lightest I had ever been.

"No more pain," I said in a dreamy way, making Jared snap,

"What did she just say!" At this I felt something seep back into my consciousness and spoke a name in question,

"Jared?"

"J, leave or I will lose my connection. Go and I will discover what she means. Go now or this won't work!" Marcus snapped, and after a deep and rumbled sigh of frustration was heard, I felt a gentle caress down my cheek. That's when I finally gathered the strength of will enough to open my eyes in time to see Jared leaning down over me.

He then kissed my cheek and whispered…
"I am sorry for this, My Wild One."

Then he was gone.

TWENTY ONE

DREAMS BELIEVED

Voices.

That's all I heard, and they started to merge, like points in time were trying to fuse together. First, it belonged to the clown. The cocky jester, only now he wasn't laughing anymore. His tone wasn't one of mockery like it had been that first night in Jared's club.

No, now it was serious.

"I don't know what to tell you, J… I can't understand why but I just know what I felt," he said in a dire tone.

"And what the fuck is that?!" Jared demanded on an angry snarl.

"A lot of pain." Marcus sighed and Jared's reply to this was a growl, one that was low and threatening.

"Then I missed something, and she needs a doctor," Jared snapped.

"That's just it, J… you didn't miss anything," Marcus replied, making Jared snarl in frustration,

"Marcus, don't fuck around!" I heard someone sigh before Marcus then told him,

"She feels pain but it's… it's like something I've never encountered before, as if her mind is used to it… the pain, it's like it's been accepted but she is not physically harmed, I checked," he said, making Jared sound furious when he snapped,

"You did what!?"

"Mentally, I checked… fuck, I am not suicidal, J. I didn't touch anything but the girl's mind, like you ordered me too, remember?" Marcus replied sharply.

"Will it hold?" Jared asked, ignoring what he just said. Marcus exhaled and Jared snapped again,

"Will her memories hold, Marcus?!"

"For now, yes, she will have no recollection of this night other than getting away from them after pulling her gun. What she does after that, if something were to trigger her hidden memories, then who knows… this isn't exactly my skill set, J… I'm not the fucking Vampire King here," he replied, making me toss around, trying to grip on to the conversation I could hear. One I heard outside my window. One I heard whilst sleeping.

Was it all just another dream?

"Have some of our men watch her. Order them to do so from afar just to be sure," Jared said in that commanding tone of his.

"I think that's wise. And well, if she goes and books a flight to London intent on hunting your ass down, then we will know for sure." Jared growled at that, like he did after almost everything Marcus had said up to this point.

"She won't remember me. *She can't!*" Jared declared, making my entire body tense. He didn't want me to remember him… *but why?* The pain increased because of it.

"Where you are you going now?" Marcus asked and the last thing I heard Jared say before even more darkness overtook me was as startling as it was frightening,

"First, I have to take care of a dead man still breathing, after that… *I have a Draven to call.*"

PRESENT DAY...

Voices.

No, not voices this time. *Just one.*

And with the sound of another frustrated voice, I opened my eyes. That, and someone was licking at my hand.

Duke.

But how? He had been at the vets. He had been sick. What was he doing here now? But wait, that had been months ago. Three months to be exact. I shook my head as if trying to make sense of what was going on. As if my memories had merged and left me feeling confused as to what just happened and what had been taken from me.

Taken from me?

"Marcus," I whispered, remembering him being there now but then... he hadn't been the only one.

"Jared." Christ, but even saying his name was painful and had me clutching at my chest, like this would help in holding it all together. I felt like I was breaking and for once, it had nothing to do with my weak body!

"Yeah, and like I fucking said, that shit you didn't think was going to happen, guess what, it just fucking happened!" I heard Orson bark out angrily, making me wonder who it was he was talking to, and it made me shake out of the lingering memories pretty quickly. This meant that it took me only seconds to take in my surroundings and realise that I was looking at my little home.

A small desk at the very end of my trailer that opened up into a pull-out sofa and a small table big enough for two sat opposite a small kitchenette. A bathroom door faced a line of cupboards and beyond that was my bedroom. Nothing had changed. So why did my eyes automatically go to one of the two chairs at my small table to find something missing.

Something I knew I wanted to find.

But it was gone.

Black leather.

"What do you think I did, asshole, invite them to a fucking tea party?!" Orson growled in an irritated manner, making me even more curious as to who it was he was speaking to. Well, whoever it was, he clearly didn't like the obvious being stated.

"Yeah, well stuff is going to have to move pretty quickly 'cos it's not safe here… not anymore," he said, making me frown in question. It was at this point that I decided to sit up, alerting him to the fact that I was awake. He was stood directly outside my window on the decking area me and Rex had built together. And as soon as he saw that I was awake, his demeanour changed, and I had the distinct feeling that this was done on purpose. He no doubt didn't want me to see him this agitated, and again I questioned the reasons why. I knew this when he purposely lowered his voice and said to the caller,

"I have to go. I will keep you updated." Then he abruptly ended the call before making his way to the door.

"What the hell happened? How did I get here?" I asked quickly, after shaking the lasting fogginess from my mind. It was at this point he raised both hands as if I was holding a gun to him, and told me,

"Take it easy."

"Take it easy, are you serious?!" I snapped, wondering how I was supposed to accomplish taking it easy after what I had just seen, that was if I had seen it at all. But then, what memory was I talking about?

"Excuse me, Lionel, what do you think this is, a damn Sunday?!" I snapped, knowing he had just eternally ruined a classic song for me. Of course, one look at his confused face and I knew he had no idea what I was talking about.

"Okay, let's try another way, leaving Lionel Richie out of this, I know what I saw… what I…" I let that sentence tail off as I frowned, trying to separate the two moments in time.

"Yeah, and what's that?" he asked, now crossing his arms over his chest and making his brown suede jacket pull tight around his biceps.

"I just saw… saw…" I stammered, suddenly not feeling so confident. Because it was true that one minute, I was staring at four guys that looked more like monsters from a horror movie, or some awesome extras from a vampire series on TV. Guys, who the moment Orson had turned up, had changed into exactly what he said they were. Four teenagers that seemed to be making a piss poor job at dismembering a buck they had taken down. And what had I done but a piss poor excuse for my job before fainting like some damsel in distress.

I wanted to kick my own ass, which was precisely why I reached back inside my trailer and grabbed my Ranger's jacket, now putting it on along with everything else that Orson had obviously taken off. Unfortunately, this hadn't been done for some romantic gesture to get me naked and underneath him, meaning that the only other thing he had taken off was my gun belt.

But then why did that thought now leave a sour taste in my mouth? It had been not even a day ago that I had wanted Orson to ask me out, to take our friendship to another level. To have him kiss me before spending the night in my bed and not on the sofa. I was about to ask myself what had changed but then I knew, didn't I?

Jared.

He had been here, or had that all just been another dream? But then if it was, why did it feel so real? And why was I only remembering it all now? Fuck! There were too many unanswered questions, and unfortunately the wrong man stood in front of me now for me to get them.

"Stay, Duke," I told my dog, making him whine but flop back down in his bed all the same.

"What do you think you're doing?" Orson asked as if shocked, which was why I frowned at him, before I barged my way past him, nudging his arm out the way quickly enough to prevent his bulk from stopping me.

"What does it look like I'm doing, my job!" I told him, using my sternest voice and one that I had shamefully practised when training for this job. Because it was all about playing a part and believing in that roll you stepped into the moment you put on the uniform. There was a lot to be said about a uniform, and I could understand why anyone who wore one would automatically feel an authoritative side of them coming out. People needed to distinguish between you and them, and the best way to do that was a uniform that spoke of the laws even before you opened your mouth.

Of course, there were those that didn't care and thought they were above the law. But most of the time, all that was needed was a stern warning to have people doing what you needed them to do to follow the rules. But one look at Orson and I knew that my stern voice might as well have been a Minnie Mouse impersonation for it did nothing for him.

"Ella… fuck sake, Ella, wait… I said wait, damn it!" This last part was snapped at me the second he grabbed my jacket to pull me back to face him, stopping me from heading down into my truck.

"What!" I snapped back, only feeling bad when his brown sugar eyes softened right into melted caramel.

"You can't go back up there," he told me, making me angry.

"The hell I can't, it's my job!"

"I know, just… just wait, wait for a little while… until…"

"Until what?" It was at this point he looked to be struggling with himself and didn't know what to say. I released a sigh and looked over my shoulder, back at the forest over the lake.

"Let me ask you, up there on Lasca Creek, do you still stand by what happened?" I asked, now folding my arms. Orson looked torn before gritting out,

"Yes."

"Then that means there is nothing for me to worry about," I said, knowing that I had to get back up there. I had to know for sure what was happening. Because right now, it felt as if I was honestly going fucking insane!

"Ella, wait… that is not what I am saying!"

"Look, I don't know what's going on with you, but I have a job to do, as not only do I still have missing hikers to find, I also now have poachers to deal with. A bunch of kids that I very much doubt have a licence and have taken down a buck. I get that, as a friend, you want to keep me safe and I appreciate that, but nothing is going to stop me from doing my job, Orson." At this it was his turn to sigh in frustration before his shoulders slumped.

"Look, I can see there's something that you're not telling me, so you have about five seconds to choose, you either tell me what it is and explain the reasons you don't want me going back up there, or I leave anyway. But the way I see it, is that staying silent might make me unprepared for whatever reason it is you don't want me going back up there, and my gut is telling me it's important enough that I should listen, or you wouldn't still be here," I said, trying to call his bluff, but then he looked conflicted, looking off to one side over his shoulder and down at the ground as if there was a place in the rocky shore that held all the answers.

"Tell me why it's not safe, Orson," I said, this time in a softer tone, hoping it was one capable of coaxing the answer from him. It was at this moment that he looked back at me and raised a hand to my cheek, before running the backs of his thick fingers down my skin,

"Ella." He whispered my name, as if it was all obvious yet we both knew that it wasn't. Then, as if he couldn't hold himself back anymore, as if he was going against some moral code set in stone, he cursed under his breath,

"Fuck it!" Then he started to lower his head, and I knew this time there was no mistaking his actions for

friendship. Not on his part. Not anymore. Because this was when he decided to make his move, and I can only say that I wished I had been ready for it as I had so many times before. But that was before that dream of Jared. The one that felt so real, I had expected to find that leather jacket still there.

I had hoped for it.

I had yearned for it.

My heart breaking a little when it hadn't been.

Which meant that had he done this under other circumstances, my internal girly side would have been jumping up and down on her teenage bed, congratulating herself on the fact that she was going to receive a kiss from someone she'd had a crush on. However, the grownup side of me knew that the reason for this kiss was wrong. A way to keep me here. A kiss granted out of some noble sense of duty that Orson believed he was responsible for. As if he knew all along that I had a crush on him and the only way to keep me here was by tempting me with something I wanted.

Something I would have taken before that dream.

But not now.

Needless to say, this thought dampened my desires for

him pretty quickly. Which was why I placed a hand on his chest, one gentle but at the ready to hold him back, silently telling him that now wasn't the time. But then he covered my hand with his own, ignoring the gesture and lowering his head further, meaning that I would have no choice but to say the words.

"Orson, I…" but then my breathy whisper became lost to another sound. The sound of a vehicle approaching that made his head snap up, and this time when he cursed under his breath…

It wasn't because of me.

It was because of someone else…

"Fuck… We got a problem coming."

TWENTY TWO

NO SUCH PROMISE

"Oh shit," I complained.

Because I knew the moment I saw the police cruiser exactly who would be inside, and if the angry set to Orson's jaw was anything to go by, I would say he was about as happy at seeing Deputy Dick as I was.

He pulled up close to my trailer before getting out and slamming the door as if to make a point. Then he straightened his gun belt like he was announcing to the world who he was, as if the uniform he wore wasn't enough.

"Great, that's all we need," I mumbled under my breath with a roll of my eyes, something that Orson didn't miss.

"Let me deal with him," was his reply. The grit of his teeth told me that dealing with him could mean a number of things, mainly something that ended in pain for the asshole.

"And what the hell do you think you're doing here?!" Deputy Dickerson snapped, directing this question at me after first narrowing his gaze at my friend. You could tell instantly that he'd got the wrong idea about us. Though making an assumption about us wasn't so farfetched, as only moments ago, Orson had been about to kiss me.

"Last I checked, I live here," I snapped.

"I'm not talking about how you squeeze the old man for favours and somewhere to live just 'cause you're hot, I'm talking about your fucking job, and why you're not where you said you'd be!" At this my mouth dropped and anger struck.

"What the fuck did you say?!" I snapped, taking a step closer and finding Orson's hand sprayed across my belly, stopping me from getting closer.

"I said, let me handle this." He then growled down at me before turning his deadly gaze on the Deputy.

"She doesn't work for you, so I really don't think she owes you an explanation," Orson said, now folding his arms, and this time he did it whilst standing in front of me, creating an even bigger barrier between me and what he obviously considered a threat.

"Yeah, well I'm a cop and I'm stood here now demanding one, asshole," Dickerson snapped back, and I felt Orson's entire frame harden in front of me as if going on to hyper alert mode. Then Dickerson seemed to sniff the air as if he could smell alcohol or something on him. But given their difference in size, then I really thought that the Deputy was just relying on his position here. That or he must have had a death wish because despite how fit he was, he was clearly no match for Orson.

"And I'm stood here telling you that she doesn't have to give you one," he replied calmly, not budging an inch.

"No, clearly too busy giving you one on the job... is that it?!" It was in this moment that I really thought Orson was going to turn around and plant a fisted 'fuck off' across his face.

"I think you will find with you just being here without cause and now having a witness to what you just said, is enough for my girl here, to file a complaint of sexual harassment against you. Now is that what you want?" Orson said, trying to be diplomatic and I had to say, I was a little shocked at being called his girl. Although admittedly it did sound good, even if I had the unobtainable on my mind.

However, deputy douchebag clearly thought he was above the law he enforced and took a step forward, now nearly shaking he was so angry.

"You threatening me, boy?" he said, lowering his face as if he was some sort of bull about the charge, giving his shoulders a jerk as if this would make him look more menacing. I looked up at Orson to see him grin, one that spoke volumes as he could clearly hold his own.

"Yeah, I think I am," he told him, making Dickerson sneer at him.

"Well, I think I'd better remind you that it is an offence to threaten an officer of the law." It was at this point that I came to stand around Orson, or at least tried to but was stopped when his arm shot out and prevented me, meaning the closest I got was standing next to him.

"This is ridiculous, you're telling him that it's against the law for me to tell you that I'm about to put a complaint of sexual harassment to your department, and you're acting like this is an arrestable offence!" I snapped, once again trying to sidestep Orson's protection and gaining the attention of the Dick deputy.

"Funny you hearing it from your boyfriend that way, as I heard it totally different." At this I rolled my eyes and groaned.

"Of course, you would… so let me get this straight, on top of being a douchebag, you're also corrupt?" I said, crossing my arms over my chest.

"What did you say to me!?" he barked, taking another step and Orson did the same.

"Look, not that it's any of your business but I was up there doing my job looking for the missing hikers," I argued, wondering if there was any point trying to defend myself with this asshole. I mean seriously, what was his problem? Of course, the guy had always been a dick, but he had never crossed this sort of line before. Was it because of Orson or was it something else? In fact, now that I looked at him, I would say that he didn't look right. As if he was sick or something. I could see the damp hair around his neck and ears, as the perspiration on his skin formed beads of sweat that trickled down the sides of his face. Even his skin was pale, and he looked sickly, with his eyes red and bloodshot.

"And what, you thought that you would stop for a

fuck break with your buddy lumberjack here?!" Dickerson snapped, making my mouth drop in shock.

"You'd better watch your mouth!" Orson warned with deadly calm.

"You see, right there, that would be a threat to me!" The deputy said, now pointing a finger at him.

"That's it! I've had enough of this shit, if you don't leave now then I'm putting in complaint against you, as you do not get to come here and speak to me like this, insinuating that I'm some kind of... kind of..." I stammered unintentionally, giving him chance to answer for me.

"Whore I think is the word you're looking for!" I gasped.

"How dare you!" I shouted, but that was when Orson was done, and in three steps he had Dickerson by his jacket collar and thrown up against the side of my trailer. It was at this point that Duke started barking inside, hearing for himself that something was wrong.

"You do not get to speak to her like that!" Orson snarled, and this time it was most definitely a threat.

"I can speak to her however the fuck I want! Whose cock do you think she was sucking before she got on her knees for you!" The deputy shouted back, moving his head closer, and it was at this point I knew he'd lost his damn mind as my mouth fell open with disbelief. Okay, so yes, he was an asshole before, but this was something else! As though some sort of damn switch had been flipped. And now, well, he wasn't the only one as Orson got closer too, only inches from in his face before he snarled down at him. Now making me question who both of these men were?!

Why was Orson snarling and growling like… some kind of…

Of HellBeast?!

No, it wasn't possible! It couldn't be!

I must have just been imagining things. Yes. That was it!

But then why did it sound like a growl I had heard before? One coming from the woods that night, and one frightening enough that it scared away a predator of a very different kind? But that had been Jared or had that just been in my dreams? Fuck! But I was so confused I didn't know what to fucking think!

Well, whatever the truth was, I still had a situation that I needed to sort out, and quickly at that! Before these two started to tear into each other, which they looked about five seconds away from doing!

"You are seriously delusional! We went on one date, and it ended with me trying to get away from you as quickly as possible. Meaning that there would be absolutely no way in hell I would suck your cock!" I snapped back and in hindsight, it might not have been the best thing to go for. Because my words only managed to send him over the edge, as he suddenly headbutted Orson, taking him off guard before then lunging at me.

"Ah!" I screamed as I scrambled backwards and nearly fell to get away from him. Something that would have happened, however, Orson grabbed him by the back of his jacket and threw him behind him. He landed near his cruiser having no choice but to go tumbling to the stone beach.

"Orson, look… what… what's happening with his eyes?" I asked, fearful in that moment as the deputy started to fist the ground, growling as if he was close to tearing out of his own skin. Orson lifted his head up a little as if trying to catch some scent on the air and when he did, his eyes grew wide.

"Impossible," he muttered before the deputy was back on his feet and now pulling his gun, telling me that shit was about to get serious.

"Get on your knees, fucker!" he demanded, which was when I decided to act in the only way I knew how. Because if I pulled my own gun, then that wasn't going to be a good enough way to stop him. So, I quickly took out my phone and start filming, threatening him in a different way...

With evidence of the truth.

Because the deputy had lost his damn mind and was so close to the edge, I knew he could quite easily go way too far. Meaning that it would be his word against mine. The word of a cop against the word of a Park Ranger... Needless to say, I didn't like my odds. He could just shoot me and get rid of the evidence for both murders.

So, I started talking quickly, after pressing live.

"My name is Ella Connor, I am a Park Ranger, and I am filming a live feed to social media of this altercation between Deputy Daniel Dickerson and Orson Esben, who did not provoke this action to be taken in any way."

"What the fuck do you think you're doing, put down the damn phone!" Dickerson ordered.

"It is my right to provide a witness account to whatever may transpire next. I refuse to stop filming as this will be classed as evidence for whatever happens. Deputy Daniel Dickerson arrived at my place of residence and demanded why I was not at work and used foul language against me and my friend. I will be filing a sexual harassment complaint against Deputy Daniel Dickerson after today's events. As for now the deputy, well, as you can see he has pulled his firearm at my friend, who is as you can also see being cooperative by getting on his knees… Orson." I said his name as a warning for him to do just that. Meaning that the deputy would have no choice but to follow through with his actions or arrest and not shoot an unarmed man live on social media.

I could tell by the way he was looking at me this wasn't over, and I just hoped that anyone watching this now could see the hatred of those cold eyes now looking back at me. As for Orson, one look at my own desperate gaze told him all he needed to know, that I was silently pleading for him to comply. Which was why he released a heavy sigh and dropped to his knees before putting his hands behind his head.

"This isn't over between me and you, bitch, as for this asshole, you're under arrest."

"On what charge?" Orson snapped.

"For pissing me off!" the deputy snapped back, making me wonder if he had even a clue at how this was going to look for him. After this, he holstered his weapon and took out his cuffs, before snapping the restraints around Orson's thick wrists.

"Let's move, asshole," the deputy said, giving him a kick and making my friend snarl back at him in anger. However, he gracefully got to his feet despite having his hands tied behind his back, and I lowered my phone, hiding it from view so that the deputy would think that I had stopped filming, now hoping that I would catch him out. The dickhead didn't disappoint.

"This isn't over between me and you, and nobody better watch that video or else," Dickerson demanded, obviously not getting the part where I had already made it so everyone could watch it. I even did it live on the town's Facebook group so that no one would miss it! Hopefully this meant his career as a cop was over as he didn't deserve to wear that badge!

"Or else what, you threatening me again?" I purposely asked, knowing he would fall for the bait.

"It's not a fucking threat, it's a promise, watch your back, Connor, as asshole here may not be there to save you next time." After this he forced Orson back to the patrol car, leading him by his elbow. But this was when he ignored his current situation and looked back at me, using the time he had left to warn me,

"Stay out of the woods, Ella."

"Orson, I've got a job to do… I can't just…" I started to argue back, but he started pleading with me,

"Promise me, Ella, stay out of the woods… don't go back there!" he continued to say this until he was sat in the car, he barely had enough space to pop his head out before the door closed to tell me one last time,

"Leave this place, Ella… run far away…"

"Orson?" I questioned, and the very last thing he said before his face was pushed and the car door slammed was,

"It's not safe for you…"

"Not anymore."

TWENTY THREE

THE THREAT OF HELP

"It's not safe for you... *Not anymore.*"

Orson's last words rang in my mind, as if hanging there like a speech bubble in the air, clinging to my aura and following me around. It was like a dark cloud, and left me slumped on the deck asking myself what the hell just happened. I mean, I knew Deputy Dickerson was a huge asshole, but I didn't think he would go that far. But then, when I thought back to that crazy look in his eyes, I couldn't help but shiver. Had he been on drugs?

And what was that with Orson, when he seemed to realise something about him? Again, just like my dreams of Jared, it left me asking myself more questions than I ever had any hope of getting answers to.

I was inclined to think it was drugs, as what else could it have been? Because even when I had got my phone out and started filming, he hadn't stopped or even attempted to tone it down. In fact, the only thing I believed my phone did was save Orson's life as I really believe Dickerson had wanted to shoot him. To shoot him and use his badge as a licence to kill for his own personal gain. I really didn't understand where it was coming from, I mean we'd had one date and it wasn't exactly like I spent it leading him on!

So naturally I was worried about Orson and exactly what was happening in that car. Would he have driven away to a secluded area, pulled over and shot him anyway? Then claim something ridiculous like Orson did something to escape or attack him. This thought made my back go ram rod straight as panic started to take over and before I could think, I had my phone in my hand and was calling the station. Then I quickly told them what had happened and how I was worried about Deputy Daniel Dickerson's state of mind. I sent them a link to the live video, hoping they wouldn't just ignore it. But then knowing that I was creating evidence by leaving a digital trail, they would know that would only look bad on the force should this whole thing go south.

But just to be sure, once I was off the call and they assured me they would check it out, I also sent it to my head office, so my own people had a copy explaining what had happened and that I was formally putting in a complaint about the deputy. I then spent the next few minutes furiously looking into the procedure on how to make that formal complaint of sexual harassment, knowing that the video would help. In other words, Deputy Daniel Dickerson was screwed and definitely not in the way he was hoping with me!

Christ, I was so angry! But I also knew that despite what Orson had said, I still had a job to do and some hikers to find. Which was why I got to my feet and grabbed the rest of my gear.

"Sorry, buddy, not this time," I told Duke, who was still sulking because he wasn't playing detective with me this time. Then I locked my trailer and headed to my truck. But then, as I wrapped my hand around the handle, Orson's words rang in my head like a warning bell, reminding me of the threat out there. Had he been referring to what had happened in the woods, had he lied to me and told me it wasn't what it actually was to save me? And why had I just passed out like that?

But then how had he made me see what I had? A bunch of kids hunched over a dead buck. At first, when waking, I hadn't believed a word of it but now, it was as if something had happened during the altercation between Orson and the Deputy.

Something in his eyes. Why had Dickerson freaked out at me so much for not being up in those woods? He seemed almost crazed but why? Well, there was only one way to find out and this time I wasn't coming back down from Lasca Creek without answers.

Many people would have thought that after what had happened back when I was eighteen, that my life would have been nothing but a constant paranoid state of mind. But in actual fact, since that night, I had never had another encounter of the supernatural kind… not unless I counted my dreams. But now, it had me questioning if that had been by design or if my luck had finally run out. Whatever the answer, Orson knew something about what I had seen up there with that gang of teens, I was sure of it!

"Well, it's time to go do my job!" I said aloud, as if

giving myself a prep talk before getting in the truck and making my way back to the last spot I remembered being in before passing out. Because if my gut was right, then I was sure that the teens had something to do with those missing hikers. But if that was the case, then why had Orson turned up? Was it to protect them?

Could he be involved somehow?

"No… no way," I said to myself after catching my own reflection in the mirror. But then I thought back to his parting words, and wondered then if the reason he was trying to keep me away was to give them chance to hide evidence or clean up the scene. And thinking back, why had Orson warned me just after getting the call not to go up there at all? Had he known something was going down or had it already happened?

Okay, so admittedly, I might have watched one too many crime shows but I couldn't help but be suspicious despite how much I liked him. I couldn't let that blind me from the truth…

Just like I had with Jared.

Who admittedly wasn't a man, *he was a HellBeast.*

This was a fact I had continued to remind myself of all these years, like some lifesaving mantra whenever I would let my mind linger too long on just how handsome he had been. Or just how affected I had been by his touch. Just like how I would wake in the night trembling from the warning he gave me. Where his words would linger like whispers taken by the wind or the remaining echo in a large empty room.

Would he really dare to keep me should he find me there again or was it nothing more than some empty threat? I always did wonder that, especially after dreaming of him and those steel coloured eyes of his. The power of that gaze had been like nothing else I had ever experienced before, and I knew I never would again. That thought was one I had battled with. One that I knew was by my own choice, as truth be told, I had thought so many times about going back there. Seeing if I could try my luck at sneaking in again and pushing him into making good on his threat, seeing if he would and what it would mean for my future.

"Snap out of it!" I shouted at myself, slapping a hand to the steering wheel in frustration as I usually did whenever my thoughts led me to him. *Always to him.* But then, as I watched my own hands grip the steering wheel tighter, I was transported back to another pair of hands. Hands that were bigger. Stronger. Tighter on the wheel. I closed my eyes for a second to try and snap out of it. A memory that was fighting to push to the surface begging me to dig deeper.

Thankfully, my thoughts soon led me back to my job as I parked where most of the tourists did, and even this triggered that same sense of déjà vu. I slammed my door and after swinging my gear on my back, I started along the trail. However, one look up and I knew that I only had a few hours of light left before I would have no choice but to abandon my search.

I wasn't going to be caught out here in the dark again… *not after last time.* Don't think about it, Ella, you pulled your gun and got out of there, I told myself. Just like I did whenever I allowed my shaky thoughts to go back to that night.

There was a growl. I pulled my gun. Then I ran. That was it.

But then, if that was true, why did I feel like this was the part I dreamed, and the dream was what actually happened?

"Head in the game, Ella," I said aloud this time. So, I continued on, but not before I radioed it in to check if there still hadn't been any sign of them, but it was a no. So, seeing as it was over half a day since they were last seen, I had wisely requested more people get involved in the search. Of course, after sending them a link to that video, I had also received a call from my boss straight after, asking if I was alright. He had also tried to convince me to stay home and let other rangers deal with it but knowing how stubborn I was, he also knew what the answer would be. Thankfully, Trent told me he would head over to the station to check and see how Orson was and speak personally to Deputy Daniel Dickerson's boss. Someone who just happened to be a good friend of his. I believe his words were, "I will have his fucking badge for this!" Needless to say, Trent felt a little protective over me and played the father figure, seeing as he didn't like that I was all alone. Just like Rex did.

I would have told him not to get involved but what was the point as he was almost as stubborn as I was. Two pig-headed peas in a pod we were, that's what Rex would say. He was right of course. Which was why I was still walking up the trail even after a few hours had passed.

But then, as I looked up at the sky, I knew that it was no use because it was time to turn back. Otherwise, I would lose the last of the light, making it difficult to make my way back without getting lost myself. I didn't fancy making camp for the night either, not after what I thought I had seen earlier. But I had to say, I was also surprised I hadn't come across anyone else, as I knew Trent had arranged a search party by now. Which meant it was time to radio in and let them know I had been unsuccessful on this part of the trail and was heading back.

"Jimmy, do you copy? Over."

"What's your status, Connor? Over," Jimmy asked, and I looked around before telling him,

"Still nothing. Tell Trent that I am calling it a night. Any luck with the others? Over," I asked, and after along moment of static, I got my answer.

"Others, what do you mean, you're the only one looking? Over." I frowned at this and shook my head a little before getting an explanation.

"What do you mean I'm the only one? I spoke to Trent earlier, and he told me he was putting Decker and Patterson on it, along with some locals. Over," I told him unable to shake the unease I felt.

"I don't know what to tell you, Connor, take it up with the boss. Over," Jimmy said in a confused tone.

"Oh, I will. Over and out," I said, before fishing my

phone out of my bag and calling Trent's personal cell.

"Hey Trent, what's this I hear from Jimmy saying you didn't get any more guys on the missing hikers, I thought I was getting some back up?" I asked, making him answer quickly,

"What are you talking about, I thought you found those hikers hours ago?!" At this I frowned, jerked my head back and said,

"Huh? Trent what are you..."

"Deputy Dickerson told me he went to check on you and said you had found them, so I..." I sucked in a quick breath before shouting,

"He's lying! Jesus, Trent, you believed him after what I told you happened, Christ, I even sent you the proof, did you not watch it?!"

"Whoa, slow down, honey, what are you talking about, showed me what?" he asked, making me shake my head in a little frantic movement as if asking myself what the hell was going on.

"You call me and... wait, what was that?" I asked the second I heard movement through the trees, and what sounded like... *laughter?* It was a creepy sound, sinister and unnerving. A sound that seemed to travel through the forest as if it were the voices of ghosts laughing at the living, mocking me for being there.

"Ella?" The sound of my name being said from the other end of the phone startled me, making me flinch.

"I can hear something," I whispered back.

"Fire a shot, scare off whatever is out there," he said in a strained voice, telling me of his own worry for me. But I had to admit, as I waited to see whether I could hear anything more, I too couldn't help but think that there was something out there, stalking me. Watching me… *preying on me.*

"Ella… fire the shot!" Trent said more desperate now, but I couldn't help but ask one thing,

"Orson… where was Orson?"

"Orson?" he asked in such a way it made the blood in my veins freeze.

"The deputy… what did he do with Orson?" I hissed, now being the desperate one.

"He wasn't there, he wasn't at the station… why… why would he be, in fact… why was I even at the station?" I sucked in a terrified breath, knowing now that something was terribly wrong. Which was why I whispered in a frightened tone,

"Because I asked you to." It was in this moment that the laughter came back, only this time it was right behind me, making me shriek out and drop the phone before spinning around.

And there, just as the last of the light fell thanks to the setting sun, I saw it. A pair of glowing white eyes staring back at me.

And then…

It lunged.

TWENTY FOUR

THE LOSS OF BLOOD AND FUR

I screamed the moment the creature lunged for me, bursting from the trees as if some blinding portal in Hell had just been opened, ripping through my reality. I barely had enough time to turn on my heel and run for it. I knew I had been merely seconds away from it jumping on me, as I felt the vibrations in my feet where it landed behind where I had just been. Even in my panic, I could hear my name being called from where I had dropped the phone, with Trent desperately calling out.

"HELP!" I shouted, hoping that he would get someone out here knowing that the likelihood of my surviving this attack was minimum. But even so, if my last act in this world wasn't to save myself then it would be to save others, because this beast needed to be caught before he could hurt anyone else!

Speaking of the beast, I turned my head enough to see that one more lunge like the first and it would be on me. But with this single look, it was enough to transport my mind back to earlier today and that's when I realised… *Orson had lied to me.*

I don't know how he made me believe what I had seen in the woods hadn't been real but there was no denying it now. This was no crazed wolf, and this was certainly no teenager with a trigger happy finger held over a shaky rifle.

This was…

A HellHound.

The image my mind had created hadn't been created at all! Because there it was, right in front of me, that demonic hound that had already torn free of its human skin. That had already broken away from the cloak of humanity it had once been hiding under. Well, it was hiding no more, as I knew that this wasn't nature fighting back after finding a human encroaching on its territory. There was nothing natural about this creature. Nothing at all.

This creature was straight from Hell.

And for some reason… *it was hunting me!*

So, I continued to run, and unfortunately whilst looking back in that split second, I realised that I was backing myself into trouble. Because now at my back was the sheer drop of a cliff face with a thicket of trees either side. This meant only one thing as the snarling creature approached… *I was trapped.*

So, with a shaky hand, I reached for my gun and lifted it to point in the direction of the hound, one that now stood there with its haunches held high and its head low, growling at me. I briefly questioned in my mind why it hadn't yet lunged for me when I realised in horror,

It wasn't the only one.

Four pairs of eyes, all glowing white, were now staring back at me from the trees and behind the hound that was leading the pack. But the moment I saw them all standing at a human's height, I knew what they were… *shifters.*

"Impossible!" I uttered, remembering what Orthrus had told me about HellHounds not having human hosts. Which had me questioning, was I wrong or was he? Because whatever they were, they definitely started out as men. This was confirmed as they began to walk closer

towards me before the shadows they created dropped to the floor on all fours. Then, one by one, they morphed into the same HellHound that was in front of them.

This was when I knew…

I was a dead woman!

Yet, despite knowing this, I also wasn't going to go down without a fight, which was why I took aim and fired my gun at the one in front. I knew I hit my mark when I heard a yelp of pain as it jerked back from the impact. However, it didn't manage to put it down like I had been hoping for. No, instead it snarled angrily before throwing its head back and roaring up at the sky, which was getting darker by the minute. This also meant that all I had achieved was pissing it off even more, giving it greater reason to tear me apart.

But then the sounds of these creatures weren't the only ones to be heard, as behind me a sound so menacing and loud rumbled through the trees, giving the creatures cause to still their steps. My head whipped around to see what had been the cause, now wondering if I had another Hellish creature to deal with. Although, if this were the case then I could potentially use it to my advantage. Because if it was my human meat they were about to fight over, then it might be enough for me to escape in the fray. That was, of course, in the hopes that I wasn't just about to face something more frightening and bigger than a pack of what looked to be HellHounds about to claim me as their dinner!

I didn't have time to wonder for long as the leader of the pack took its chance and leapt at me, making me take a step backwards, forcing me to get closer to the cliff at my back. I knew then that there was only two ways this was going to end, and neither looked good for me. As I was either stepping off this cliff and taking my chances in praying that nothing important broke, like my neck, or I would find myself caught in the teeth of those snapping jaws. Which meant I was presented with the very real saying, being between a rock and a fangy hard place.

However, just before I could take that plunge to certain death, a flash of darkness came barrelling through the trees and straight into the HellHound, taking him off his feet before he could get to me!

"Ah!" I screamed as the largest bear I had ever seen started tearing into the creature beneath him, making short work of biting limbs from a screaming man's torso. This was because the creature had shifted back to that of a human, making me wonder if this was what happened to all of them when being attacked. Like some sort of default mode.

All four of the HellHounds now howled in anger, before they worked as a pack to try and take down this new beast by circling him. A bear unlike I had ever seen before, which now had me asking myself if it was some sort of demonic version of what I once considered a majestic animal of the forest.

Its huge body consumed the sight of its dying kill beneath it and once it was dead, the bear raised its massive size up to standing. Its height was easily over ten feet tall, made to look even bigger when it threw its head back and roared first at the sky before then at the direction of the others, showing its thick white fangs. They looked wider than what I would have been able to get my fist around! Two gleaming fangs that were larger at the top, with two shorter ones at the bottom, all of which had a line of razor sharp teeth in between.

Then, as it dropped its heavy bulk back down to the earth, with its huge paws making the ground vibrate with the impact, a set of glowing yellow eyes pierced the dark, they were like twin burning hot coals set under two brows of spiked fur.

In fact, all of its midnight black fur looked interlaced with long needle like spikes that you would have expected to see on a porcupine. They were each tipped silver as if they had been dipped in metal, flashing with its movements. And as it twisted, I could see there were shorter needles that framed its neck, along with thick stripes of them running down its legs and along its back. The same silver also tipped those deadly claws that curled from its paws, protruding out from clumps of black hardened fur that looked like a mangle of thorns.

He was a beast!

One who charged and swiped out at the HellHounds as they attempted to ambush him from behind. Snarls of anger ripped through the air as the bear fought against the attacks, striking out its large talons three times the size of any normal bear. In truth, they were sharp enough that they cut straight through bone as if it had been butter, rendering one of the hounds completely severed in two. Another one lost its hind leg as it tried to escape, now dragging itself back to the safety of the trees after losing its limb. As for the other two, they were making deep, damaging bites after they had jumped onto the bear's back, clinging on with their fangs and claws embedded in its flesh.

I sucked in a frantic breath, in fear now for the bear, despite knowing whether it was friend or foe. Yet it continued to fight, doing so in furious anger whilst twisting its body and then rearing up on its hind legs, trying to dislodge them both from its back. One was furiously scratching at its flesh with its back legs, tearing into it and making me gasp in horror.

But this was when I knew I had to run. I had to try and get past the fighting! However, my legs refused to move. But it wasn't through fear, it was something else. Something deep inside was speaking to me, telling me that the bear needed my help. So, without another thought, I aimed my gun again and shot at the one that was doing the most damage. Three bullets was what it took and was enough to dislodge him, making the hound fall to the ground, now trying to shake off the shots.

Thankfully, this gave the bear long enough to turn and swipe at him, and I felt sick the moment I saw the hound's jaw severed from the rest of his head. It had been sliced through and flew at me, only to land at my feet in a mound of bloody flesh, teeth and bone. After this the bear gripped onto the other hound's head, holding it in its massive paw, curling its talons around its skull before lifting it up. It tried to twist free, desperately trying to scratch at the bear's long arm, but it was no good. The twisting stopped when the bear roared furiously in its face, inches from what would soon be the dead carcass. A second later, this happened when its head was crushed in his meaty paws. He dropped the dead hound before falling to his back, purposely crushing the one still clinging there.

This meant the fight was over as the one with the missing leg was long gone after limping into the woods. But it also meant that I was now stood alone with the bear who was only now getting back to its feet. And with the rest of the twilight still allowing that dark blue of the sky to show enough of my surroundings, I could see the damage the bear had taken. Because he might have won but it wasn't without its sacrifices, as his fur was now wet and gushing with blood, the worst of which was at his back. I held up my hands, dropping my gun and trying to show the beast that I was no threat. A laughable notion but I was taking no chances with me still holding a weapon because I knew now that the bear had come to my aid.

I knew this when all aggression seeped out of it, and it shuddered as if only now feeling the pain. Yet despite knowing it had saved my life, I still held myself perfectly still, remembering that I was only a footstep away from plummeting to my death. But I waited just in case, seeing what it would do next. However, as it stood there panting, a wheezing sound came from its chest before it suddenly crashed to the floor. Then I watched in astonishment as a darkness started to seep from beneath its fur, swallowing the body whole.

"What the Hell?" I muttered before it started to clear, only when it did, I cried out in shock and horror, as I could now see the truth.

The bear had also been a shifter. As now left in its place was the naked body of a large man.

A man I recognized.

"Orson!" I shouted his name before running over towards him, cradling his face and patting his cheek to try and get him to come back around. I sucked in a breath of relief the second his eyes flickered, awarding me that brown sugar, but instead of the kind eyes of the man I knew, instead they were now pained and unfocused.

"Orson!" I shouted his name again in panic, hoping that he would be alright and that more of those creatures wouldn't come back to try and finish the job. But then with a croaky voice, he told me,

"Ella… go."

"I am not leaving you!" I shouted back down at him, and he started to shake his head.

"You can't help me. I'm out of time… go… you have to go… you're too important to his world… go, Ella before it's too late!" he shouted frantically between laboured breaths. Then, before I could try anything more, he closed his eyes and I cried out as his breathing stopped.

"No! Orson!" I shouted but it was no use.

Because that's when I knew…

My friend was dead.

TWENTY FIVE

A CALL FOR HELP

"No!" I shouted as I buried myself in his chest, holding him to me, crying for the loss of someone I cared for.

"Orson." I whispered his name as I cupped his cheek, feeling no life beneath my palm. I even checked his pulse but there was nothing…

He was gone.

A sob tore through me as this knowledge slammed into me, that he wasn't coming back. He had died saving me and he… he wasn't coming back.

"This is all my fault… all… my… fault," I cried, holding

him closer, feeling myself breaking under the weight of my guilt. I should have listened to him. He warned me not to come here but I did anyway. Why didn't I listen?

"Why didn't I listen to you!?" I chastised myself, letting my forehead fall hard to his chest. I didn't want to let go. I didn't want to leave him, but I knew the moment I heard the movement in the forest that I needed to move. I needed to do as Orson told me or I would be making his sacrifice a pointless one. A loss of life in vain as he had to die saving me and what was I about to do, stick around and let myself get attacked again.

He had wanted me to run, and with there being nothing more I could do to help him, I knew I was out of options. So, I cupped his handsome, rugged face and whispered down at him,

"I'm so sorry... so... so sorry... my friend." Then I kissed him on his lips and cried, letting my tears fall on his lifeless skin. Then, after putting my forehead to his, I told him,

"I will never forget you... Never."

After this I forced myself to move, grabbing my gun off the floor and then... *I ran!*

I ran and I ran, and I didn't stop running. I didn't look

back, not once, knowing that I would crumble if I did. If I looked back and saw him lying there in the forest, where I had no choice but to leave him, I knew I'd break. So, I kept running, trying desperately to keep to the trail I knew and forming a plan in my mind as I did. But with only three bullets left, I only stopped long enough to fire behind me when the sounds got closer, trying to deter them from attacking. I just needed to get to my truck, which meant that by the time I did, I was running on empty, both bullets and energy. My bones felt as if they would snap at any moment, and I knew that for my condition, I had pushed it way past my body's limitations.

I hurt.

I hurt everywhere.

And as soon as I was in my truck, I finally let myself react in a way that couldn't be held back. I screamed out an agonizing sob before it turned to anger as I smacked my hand on the steering wheel. A sound that echoed by the sound of a hand being hit against my window.

"AH!" I screamed and then saw who it was, and my heart started to pound harder in my chest.

Deputy Daniel Dickerson.

He rapped his knuckles on the window and made

a motion for me to bring it down, something I did after turning the ignition. But I made sure to only do it enough to hear what he had to say. However, when he ordered me to do much more, fear struck me. I then remembered what had happened with Trent and my distrust of him doubled.

"Open the door."

"What do you want?" I snapped, ignoring his order.

"For you to open your fucking door!" he snapped, making me flinch at the threat in his tone.

"I am not going to do that," I told him, trying to keep my tone calm even though my hands were shaking as I wiped my tears away. But then I saw that same look in his eyes that I had seen when facing the teenagers earlier that day. The moment they had turned blood thirsty and cold. That was when I knew the truth. As, just like them, Dickerson was not what he seemed to be. It was as if the people I knew had been taken over by some alien race making them act bat shit crazy! Even the deputy who had been an asshole, yes, but he had never once looked crazed out of his mind.

Speaking of which,

"Get out of the car, Ella, I won't ask you again!" he demanded, and this time his voice took on a sinister depth

that I had only heard in Jared's club. In fact, if I had the time, I might have wondered what the hell was going on but the moment I shook my head, he snapped, leaving me no reason to wonder anymore. This was because he now grinned at me, as if this was some sick game he was happy to be playing with me. Something that started when his hand rose up to the small crack I had opened my window to. Then he curled his fingers over the edge, and this was when my fear doubled as he started to bend the glass backwards as if it had been made from dough.

I sucked in a startled breath as he made the opening bigger and bigger, pealing it back like a roll of clear paper. And as he did, his fingers started to change, morphing into demonic hands, as if his flesh was now burnt, with his skin turning black and charred. Then yellow claws started to push from underneath his human nails, making me want to gag when the skin split to accommodate them. This was when the same shadows I had seen sweeping over Orson's shifted form, started to do the same to the deputy, leaving me with a cloud of darkness cloaking his features.

Thankfully, it was in this moment I reacted, grabbing the first thing out of my spare backpack that I could reach as his eyes started to seep back through the fog. Eyes that seemed to have absorbed part of the darkness as no whites remained, making them looked as if you were staring into oblivion. An abyss of obscurity that you couldn't break free from.

It was terrifying!

However, just because my gaze was locked to his, it didn't mean everything else was. So, I scrambled in my bag, and the moment my fingertips felt what I was looking for, I grabbed it in a death grip. Then I swung the bear spray in his direction an inch from his face and sprayed it direct in his eyes now the opening was big enough, making him scream out. Then, as soon as he let go of my window, I put the car in drive and started to back out of there!

"Fuck!" I shouted just as he lunged for me, grabbing me by the jacket. I screamed, this time in pain as his fingers curled into a fist, ripping through the material and straight down into my skin, slicing his talons through my flesh in four lines at my shoulder.

"AHHH!" I shouted again as the pain cut through me, but my quick actions meant the car swung around and was enough to force him to let go, taking with him a chunk of my jacket.

After that, I hit the gas and didn't stop. I didn't stop for anything. I just kept driving until I was out of that town and into the next, only pulling over when I saw a gas station. By that time my adrenaline had run dry and all I felt was the pain at my shoulder, the fear making my hands shake.

"Oh my God… fuck… FUCK!" I screamed after I'd made sure that I hadn't been followed for the millionth time. I knew then that I was way over my head in all of this. I knew that I couldn't rely on calling the police or the authorities or even my own boss for help! For starters, I didn't even have my phone on me, one that had been lost back up at Lasca Creek.

I also knew then that I needed to get to a hospital and get medical attention as I could still feel the blood trickling down my skin, knowing that I needed stitches.

It was deep.

I knew that with how quickly my shirt and jacket became soaked.

"Okay… okay… time to calm the fuck down, Ella… time to think!" I told myself seconds before I started to formulate a plan in my mind, because I couldn't afford to lose it. I couldn't afford to lose my sense of focus or the strength of bravery I knew I had deep inside of me. I also knew there was only one person in the world that would know how to deal with something like this, and for that I needed to get to a phone. But that was the problem with today's society of modern technology, everyone had a cell phone these days. which sucked for me as it made payphones a long-lost redundant thing of the past.

Which meant that in cases like this, I was screwed as it also meant that people rarely memorized numbers these days, me included!

"Think, damn it!" I shouted at myself, letting my head bang back against the headrest and stayed there as I closed my eyes. My shoulder hurt like a bitch, I had no phone, and I couldn't risk going back to my trailer.

"Okay, so time to focus on what I do have," I said aloud, finding comfort in that. I still had most of my gear, which included my radio but then I also knew that if the psycho deputy demon was still looking for me, then he would be listening in, so I couldn't risk it... wait... *unless I threw him off the scent completely.*

"Okay, so that might work," I muttered, grabbing my radio and calling into the office.

"Ella is that you, over!?" Trent said in a panic and taking over from Jimmy, which meant he was obviously worried about me since hearing me scream when I dropped my phone.

"Listen, I can't talk for long, but you've got to know I am safe. I got out of there, after…" I paused, wondering how much to say and remembering my cousin's words that day…

'You can't tell anyone, Ella, not even a soul… it's the biggest rule they live by… our family lives by.'

I released a sigh and continued,

"…wolves attacked. Orson he… oh God, Trent, he got in the middle of it, and he was… he…" I couldn't finish it… it was too damn painful and, in the end, leaving my heartbreaking reality with radio silence.

"We have a team out there now… were you hurt, where are you? Over," he asked after giving me a few seconds, and the emotion in his voice was easy to hear. He had liked Orson too, often making comments like how I could do worse. It seemed everyone had been eager to see us get together. Well, other than deputy freak!

"I was pretty shaken up, but I am okay and just got in my truck and kept driving. I'm somewhere on highway 3A just past Willow point but I am heading back now. I lost my phone. Over," I said, giving him the totally opposite position to where I actually was.

"And the deputy? What was all that earlier? Over," he asked, making me tense as I didn't know what to say, as the last thing I wanted was to put anyone in danger. No, I needed to hand this over to the right people as they would know how best to deal with this. Then hopefully I could go back to my normal, safe, supernatural free life.

Yeah, right, Ella.

"I'll explain when I see you. Do me a favour, ask Rex to look in on Duke and take care of him until I get back, he has a spare key. Over," I said, knowing that he would look after my dog until I returned and that at some point when it was safe to, I would explain everything, including why I was having to lie now.

After this I said goodbye, now knowing that I needed to lay low and think of my next move. Ideally, I needed to find a hospital, but then would that be the first place the deputy would look? It was clear he was out to get me, and I had no choice but to link him with what happened in Lasca Creek. Because really, just how freaky could one person's day be?! What with finding themselves with a crazed cop stalker and being attacked by HellHounds hours later!

I didn't believe in coincidences and even if I did, I wasn't stupid enough to believe in that being one. The deputy hadn't been human and neither had those teens! Which meant that I couldn't trust going to hospital, and neither could I continue to drive around aimlessly. I looked down at myself and realized that I needed to use my greatest asset right now, which was the fact that I was a woman hurt and in uniform. People tended to trust the word of someone in uniform and at the very least, I knew that places like gas stations had first aid kits.

So, I filled up my truck, grabbed my purse from my bag, thankful that that wasn't another precious item I had lost. Then I made my way inside. I sighed in relief to find a middle-aged woman behind the counter stocking up the cigarettes. The very last thing I needed was another asshole. She turned to face me when she heard the bell at the door. Then she took one look at the blood beneath my ripped jacket and alarm took over her sweet features.

"Oh, Christ almighty, what happened to you?"

"Animal attack, I'm alright and I'm on my way to hospital but I wanted to know if you had a first aid kit I could use first?" I asked, holding up the hand of my uninjured arm, which seemed to put people at ease, seeing as it was a universal signal for, I come in peace. After this, things happened pretty quickly as she let me take the first aid kit into the bathroom along with allowing me to borrow her cell phone.

It was crazy how one minute I was waking up to my normal routine going to the coffee shop, grabbing my usual order and sitting down next to my friend like every other day, and then suddenly my world was turned upside down. And I now found myself living out some damn real life horror movie where I was looking over my shoulder and trying to elude the bad guy chasing me.

I released a shuddering sigh, one that nearly had me in tears again. Because once inside the bathroom, I locked the cubicle and went to work trying to remove my jacket, biting my lip so that I wouldn't cry out and cause the poor woman even more worry. I'd had a job from stopping her calling an ambulance as it was, and I was forced to try and pass off my injury as a lot less serious than it was.

"Ahhh…esss," I hissed in pain as I took off my torn shirt, gently peeling it away from the torn edges of my skin where it stuck to the blood there. I stood there in a white tank top that was mainly now crimson thanks to the loss of blood. Blood that had poured freely from the four long jagged slices in my shoulder.

"What a mess," I said, talking to myself and finding

some comfort in it. Then I opened up the first aid kit with shaky hands, grabbing what was needed and remembering my training, treating it just like any other wound inflicted by an animal. The main thing was to get it clean, and thankfully I found the right stuff in the kit, otherwise I would have bought myself a bottle of vodka and finding myself a damn stick to bite on.

I poured on the solution, letting the sting burn through me and gripping on to the edge of the sink to prevent myself from falling to the floor. However, I just gritted my teeth and persevered until it was clean before I started wrapping it in gauze and strapping my shoulder the best I could with the bandages that were available. After that I eased one arm into my jacket, knowing that my shirt was definitely a lost cause. But as for the jacket, I would definitely need it to keep warm despite the large gaping hole at the shoulder.

"Jesus," I muttered, as I sat down on the toilet seat and scrolled through the woman's cell phone using the Internet to find the numbers that I needed. Thankfully, I always kept a notepad in my chest pocket of my jacket in case I could provide any evidence to any crime I came across. License plate numbers, descriptions of people, that type of thing. I wrote down all the numbers that I thought I might need, and the first number I typed in was one I cancelled three times knowing that I couldn't ring it.

I couldn't call him.

So, I cancelled the international number for London and instead rang a very different club instead.

And one that I knew held a *very different king inside.*

It rang six times and then after the seventh, a voice finally answered…

"Club Afterlife."

TWENTY SIX

DANGER AT THE DOOR

Deep breath, Ella.

"Club Afterlife, Mike speaking," a man answered.

"Is this… erh, is this the manager?" I asked in an unsure tone, having never called the club before.

"Yeah, I'm the manager, can I help you with something? Only we don't open for another twenty minutes," he informed me, telling me how late it was, as Afterlife opened late some Fridays, especially if something was going on with my aunt and uncle, and they were three hours ahead.

"I'm trying to get in touch with Keira Draven," I told

him, making him scoff,

"Yeah, good luck with that." I released a frustrated sigh, wincing in pain and pleaded,

"Please, it's important."

"Look, I've been working here for a very long time, and in those thirty odd years how many times do you think I've had someone ring up here and want to speak to one of the town's most famous couple?" he asked, and I had to admit he certainly had a point. My auntie and uncle were the equivalent of having some Hollywood couple living in a small town.

"I get that, but I'm family. I don't want to get into it but I'm Keira's niece, Ella, and I'm trying to get in touch with Amelia. I lost my phone and I just need her cell number… trust me, she's going to want to give it to me." After this, and mentioning the right names of people, I heard him release a sigh and tell me,

"Okay, Ella, just give me a minute to verify this," he said, before putting me on hold and just like I had in my truck, I let my head fall back against the wall, holding it there as I counted the minutes that went past until finally,

"Okay, I'm going to put you through," he told me, making my heart beat quicker.

"Thank you," I replied, this time with a grateful sigh before seconds later and my auntie's happy voice was on the other end of the phone. Meaning that this was when I knew I would have to act out the next part of my charade, because I still wasn't sure whether my uncle and auntie had any idea what I knew of their world, and the last thing I wanted to do was get Amelia into trouble.

"Oh, my Gods, Ella! How long has it been?!" Her excited voice came on the other end, and I couldn't help but smile. My auntie Keira just had that way about her that drew you in and made you instantly like her. She was friendly and kind to everyone, which I think was why it was so shocking when it came out who she was dating. My mom often told me stories about it, how her little sister had managed to catch the eye of the town's most eligible broody billionaire bachelor. A man who had not taken notice of anyone else before and only I knew why.

She was his Chosen One.

Not that I knew exactly what that meant when Amelia had told me, only that my uncle Dominic had become obsessed and besotted with her the moment he first saw her, knowing instantly that she would become his. I admit it sounded a little barbaric to me, but the way that Amelia had said it in an almost dream like fashion made me believe that this was to be more romantic than anything else. It made me wonder if this was why she was so obsessed herself with a man named Lucius Septimus, the Vampire King.

In truth, it made me feel a little bit guilty as it had been some time since I had last spoken to my cousin, having no idea what she was up to and I wondered what she was doing now. It was weird, as it felt as though I already knew, but then when I tried to think what, I came up empty. It was almost as if someone had told me, but who? I couldn't remember. Had it been my mom? Has she mentioned something the last time I called?

Well, whatever it was, there was no getting away from it, as I missed her. Because it had been years since I had seen her and right now, I also knew that she was the only one who could help me. Which was why, after a brief conversation with my aunt about how life was perfectly boring here, I got to the part of the real reason I was ringing.

"I had an accident with my cell, let's just say trying to take a selfie with the lake in the background doesn't always work out for the best. It also means that I lost all my numbers, and I haven't spoken to Amelia for a while…" I let that linger on so that my auntie could get the message loud and clear.

"Is this your new phone, why don't I just go ahead and send you a message with all of our numbers on," she offered, making me laugh once in relief, as if this was all just some silly mistake of mine.

"That would be perfect, and I promise the next time I call we can have a proper chat. Unfortunately, I'm about to go to work the late shift, but soon, Aunty Kaz, definitely," I said, knowing that if I didn't say that now, I would end up being on the phone for another twenty minutes. So, after promising to call again, I hung up and waited for those numbers to come through. Then I made a note of them all before deleting the messages so that the woman didn't have them.

After this I thanked the woman, paid for my gas and a bottle of water before heading back to my truck. Then I carried on driving, intent on making my way to Vancouver, which was a long and grueling seven-hour drive away. In the end, I made it all the way to a place called Hope, which I thought, given my current circumstances, was a good omen. So, I pulled into a hotel just on the outskirts, by that time near dead on my feet and weak from blood loss.

I also tried to ignore the strange look I received from the girl behind the desk, and told her,

"It's been one hell of a day." Then I paid for the room, took my key and dragged my feet down the hallway. Once I was inside my room, I wasted no time, and I went straight over to the phone, getting out my notepad and dialing Amelia's cell number. My auntie Kaz had told me that it had changed recently so it was lucky I called. I was even luckier that it answered on the third ring.

"Who is this?" a man's stern voice answered, making me frown, as it wasn't exactly friendly and most definitely had an authoritative air about it. It was also at this point that I heard my cousin's voice in the background complaining,

"And who said you could answer my phone?" The man's answer came with smooth tone this time, and one filled with amusement,

"The man who has your backside in the palm of his hand… and, sweetheart, *it's twitching,*" he replied to her, making my mouth drop in shock. Did Amelia have a boyfriend? Thankfully I heard laughter in her reply, realizing that he must have been teasing her, and I had to say it was a voice that sent shivers down my spine.

"Who is it?" I heard her ask after giggling.

"I'm yet to find out, my love, if of course you would let me continue," was his silver-tongued reply.

"It's Ella, Amelia's cousin," I replied, wishing I had started with that to save myself from the explicit sex talk.

"Ella!" I heard being shouted, before suddenly the phone must have been grabbed from her boyfriend's hand.

"Feel free to climb over me anytime, especially in that dress," I heard being said in the background by Mr calm, cool and obviously besotted with my cousin.

"Oh shush, Mr grabby hands…" she whispered, and I had to say it was a bit pointless considering I heard it.

"Oh, I will show you just what Mr Grabby hands can do, phone call or not," he replied, making me groan and ask,

"Erh, is this a bad time?"

"Ella, is that you?!" she said in a serious tone, and I couldn't help but smile.

"Yeah… *it's me.*"

"Wait, what's wrong?" she asked, instantly knowing something was wrong from my tone but then again, I wasn't surprised as no one knew me like Amelia. Which was why just hearing her voice opened up the flood gates and I found I couldn't contain it any longer!

"Oh, Fae!" I shouted, suddenly finding myself in tears and telling her,

"I'm... I'm *in trouble.*" This was all I needed to say, before she was barking orders at the people around her, one of which was obviously her boyfriend who took her tone as being as serious as she had taken mine.

"Tell me exactly where you are, Ella," she demanded, making me sniff back my tears so I could speak, telling her,

"What good would that be, you're in London or Jerusalem or wherever and I'm... I'm in Canada."

"Just trust me, Ella, you need to trust me now and tell me exactly where you are." After this I told Amelia everything that had happened, finding myself in even more tears doing so, especially when telling her about what happened to my friend. About what had happened to Orson... *because of me.*

Fae only stopped asked questions whenever she relayed a piece of information on to who I was still guessing was her boyfriend. God, and I even felt guilty that I didn't know who that was. Meaning I could add shit friend onto being a shit cousin!

Yep... this just made me cry even harder.

But then, by the time I had finished, it was thirty minutes later, and I shrieked in fright the moment there was a knock at my door.

"Ella! What is it! What's happened?!" Fae asked in a panicked tone. But I covered my mouth trying to stop the sound of my frightened, panicked breathing.

This was when I crept to the door and looked through the peephole to find my worst nightmare stood on the other side. A man turned away from me, but the uniform he wore could not be mistaken.

That's when I whispered in a fearful tone back to Amelia the depth of my dire situation,

"He's here…" I then swallowed hard and forced out the words,

"The Deputy… he's found me."

TWENTY SEVEN

FOUND

The man at my door knocked again, making me nearly jump out of my skin, which after tonight was definitely the wrong saying.

"Ella?" I heard Fae say my name, but I kept my eye to the peephole, watching to see what he was going to do. He was still looking the other way as if keeping an eye out for witnesses. Seconds later I heard Amelia whispering to what must have been her boyfriend,

"She says he's at her door." This was when he lost that playful side and told her,

"Hand over the phone, sweetheart." Then a moment

later he was back to being in control.

"Listen to me, Ella, the man at your door is an officer I called. He is someone you can trust. He is there to take you to the airport where you will find a private plane waiting for you." I gasped at the idea and argued,

"What! I can't leave... I mean, I don't even have my passport. I don't have anything on me... I..."

"You don't need anything. You just need to get on the plane and that's it, everything else will be taken care of. Now, are you hurt in any way?" the man asked with a calm tone that still held an edge of command to it. Let's put it this way, it wasn't one I would have braved saying no to. A little like Jared in that way.

I heard Amelia suck in a quick breath at this question, making him whisper back at her,

"Easy, my girl." Ah, so here was another guy telling a girl to take it easy. The thought was a painful one as it made me think back to Orson, who I had painfully explained had died in the attack. I shook the guilt from my thoughts because I would have time for that. I would have time for mourning his death and now... well, now was not that time. This was when I heard Fae speaking to him in the background.

"But the threat that was made, we have to tell him, he has to know and..."

"And he will, that I promise you. But for now, let's get her safely away from the threat. It will be fine, love, trust me, we will deal with it," I heard him reply, making me want to question them further, but the man came back on the phone and asked me again,

"Ella, please answer me… are you hurt?" I released a sigh and knowing there was no point in lying, told him,

"My shoulder, he grabbed my shoulder, sliced through into my skin and…"

"And?" he pushed,

"It's okay, I think", I told him, but he wasn't convinced.

"Has the bleeding stopped?" Again I heard my cousin's worry on the other side as she hissed,

"Gods."

"Yes, it's stopped," I told him, after looking at my shoulder and seeing that at least no blood had seeped through the bandage.

"Good, that's good," he said, making me hit my limit,

"Look, no offence, but who the hell are you? I get that you're trying to help and you're obviously Amelia's boyfriend and all but…" at this he scoffed, and muttered to my cousin,

"I have just been called your boyfriend."

"Ha! He wishes!" I heard Amelia shout, before hearing the playful growl in return and obvious rustle as she must have wrestled the phone out of his hand again,

"Look I know this is hard, Ella, but you have to listen to us and open the door, what he says is true," she told me, making me suck in a breath and tell her honestly,

"But I don't know him, Fae."

"No, but I do. And you have to believe me when I tell you that you can trust him as much as you can trust me. We just need to get you out of there and somewhere safe where we can figure all of this out together. You're not doing this alone," she said, and I knew she was right, if she trusted him then I needed too also. So, I unlocked the door and opened it, nearly sagging in relief when I found myself staring at the face of an officer I had never seen before.

"Whoa!" The officer made a sound of shock before grabbing me and holding me upright, so I didn't just fall. Then he took the phone and held it to his ear, wedged against his shoulder.

"She's fine, she's got an injured shoulder and looks exhausted, but she's okay… no, don't worry, I understand

and will protect her with my life. Trust me, sir, I will get her to the airport… I will tell her." After this he hung up the cordless and threw it towards the bed before leading me to a seat.

"I'm Noah Simmons… It's Ella, right?" he asked, making me nod my head.

"Your cousin told me to tell you that everything will be fine now. She will take care of it, and she will see you soon." At this my head snapped up.

"She did?" He gave me a smile and I had to say, he was cute as he had deep lines either side of the smile. He was also in his early thirties, had dark blonde hair that was cut with his profession in mind. Meaning he was as clean cut as you could get. But he had kind blue eyes that were as unthreatening as you could get and had a medium build.

"She did, and I am to inform you that you don't have to tell me any details… in fact, you don't even have to talk if you don't want to. Just know that you're safe and my only job right now is to get you there safely and on that plane. No questions asked, okay?" I nodded, feeling as if I had an inflated balloon inside me that had slowly been letting the air out and now there was barely anything left keeping me upright. He helped me get back to my feet and I told him I was okay to walk. So, with a nod he led me back through the hotel into the parking lot, making it officially my shortest stay anywhere.

"What about my truck?" I asked now looking concerned.

"Don't worry, I'll make arrangements to get it back to your address. It won't get towed. Now, is there anything you need out of it?" I shook my head telling him I had everything in my backpack, which was basically a piece of paper with numbers on it and a small wallet in my jacket pocket. I let him lead me into the passenger seat of his cruiser and found myself falling fast asleep within minutes.

In fact, it was only when I heard my name being called softly did I realise that we were almost there. He had driven the rest of the way to Vancouver, meaning I had been asleep for hours. But I knew we were only minutes away when I started seeing signs for the airport.

And Noah had been right in saying that there would be no questions, which I found odd coming from a cop. And as if he knew what I was thinking, he told me,

"Believe it or not, right now I'm getting paid not to ask those questions." I shrugged my shoulders, wincing in pain and making him nod towards the glove compartment, telling me,

"There should be some pills in there... I get migraines, so it should help with the pain." I fished around and found the plastic tub of pills and popped two in my mouth to swallow whole.

"Thanks."

"Don't thank me, I should have told you sooner but damn, you passed out before I barely pulled out from the hotel parking lot," he told me, making say for the second time,

"It's been a hell of a night." He nodded to my shoulder and said,

"Yeah, I gathered as much."

"So, you really don't want to know what happened?" I asked, finding this hard to believe, especially for a cop.

"You gonna tell me it's life threatening?" he asked, making me reply,

"No."

"Then nope, I don't wanna know." After this I took his answer for what it was, he wasn't being paid for asking questions, making me wonder... just who was this man who was dating Amelia and how powerful was he? But more than anything else... was he also like the rest of her family, *a supernatural?*

Minutes later and I could at least say he was most definitely rich, as I now found myself staring at what a billionaire lifestyle bought you. Something I knew thanks to my uncle who had a few private jets himself. In fact, I had been no stranger to them myself when I was younger as my uncle often flew us all back to the UK for special occasions. This was so we could spend time with my grandparents who still lived in Merseyside, England.

But it had been a long time since ,and now being an adult and someone who could only afford to fly coach, then I knew what a luxury this was.

"Good luck," the officer said and before anything more could pass between us, I got out of the car and watched as he started to make his way back to wherever it was he had come from.

"Miss Connor?" I whipped around when I heard my name being called from behind me.

"Yes, that's me," I said in reply, seeing a man dressed as a pilot stood at the plane's entrance with his hands tucked under his armpits as if trying to keep warm.

"Very good, miss, if you would be so kind to come aboard, we can then be on our way." I nodded, feeling this surreal sense wash over me as if still questioning if this were all really happening. If I was, in fact, being whisked away in the middle of night like some injured damsel having already lost her hero to the fight.

That was a painful thought and far more so than my injured shoulder. Because even though I hadn't known Orson long, only three months, I still felt the loss pierce my heart, knowing full well that I'd had a large place for him there.

I also climbed those steps wondering when it was I would be back and how long it would take for this ordeal to all be over with. When would I see my dog again or how many nights would it be before I was once again sleeping in my trailer? But more importantly, what would be done about Deputy Dickerson?

As soon as I was on board, I found a woman sat there, who obviously wasn't part of the crew. She was dressed as a lawyer in her black tailored suit and perfectly styled hair, that was twisted into a perfect blonde bun.

"Hi there… Ella Connor, I presume." I replied with a curt nod before her eyes travelled to my injured shoulder.

"Don't worry, I am a doctor and I have been instructed to take a look at your injury… after take-off of course," she told me with a smile and a friendly manner that didn't seem faked. She was pretty, even if she wore a lot of makeup that darkened her brows and created a smokey effect over her eyes that complimented the sage green in them.

"Wow, cops and doctors on the payroll, makes me wonder if this guy my cousin is dating is in the Mafia," I said, making her laugh and say,

"The rich billionaire part is right but just with less swimming with the fishes and meatball sauce." I laughed and remarked,

"Wow, someone obviously watches more crime movies than I do." At this it was her turn to laugh before she held her hands up and replied,

"Guilty." After this I took a seat opposite her in what could have quite possibly been the comfiest chair in existence, picking this one so as not to think me rude. Then a stewardess came with drinks before take-off, that I downed in one.

"Rough night?" the doctor asked, who I noted still hadn't give me her name. I laughed without humor and replied dryly,

"Something like that."

Fifteen minutes later, I found myself being led over to

a sofa, playing patient, as she got to work stitching me up and making me wince at the injection. But like the cop, she too didn't ask any questions unless they were medically relevant, and when I quizzed her on why, she shrugged her shoulders and said,

"Not to sound too mafia cliché but I am not paid to ask questions." Then she winked at me and suggested that I lie down and get some rest. She also said she would check on me in a few hours, making me now question if she knew where we were headed.

"That is also not part of my pay grade I am afraid, but I am holding out for it being somewhere sunny." I laughed once before doing as she suggested, making my way to the back part of the plane where there was a bedroom with a bathroom attached.

And despite the nap I had already taken in the cop car, I still couldn't help but take one look at the bed and sigh with happiness. Because it took me all of five seconds to realize that all my energy was spent as I collapsed onto it, with my last thoughts of HellHounds, creepy cops and mafia style mob bosses meeting me at the end of my weird ass journey to God only knew where.

And in all honesty, only half of me wished there was

one face I wouldn't be seeing at the end of it...
And as for the treacherous half,

It wished for his face to be the first.

TWENTY EIGHT

THE TREACHEROUS HALF.

I checked the doc's handy work in the mirror after a stewardess knocked on the door to wake me up, letting me know that we would be landing soon. She also let me know there was a bag of new clothes by the bed that I had missed, so I could change if I wanted. And well, considering I was still covered in my own dried blood, then yeah, I wanted to change. I had no idea how long I had slept for but as I rolled my shoulder, I knew it was long enough for the pain killers to have long ago run their course. They obviously were now out of my system making me wince at the pain.

"Okay, too soon to start with the star jumps," I told myself, before taking off my tank top and washing myself the best I could… without having the time to jump in the shower I was amazed to see was in this bathroom. Boy, did I wish I had woken up sooner. So, I quickly grabbed the bag full of clothes, seeing that they were all brand new, with tags on that I refused to look at to see the price. I was already racking up this rescue Ella bill, and would no doubt be eating noodles for the next six months so I could pay it off.

Now why did the thought of noodles make me think of Jared?

In the end, I had no answer to that one, so shook my head as if this would help rid me of the memory that wasn't even there. I pulled out a pair of light blue jeans, that were tighter than I would normally wear as my thighs weren't exactly skinny and neither was my ass. But they were made to look even less skinny thanks to my slim waist that gave me an hourglass shape, which I found hard to buy dresses for.

Thankfully, the other items in the bag were a tank top in black, and an over-sized, grey knitted sweater with a wide cowl neckline that slipped off the shoulders. It was also open at the back, but to stop it from slipping off completely, it had a knitted black ribbon attached to the shoulders. One that I tied into a tight bow in hopes it would only show one shoulder, choosing to keep the injured one covered. It also had a stretchy ribbed band at the waist that fitted snug to my hips, which also matched the same at the wrists, creating bell shapes as the baggy part of the sleeves hung over them.

I then washed my face and tried to tame my curls the best I could before tying them back up off my face, using one of the hair ties from the pack I had also found in the bag. This was what made me smile, as I knew then that Fae definitely had a say in shopping. She would have known my hair would have driven my crazy wearing it down for too long.

"Well, that's gonna have to do," I said to myself, before kicking my feet into the black, soft leather ankle boots, that had a tasseled trim up the zip. So, with nothing else to do to my appearance, I left the room and took a seat ready for landing.

"Any idea's where we are at yet?" I asked, making the doctor shake her head before telling me,

"Nope but I can tell you one thing… *it isn't sunny.*"

I laughed, seeing as it was clearly dark outside.

We landed shortly after, and before I got off the plane, the doc handed me some pain killers and checked my bandage one more time. She also told me to change it regularly and keep a look out for signs of infection. Basically, if there was any swelling or discharge, I should get it checked out straight away. Only then did she give me the all clear. But after saying all this, I could tell that she thought it was an animal attack, because she also advised that I get a shot just to be sure.

Of course, if she knew what kind of animal it had been, being that of the Hell variety, then she most likely wouldn't have bothered. No, I think telling me I was already screwed before she went running as far-away from me as possible would have been the likely response to that. I mean, did demons carry rabies? I also wondered just how many people on Amelia's side of the family I would have insulted with that question?

But this had me questioning what the hell had Dickerson been exactly, as I knew that for sure as a heck pecker, he was not human. It was in that moment that I started to question everything. I started to question why Orson had said the things he had said, and why he had been there.

Had he been tracking those things, those hounds of hell? Had it been his job to stop them and if so, had that been why he had warned me from going up there to look for the hikers?

He was a shifter…

He had been a shifter… I corrected painfully.

But what he had been was something I didn't care about. I didn't care if he had been a shifter, he had been my friend and he had sacrificed his life to save me. And now he was gone.

Orson was gone.

My friend was gone. The pain of that was still raw, and I knew it would be for a long time to come. All I had left was trying to figure this out and find out the truth of what was really going on.

Something I knew started with saying goodbye to the doc and leaving the plane. So, I walked down the steps and instantly took note of the fancy car that was waiting for me, one that came with a man who I assumed was my driver.

"Welcome to Munich, Miss Connor." I frowned for a second and looked around, not that this would give me much clue as to the place but still, I guess it was human nature.

"Thanks," I said, before getting in and wondering aloud as soon as the door was closed,

"Now what the hell am I doing in Germany?"

Without any way of telling the time, other than it was dark out, I didn't know exactly how long it took us to get to where we were going. But as we drove through a busy city, I knew it couldn't have been too late as there were plenty of people walking along the well-lit streets. We also seemed to be making our way through the centre of it all, with the driver beeping a few tourists out of the way, whilst he hissed out words I didn't understand in German, which I gathered was him cursing. Something that only stopped when he pulled the car up next to a historical building. It also didn't look like we were allowed to park here as the building sat in the corner of a busy square.

It was huge, and by all the warm lights coming from the different shaped windows, it also looked to be on four floors. Most of the building was painted white, with the exception of a corner section that looked like a stone turret had attached itself there. It looked out of place as much as it didn't because it created a charm that drew your eyes to it. Two rows that held five square windows sat on decorated ledges of carved stone, making me wonder what these circular rooms looked like from inside.

"What is this place?" I asked the moment my door was opened, something that caused a stir as a mass of tourists stopped to have a good stare. But then again, I guess most people always assumed when a fancy car pulled up with a driver opening the door, the chances were high that a celebrity would be seen getting out. *Oh well, sucks for them,* I thought, as it was only little old me. The driver shut the door for me and I was just about to ask what to do next, when he held out something for me to take.

"Give this token to one of the bar staff and they will show you the way." He handed it to me and before I looked at in more depth, I asked again,

"Where are we?"

"This is Hofbräuhaus," he replied, making me look up again and remark,

"It looks like a pub."

"That's because it is, the oldest one in Munich in fact," he told me, before nodding his head as a way of goodbye and leaving. Then I looked down at the token in my hand and sucked in a shuddered breath when I saw what it was.

"The three headed beast… *Cerberus,*" I whispered to

myself, hoping this didn't mean what I thought it meant. But then, one look up at this clearly lively place, and I knew it was totally different to the last pub he obviously owned in London. No, in fact, this place looked more like a tourist attraction than a quiet place to enjoy some local beer.

Nevertheless, I walked inside seeing that I had very little choice to do anything else, knowing that I had to trust that my cousin knew what she was doing and wouldn't put me in a dangerous situation again. Although the first time had kind of been on me considering I was the one who followed her. Then again, I knew nothing about her world and honestly, just thought she was trying to sneak into a pub for a little underage drinking. Boy, how wrong had I been? Well, I just hoped that I wasn't as wrong this time, and inside I would find my cousin waiting for me. Although what she was doing in Munich was anyone's guess.

Because it had been years ago that I had convinced her to follow her dreams and come here to study. Although we both knew there had been an ulterior motive for that choice, and it had to do with one bad ass Vampire King who was supposed to have owned a club here…

Transfusion.

That was what she told me it had been called, making me wonder now if the guy on the phone was none other than the man himself. Had she finally managed to break through the ice-cold shell she had once accused him of having? In all honesty, she hadn't told me all the details surrounding why she came back heartbroken, only that she had, and it had something to do with his cruel rejection of her. How she went to his club one night and requested to speak with the lord of this hidden Vampire world, and how he humiliated her. After that, it was difficult to witness but she never seemed the same. Like that night she left something behind…

A broken piece of her heart.

Well, that must have been about seven years ago now, so I couldn't help now wonder what had changed and if he had been the man on the phone? In the end, Amelia had chosen to study in London, moving there shortly after and creating a life for herself. One of independence and making her own way despite the extreme wealth of her parents. I always respected her for that. I respected her a lot.

I also knew it had been far too long since I had seen

her and I found myself looking forward to it, hoping that she was in there. but then the moment I walked inside and saw a room big enough for what must have been over a thousand people, my mouth almost hit the floor.

The place was huge!

It looked more like a hall than a pub, with sections partitioned by the arched ceilings attached to decorated pillars, and the positioning of the long tables and bench seats. Red mahogany wood panelling framed the lower walls complimented the pale-yellow tiled floors laid in a diamond pattern. But as beautiful as the room was, it was nothing compared to its incredible ceilings that had been painted with elaborate frescoes. Pictures of bountiful food and wine were everywhere, from bunches of fruits, vegetables, to seafood on plates and poultry and meats on platters. There was even a pig's head on a large silver dish painted at the curved part of the arch. These were all complimented by a diamond pattered that looked like it could have been some type of flag.

As I stepped further in the large open space, I noticed the large glass and metal lanterns hanging down from the centre of these domed sections of the ceiling. I also knew it would take me a small forever trying to find Amelia, as the place was packed full of people. The noise was almost deafening.

So, I walked over to the bar area and did what the driver had instructed me to do, seeing as just standing there looking around like a lost red-headed puppy would get me nowhere. However, the moment I handed the token over, that in truth looked more like some ancient coin found in a pirate chest, the barmaid's eyes widened before snapping back up to look at mine. It was an unnerving look to say the least. Especially considering just moments ago she had been smiling, a look that had been more in keeping with her buxom beer maid outfit. It was also one that looked traditional and not something you would wear in the bedroom if you fancied a bit of role play.

She nodded her head in a direction she wanted me to follow, and we weaved in and out of the long tables that looked to be ones you would share with people you didn't know. No doubt a great way of chatting to people of all walks of life and meeting new friends, with that main question being,

"So where are you from?" I heard it asked at least three times by the time we stopped. To be honest, this had been the first time I had ever been to Germany but being in this place now, with its local people wearing their traditional Tracht and lederhosen, I would have liked to have spent time here sightseeing. Like getting to try the local cuisine, and the plates full of large Bratwurst sausages. Or take from one of the baskets of giant pretzels being handed out. In truth, seeing the tankards of beer thick with white froth, and the traditional outfits, it felt more like stepping into a movie set trying too hard to depict this as being a place in Germany. In fact, it was surprising in a good way as I thought it was great to see such strong traditions not lost to modern age.

"What is this?" I couldn't help but ask the moment I stepped behind a corner and was faced with walls full of what looked like grey ceramic tankards, locked away behind their own little cage.

"This is where we keep the storage lockers for the steins that belong to regular customers," she answered in perfect English that had a distinct German accent.

"I don't understand," I answered honestly.

"It is a long waiting list to get one, most are handed down the generations but if you possess a token, then you have a stein to use that no one else can own."

"And is that what that is?" I asked nodding at the token

I had given her. She grinned down at it as she flipped it between her fingers like a pro and then said,

"Oh no, American, this... *this is something much more,*" she said, before turning around and slotting the coin into the only black tankard there, and this was behind a gothic looking metal cage of its own. In fact, it was one that held a crest at its center, and I sucked in a quick breath when I realized where I had seen it before.

The elevator at Jared's club.

After she did this, a band started up from the small stage area, which also meant that the sounds of many locks turning was drowned out for anyone who might have been close enough to hear. Locks that released enough so as a hidden door was revealed behind the cages, and one that was big enough to slip through unnoticed.

"I can't go in there," I said, shaking my head and wondering if I wasn't now about to walk into some kind of trap. But the woman just shrugged her shoulders and said,

"Suit yourself, but they automatically lock again in ten seconds, so you have five more to decide."

It only took me two before I stepped inside, knowing I didn't have much choice. The sudden sense of déjà vu was near overwhelming as it shot me straight back to that night

I had stepped through another hidden door. Only this time, instead of being faced with an old elevator, I was faced with a large gothic looking door.

One that had a sign above it saying,

'Club 666'

"Oh, shit no... this was a mistake!" I said to myself, before turning around and trying to get back to the human side, only it was like she said it would be... *it was locked.*

"Fuck... fuck!" I hissed before accepting that I had no choice, just like the last time.

"Please don't be in there... please don't be in there," I whispered over and over before finally...

I turned the handle and stepped inside, knowing deep down that...

The Beast King was in there.

TWENTY NINE

A ROYAL ENTRANCE

Stepping inside now was a bit like stepping back in time, to some Victorian era that hadn't been touched since the first time it had been decorated. The main theme of this was dark wood, which was everywhere. It paneled the walls from floor to ceiling, which meant that without any windows it also made it a dark space, even with the wall lights. These were twisted wrought iron of thorned vines, wound around giant claws that held a flaming bulb at the top.

As for the size and shape of the room, it was a wide-open room with a small, raised area, which was blocked off by the thick wooden balustrades that surrounded it, filling up the entire back end of the room. Two huge guys could be seen guarding the small staircase that led up to the platform, meaning there was no mistaking that this was the VIP.

A huge, carved wooden bar ran along the right side, and it looked as if it belonged in a cathedral, with its ornate arched shelving and its spire spiked corner posts. A row of worn bar stools were mounted to the floor, and all had cracked leather seats that at one time might have been a bright red colour.

Opposite the bar was a raised dais for the band, who looked like bikers with instruments and were playing some heavy number, where the lyrics were about monsters.

"But of course," I muttered to myself as I walked further inside, glancing around until suddenly a flash of colour was all I saw before a body barreled into me. I barely had enough time to brace, as the person threw themselves at me with enough force that I ended up going back a step just so as I wouldn't fall on my ass. But then the second I heard my name being whispered and the deep emotion that came with it, I finally gave way to all my fears, having them replaced with pure relief and happiness.

"Amelia!" I shouted back, now hugging her with just as much force as she did to me.

"Gods, I have been so worried!" she said before releasing a hiccupping sob, and, soon, tears were streaming down my face. It felt so good to hold her, so good to be held by her, like I had a sister back in my arms. That was when she noticed my injury and pulled back, before nodding to it,

"Are you okay? Gods, I could kill the bastard!" she said, referring to Deputy Dick!

"It's been a long, never-ending day," I told her, now rubbing my eye with my sleeve.

"Yeah, I bet, and one that will only get better with a drink… come on, hope you still drink beer, 'cause you know I hear no one makes it like the Germans." I laughed and nodded, letting her lead me over to the bar area. Talk about gothic, it was the epitome of it!

"Okay, so you know what happened to me, now it's your turn to spill," I said, making her blush and trip a little as she took a seat on the bar stool. But then this wasn't surprising as she had always been really clumsy. Of course, she was also stunningly beautiful, which wasn't exactly surprising with her parents. There was a reason my uncle made the female population swoon, as even for an older man he was the very meaning of tall dark and handsome. He was also a powerhouse of muscles and when you were old enough not to swing from them like I used to as a kid, then he was as intimidating as… well, Hell. Obviously, I now knew the reason for that, seeing as he was a demonic King.

As for my aunty Kaz, she was a blonde beauty with the right amount of curves, pretty blue-grey eyes and naturally red lips that she would bite out of habit, especially when my uncle was around to tease her.

Amelia had inherited her father's black hair, that flowed down her back, ending at the base of her spine. She had stunning blue eyes and her father's sun kissed skin. She was a little taller than I was, and whereas I had a bit more ass than she did, she had more to fill her bra than me.

Of course, she was also a mega geek and was currently wearing her glasses, a pair of jeans and a red T-shirt that said,

'I saved Hell and all I got was this crap T-shirt'

I couldn't help but laugh, nodding to it.

"Let me guess, another from your aunty Pip?" I asked, knowing she was the crazy cute one in Amelia's life and made it her mission to buy her niece every funny T-shirt ever created. She laughed and said,

"Oh, now that's a way longer, loooonger and even longer story, and would require a lot more than beer," she answered with a shake of her head.

"Would it have anything to do with how you got yourself a sexy sounding boyfriend by any chance?" I asked, making her blush and give me only of those 'I am totally loved up' kind of sappy smiles. I laughed.

"Now that is a crazy long story that needs a whole night of drinking wine and stuffing ourselves stupid on pizza after," she replied.

"After what I just went through, that sounds like heaven right about now," I told her, making her give me a warm look. Although that type of night would have to wait, as suddenly there was something happening at the other end of the club.

This was when I soon realized the way I had come in must have been through a back door of sorts… *Maybe the lowly human entrance,* I thought with irritation. Because just like everyone else was now doing, my eyes automatically turned to where a huge set of doors suddenly opened at the far end corner. Double wooden doors covered in twisted iron hinges and riveted pins were set further back in a grand stone arch that echoed loudly as they were thrown wide. My eyes then followed the parted sea of people as they quickly moved to allow the newcomer to make his way through the club with ease, as if the president of the United States had just walked in.

But no, that wasn't quite right. Because it wasn't someone that would be important in my world, it was someone that was important in Amelia's. Which meant only one thing...

It was royalty.

It was their King.

The entire room full of people all stopped what they were doing, and all conversation ended in a hush of shock. Only the music continued, turning to a heavy base that matched the sight of the person's entrance, making more of a commanding impact. And even though I could only see hints of him through the thickness of the crowd, it was enough to have my heart trying to pound its way out of my chest!

Christ, but he looked so tall and intimidating, it was

honestly hard to look at but even harder to look away. Flashes of those silver-grey eyes could be seen as he scanned the crowd as if looking for something. I even watched as his nostrils seem to flare as if he was trying to discover some scent in the air, and I don't know why but I had a dreaded feeling… *it was me.*

I sucked in a sharp breath the second I saw that thick leather jacket of his tense around his massive frame, and the second his head slowly turned in my direction, I freaked, turning my own quickly and ducking lower.

"Oh God no!" I hissed aloud, making Amelia glance down at me now trying to hide, and I didn't know whether she expected the panic she saw on my face or not. But it was there regardless, and she uttered a curse under breath because of it.

"Ah shit… okay, Ella, look at me, it's okay… it's going to be okay… Ella!" she shouted, dragging my attention away from the way I seemed to sink down to the ground and away from the magnificence that was also the ultimate predator that had entered the room. This was when she crouched low and told me,

"Don't worry, I am here this time." My fearful gaze shot to hers and she cursed again.

"Fuck... okay, I know this is hard but you're going to have to trust me. This is not like the past... it won't be, I promise." I shook my head as if telling her silently that I couldn't do this, but she placed a hand at the top of my arm and gave me a reassuring squeeze.

"I promise," she said again with a dip of her head.

"But..." I tried to argue against this, seeing as it had been eleven years since I had seen him, as dreaming of the guy really didn't count! I would have reminded her of the threat he made if he ever saw me again. In fact, I would have reminded her of a lot of things about that night and how afraid of him I was... if she had let me of course.

"Ella, stop and listen to me, it won't be like last time so don't even go there," she said and again, this only made me want to argue against how she could possibly know that. How she could know that he wouldn't just take one look at me and decide that one warning over a decade ago should have been enough. And in all honesty, it had been. It had been more than enough, as I had never gone back... *ever!*

No... only in my dreams had I gone back to him. *Only in my dreams had he come to me.*

Because that was all the bravery I had for this man...

for this beast. The bravery to dream. But I wasn't asleep this time, and this HellBeast King was nothing but a real threat. He wasn't the gentle lover I had made him out to be in my fantasies. They weren't real and I couldn't trust them. And speaking of trust.

"Ella, you need to trust me. Jared won't hurt you," Amelia said again, making me shake my head and whisper,

"You don't know that."

"Yes, I do," she stated firmly.

"But how can you be so sure?" I asked as she reached for my arm and started to pull me back up to standing.

"Because you have no idea who you really are," she said, startling me.

"What is that supposed to mean?" I asked after jerking back a little. She released a sigh and looked back over to Jared, who had seemingly disappeared from sight and no doubt had already passed us on his way to wherever it was he was going. Most likely the VIP.

"It's hard to explain right now but I will tell you this…" She paused so as she could take a step closer and tell me,

"You maybe a Connor but you are also a Draven and that, my dear cousin, makes you… *untouchable,*" she said, whispering this last word before kissing me on my cheek. I sucked in a deep breath and allowed her words to calm me down, feeling them take root down to my bones. That was of course until she said,

"Now I am going to leave you here for a minute…"

"But…" She held up a hand and quickly said,

"Just so as I can explain things to Jared so there are no surprises this time," she said, and it made sense, despite the fact that I wasn't exactly feeling great about being left alone in this club. Not when it looked like a biker convention got their days mixed up with the group celebrating for Vampire appreciation day. Basically, the dress code was leather or anything black. Thankfully though, it was a lot easier to deal with than the creepy carnival freakshow.

"Yeah, that might be a good plan," I agreed after my fearful glance at the people closest to us, because I knew the last thing we needed was a repeat of last time.

"Now wait here and if anyone gives you shit, you know what name to give them," Amelia said,

"So not Miss Human Snacky pants then?" I joked, making Amelia smile that incredible smile of her that lit up her beautiful face and had the power to bring men to their knees. Not that the girl knew it, too busy with her head in a book most of the time or dusting off old bones.

And if it wasn't that, then it was watching anything Sci fi or playing with Lego. In fact, she was probably the easiest person to buy for as all I needed to do half the time was walk through a toy store or look for movie figures on the internet. Basically, Amelia in a nutshell was the most beautiful geek in existence, and knowing that she was a part of this hidden world actually didn't surprise me. No, what had surprised me was how she had survived it but then again, I also knew there was most likely a lot about my cousin I didn't know. Although, after that one and only conversation about her world, shamefully, I had never asked.

I had never wanted to know.

Which now made me feel a bit sad. As if I had let her down. Because surely carrying knowledge of the world she was born into was a heavy weight to hold alone. Of course, I knew she had her family but what about her friends? What about Wendy, a girl I knew she spent a lot of time with in London or that guy that lived opposite her, what was his name, Ben I think? The secrets she had to keep, and the one person she didn't have to keep them with was me, because I knew. And what had I done… turned my back on it all.

I felt, well... honestly now I was here, I felt a bit ashamed. Like I had only thought about myself and not of what I could have offered her. What she may have needed.

A friend that knew.

Someone she could have shared that weight with. And instead, all she had gotten was a selfish cousin who had run away scared. This thought made me feel sorry for the past I had wasted by not being there but before I got chance to tell her any of this, she laughed and told me,

"No, probably not the best name to give but you get an A star for humour, and I would love to see their reaction, so do me a favor, if the insane moment takes over, then just don't do it without me around." She chuckled before she turned to walk away when I stopped her, and pulled her in for a hug, whispering only a small part of my feelings,

"Thank you, Fae Bear... and I... I'm sorry," I told her, making her tense when I said this before pulling back, and with surprise in her stunning blue eyes, she asked,

"Why are you sorry?"

"For so many things," I answered with a shake of my head, looking shamefully down at my feet and seeing boots that didn't belong to me.

"Oh, Ella Belly... we will talk about this but right

now I got a big bad wolf to approach… sorry, sorry… bad joke," she said, holding up her hands in surrender and laughing when I scowled at her. Because she had teased me in that hotel room when I had called him this. But then seeing as I had been dressed like little red riding hood, then what had she expected? Of course, we had laughed about it afterwards but just hearing her joke helped my nerves, and was exactly what I needed in that moment.

After that, she left, leaving me at the bar and with a mammoth sized glass of beer in front of me. I mean, I liked beer, but I couldn't drink a jug of it to myself and that was what those glasses looked like they could hold. I mean the froth alone was the width of my thumb, what did they expect me to do with that, spoon it up with my tongue? If I tipped that thing to my mouth, I would come away looking like Santa Claus.

I scoffed a nervous laugh, as here I was worrying about the beer, when what I should have been worrying about was what could be in this bar with me. And honestly, it was no wonder I had been terrified of my cousin leaving. But I also had to admit, Amelia's words had definitely helped ease my fears. Although when I heard someone approach the bar next to me, that ease started to slip away and I could feel myself tense.

I purposely didn't look, not wanting to draw attention to myself, although when he spoke, I realized there had been no hope of that. After all, I wasn't blind to all the looks I had been getting since stepping foot in here.

"Du gehörst jemandem?" said a deep voice next to me, meaning I had no choice but to acknowledge him.

"I am sorry, I don't speak German," I said, then glanced at him to see he was huge guy with a shaved bald head, and like most other people, was dressed in leathers. But unlike Jared, who admittedly made it look effortlessly cool, this guy just made it look cliché. Like some kind of biker henchman or something.

"That's alright, food doesn't need to speak at all, although I like my playthings to make all sorts of noises," he said in English, making my mouth drop open in shock.

"Are you serious?" I hissed, making him laugh before leaning closer to me, and after his green eyes started to glow white, he said in a husky voice,

"Most definitely." I swallowed down a fearful lump, now praying Amelia would come back and save me. I felt so weak, and I hated it!

"Now I asked you a question, do you belong to

someone?" he asked, which must have been what the German had meant, and I nodded quickly, telling him yes. His eyes glowed brighter at this.

"Good, I could do with a fight, now tell me who the dead bastard is, so I can get on and claim my new plaything... you look fucking tasty." I tried to pull away at that, but he grabbed my arm, holding me in place, and that's when I panicked. This making me say the first name that foolishly came to mind, and unfortunately it wasn't the one that Amelia had told me to use.

"Jared... Jared Cerberus," I said, knowing that was it, I couldn't take back the name that had automatically slipped through my lips. But of course, the guy knew who he was as his eyes widened for a moment in obvious fear. Telling me that if a guy this size and scary could be afraid of Jared, then Christ, just what was I about to get myself into by even being here? His hand quickly let me go, as if even being caught touching me was enough to get him killed. But then his eyes narrowed on me, and he looked around as if thinking more about my claim. This was when he started laughing, and I knew he was about to call my bluff.

I knew this for certain when he suddenly got closer and whispered,

"I smell bullshit, little girl." I swallowed hard and put my shoulders back, knowing I had to play this claim out or I could be in real trouble here.

"It's true," I stated firmly.

"Is that right? Well that might have been true had I not known for a fact that if you belonged to him as you boldly claim, then he would be right here now, as I know he wouldn't be so foolish as to let such a tasty fuckable snack out of his grasp for long." I sucked in a breath and tried to argue such a point, even though it felt like trying to swim though glue. I was drowning, regardless of trying.

"He will be back in a minute and won't be pleased to see you talking to me," I said with a tremor in my voice I stupidly tried to hide, one that made him grin even more.

"I might have run in fear if it was true, but I know for certain that it isn't, and do you want to know how?" he taunted with that grin getting bigger. I shook my head telling him that I didn't, but regardless, he would tell me anyway, as he closed the space between us and whispered,

"Because I know for a fact, just like all of us do… *the King fucking loathes humans.*" At this I yelped as he opened his mouth and fangs started to extend as if he was getting ready to take a bite out of me. But then something totally unexpected happened, as suddenly a large hand came from nowhere and grabbed his head before smacking it down on the bar top. It was done so hard that it cracked the surface, making me cry out in shock.

But then before I could move out the way, another hand came to the small of my back and pushed me forward, now holding me pinned to the bar, making me put my hands down flat on the cool surface. Then a deadly growl rumbled at my back, followed by a demand that crackled the air around me,

"Stay where you are."

"Oh no," I whispered in dread, meaning that this time I knew what true fear was, as I recognized that voice behind me and once again,

The HellBeast King had found me.

Something that was confirmed by the next words that were whispered dangerously against my ear…

"Back again, My little Red?"

THIRTY

PROMISES WERE MADE.

The moment he said this, I seemed to sag against the bar, knowing that if his hand hadn't been there, I might have shamefully sunk to the floor as my legs didn't seem to want to keep working. Because this man, *this King...* had been the very same one that I had been fantasising about all these years. Years of happily fooling myself that I would never see him again, whilst secretly cursing that fact as well. And now, well here he was, currently stood at my back and holding me captive, where he wanted me.

And all I could think was...

How I was to survive a second time?

"Now ask her again," he growled out the question, jarring me from my thoughts, knowing the demand was meant for the sorry state of a man next to me. Someone, who I have no doubt had deadly things planned for me.

But then with his head still pinned to the bar with a pool of blood getting bigger under his head, I couldn't help but wince. I also noticed that most people around us had given us a wide birth, whereas others had literally scrambled out of their seats to get away from what was going on. And here I was still held to the bar by his large hand, one that I swear felt like it was so big, it spanned nearly all of my lower back.

"M…My L…Lord?" The man mumbled, which looked difficult considering his mouth was half pressed and smushed against the bar, spluttering in his own blood.

"Ask. Her. Again," he warned in a demonic voice, one I couldn't help but shudder from, making me flinch under his hand. Something he felt and the moment he did, he started to draw comforting circles on my back with his thumb. This shocked me more than what was happening now with the guy's leaking head.

Why did he do that?

"Ar…are you… do you… belong to anyone?" the

bald guy asked me, pushing the painful words out through gritted teeth, making me swallow a fearful lump knowing now that Jared had heard everything. Oh shit, *I was fucked.*

But once again, this was when he shocked me to my core, starting with seeing part of his face for the first time. Because as he got closer to the guy from where he still stood behind me, he lowered that handsome face before snarling down at him,

"Yes, she fucking does!" Then he straightened back up, and I watched in astonishment as his now bare arm started to transform into a hellish version of itself!

A rippling effect rolled over his skin as if was heating up from the inside, and it seeped through his flesh as if his bones had become a heat source. As if they had ignited like the glowing ambers or hottest part of the fire. Now charring his skin, before what emerged was the hand of a monster. A hand that grew bigger and longer, with thick silver talons that pushed their way through where his blackened nails had once been. They were so big, that they curled around the bald guy's head, reminding me of a giant bird of prey that had just caught its next kill by the skull. Thick fingers with added knuckles, making the glowing red skin crack, but no blood emerged. Just the flicking of flames could be seen before black scales started to push through.

Which meant that if I thought I was shaking before, then now I was gripping onto the bar just to stop myself from trying to run, knowing I wouldn't get far. Jesus Christ...

I was fucking terrified!

This was made even more so when Jared growled down at him,

"The girl is mine!" Then he tightened his fist, making me cry out in shock before he twisted the guy's head in an unnatural way, snapping his neck. After this he simply let go so as the guy dropped to the floor with a sickening thud. Then as if the incident had never happened, he stepped up closer to me, now caging me in completely with his massive body. His hand sliding from my back and snaking its way to my side, keeping his hold on me.

I sucked in a frightened breath as I tried to press myself even closer to the bar, but other than climbing the damn thing like a monkey, then I was trapped. Although the most shocking thing came next as he crowded around me so close, I almost wondered if he had actually forgotten that I was here. Especially as he reached around me and grabbed the massive beer in front of my chest, that was nearly fully smushed to the bar. But then with him being so much taller than me, it wasn't hard for him to do. The guy was even bigger than I remembered!

So, with little choice to do anything but just stand there paralyzed, I watched as he took possession of my drink with his demonic hand, and raised it to his own lips until it was out of sight. This was because he was over a full head height taller than me, as I knew the top of my head barely came up to his collar bone. He started drinking and with being this close, I could hear every strong gulp as he started downing the entire contents.

But then the moment I tried to slip free, was when his other hand gripped my waist tighter, effectively holding me captive and silently commanding me to remain still. He didn't say anything but just continued to drink until it was all gone. Meaning that when he slammed down the now empty glass, his hand was back to being that of a human.

I couldn't help but release a breath of relief at the sight, despite knowing full well the threat was far from over. I knew this when he lowered his head closer to mine before I felt his words vibrating through me, reminding me of a promise made all that time ago... *one neither of us had ever forgotten.*

"Didn't I tell you what would happen should I ever find you in my club again?" he said, and now he was no longer dealing with the guy, it was a far softer threat. At least of that I could be thankful of. But then even the only thing that came to mind to say sounded like an excuse to my own ears,

"This isn't your club," I said, hoping this was true, as why would Amelia do that to me without telling me? No, she knew how scared I was of him, as she had been there that night… she had heard his threat. But then as I heard and felt him scoff a laugh behind me, I knew in that moment that this had all been a huge mistake.

I should never have come here.

"Isn't it, little Red?" he hummed in my ear, using his nickname for me. But then as he inhaled deep, he paused his amused sigh, cutting it dead and stilling at my back as if something had just hit him. I didn't have to wonder long.

"You're hurt… did that fucker touch you?" he growled, making me flinch and question why he seemed so angry by that thought.

"I…I…"

"*You* will answer my question… *now!*" he demanded, making me jump this time, and despite the anger in his voice, his hand started stroking the length of my side as if he couldn't help but try to comfort me. Even against his own harsh words. It made no sense and only ended up adding to my confusion. But then he growled in warning, which was enough to get me talking… and quickly.

"No, he just grabbed my arm, but he didn't hurt me," I braved, barely trusting in my own voice to speak the truth which was why it was barely whispered. It was then that he leaned further into me, and inhaled again, as if trying to pick up the scent which, well… I gathered was exactly what he was doing. I knew this when he picked up my arm, taking it in his and lifting it up so as he could smell it better before pushing back my knitted sleeve. I couldn't help but close my eyes as I felt his skin come into contact with my own, trying to make sense of how it was that he was able to affect me so much. It was literally like feeling a burn I craved. A touch that seemed to have the power to ignite my skin and every nerve ending that lay there. A million people could have done the same thing he was doing now, and even with my eyes closed I would have been able to tell you which one was him.

It was that powerful.

Of course, this made me wonder if this wasn't part of his

power. Did he have the ability to capture people with just his gentle touch? Could he hypnotise them, immobilizing them for a deadly purpose? Fuck! But I had no clue, and now I felt like an idiot having not tried to find out in all those years before this point. Because what help had my cowardly actions given me? What true protection had come from burying my head in the sand all these years?

I felt like I was stood here with a storm at my back, just waiting for it to catch up to me, before it had the power to sweep me away. But hadn't it always been like that with this man…? Had I really thought he wouldn't one day find me again? Had I really been that foolish?

"Lucky for him," Jared said, and I finally reacted and nearly choked when I replied,

"Lucky…? He's…he's dead, how lucky can he be?!" This was when he chuckled… actually fucking chuckled!

"There are worse things to face than death," he told me, and I shook my head a little and stupidly asked the question,

"Like what?"

"Torture at my hands for one, something he would have experienced had he been the one to inflict harm on you," he told me, making me swallow hard and before I could ask him why… why he would want to protect me, a human he hated, he drew in another deep breath. This time I felt his lips on my skin as he shifted over to my other side. Then I felt my injured shoulder come into view, and the next growl of words made me suck in a startled breath.

"Speaking of which… *who do I have to kill for this?"* he asked, and I could hear the deadly calm he was barely keeping in check the second he pulled at my sweater, making it slip off my bandaged shoulder. Again, it was confusing, as I wondered why he would care enough to do something about it. Was there something Amelia hadn't told me?

"That's… that's why I am here," I said, only managing to make my voice sound even after first clearing my throat. He inhaled again before telling me,

"It's fresh… when did this happen, Red?" He finished off this claim with a question. I paused too long after I tried to work out how long ago it had been, totally losing track of time.

"Tell me," he growled impatiently.

"Yesterday…I think," I replied unsurely.

"You think?" he snapped, telling me he was angry at my reply, along with the way he tensed his hand at my side.

"I have been travelling and I...I lost track of time," I admitted, feeling like a fool. But at the very least, my reply appeased him as he released a sigh. And again his reactions were so confusing, as I felt as if my head was spinning! This was down to his other hand that gently brushed back my hair from my injury, so he could run his nose along the seam of where my neck met my shoulder.

"Ah, that explains the Vampire I can smell in my club," he said as if more to himself, as I had no clue what he was talking about! But then again, had I been right...? Had Amelia caught the eye of the infamous Vampire King, Lucius? The one she had told me about? The man she had admittedly been obsessed with and the one who had broken her heart all those years ago?

But then I also had to admit to knowing barely anything of this world, so just how many Vampires she knew could have been in the hundreds for all I knew.

Suddenly my thoughts were slammed back into reality as I felt his hand pealing at the edges of my bandage, making me flinch and try and get away from him, hissing,

"What are you doing!?" His gentle hold on me tightened in an instant, and tugged me back to his chest in a forceful way I couldn't escape.

"Silence, girl!" he growled, making me still at his tone, one I knew not to mess with, despite up until now him not hurting me. No, in fact he seemed more angry that someone else had, and now here I was trying to squirm away from him. Trying to prevent him from discovering the extent of it was what only pissed him off more. But once again, the biggest question of all was a simply… *why?*

Naturally, after this threat I remained still, and after he was assured that I wouldn't try and pull away again, he went back to his task of discovery. He eased his tight hold on me, making me let out my held breath. Then once he had pealed back the bandage, doing so enough so as it was held on by only one side, he sucked in a ragged breath. One that sounded angry and unlike the reasons I did it, which was mainly out of fear and shock at this point.

Then I felt him run his fingertips so very gently over the four stitched lines of cut skin, as if going through the motions and knowing exactly what had done this…

A demon's claws.

It was at this point that he released a rumbling growl so deadly that it had me squirming once again in his hold, nearly begging him to let me go.

"Please…please…" I said twice, making him step into

me so as I was locked in place by his body, one full of solid muscle as his whole body had tensed as he snarled a question down at me.

A deadly question that masked the real question beneath the words he growled…

Who else did he have to kill?

"Give me his name."

THIRTY ONE

BAD ASS RED

My mouth went dry as soon as the question was growled down at me with its deadly intent so obvious. I wondered if his eyes matched his words, because I was yet to see him fully, seeing as he had stayed at my back this whole time. But that seemed to make the whole situation more dangerous because I had no warning as to what would happen next.

Like having the Devil at my back and praying for him to play nice. The expectation was almost laughable.

"I am not accustomed to waiting, little Red," he warned sternly, telling me his patience was at zero, making me wonder if his jaw was set tight with his eyes narrowed. But instead of being brave enough to try and turn around in his arms, I lowered my eyes to the bar top like the coward I was.

"Like I said, it's why I am here," I told him again, and I felt him sigh before what he said next was even more confusing.

"It never should have happened." However, he said this more to himself than to me. I could tell by his tone before he then started to replace the bandage, taking his time to smooth the tape back over my skin and making me shiver at his touch. This was something he didn't miss either, as he scoffed a gruff 'umpf' sound in the back of his throat in an almost mocking way.

Well, what the hell did he expect I would do when his hands touched me that way! God, if only he knew what had been in my dreams, then he would understand. But then the next words out of his mouth were like being injected with liquid nitrogen.

"You can fuck off!" he growled, making me suck in a painful breath before I let my anger take over, doing so by suddenly barging out of his hold. Something I should have done the moment it happened. My sudden movements surprised him enough to be pushed back a step, and it was all I needed.

"With pleasure!" I snapped, letting my anger fuel my actions and burying the fear I knew would be smarter for me to feel. Then without looking at him, I made my way past him when suddenly I was transported right back to that moment all those years ago. That single moment that even then, I knew would change my life forever.

He grabbed my hand, shackling my wrist with his hands as if taking the place of the metal that had once bound them back when he first found me on that stage. Then he tugged, making me spin once more straight into his arms. Arms that circled around me before I could fight to get away. Before I could take a step away from him, before I could do anything to put space between us! But that didn't mean I didn't try, as I started squirming the moment I realized what he had done. Which was when history repeated itself for a second time.

"Easy now, Red," he whispered gently down at me, before turning his head to the side and growling,

"I told you to fuck off!" My eyes snapped to the side to see that he was referring to one of the men I had seen him walking in here with. Someone who just shrugged his shoulders and walked off, muttering about a Vampire getting antsy. But this just made me realise that his fuck off hadn't been for me.

It was with this realisation that I stopped struggling and finally braved looking up, but the second I found those silver depths staring back down at me, I lowered my gaze quickly, fearing the power he held over me. However, this wasn't good enough for him, as he took possession of my chin in his thick fingers before raising my head up to meet his intense gaze once more. That handsome, rugged face that both kept me up at night and had me sleeping in sexual contentment thanks to my fantasies of him. The scar that I wanted to run my fingertip along and ask in a soft, sweet voice for him to tell me how he got it. I wanted to ask him about each part of his painted skin that I could see now was a whole sleeve tattooed. I wanted to run my hand down those buldging muscles and see for myself if there was any softness under all those layers of hard. I wanted to get to the root of him like no one else ever had.

That was the impossible dream.

To have the freedom to brush his full lips with my thumb before kissing them. To feel for myself what that beard of his felt like against my skin, and if those hard grey eyes would soften under a gentle touch? His raw beauty was almost too painful to look at knowing that I had no right to it.

A right I craved to own.

"You're going nowhere, Red, you got that?" he stated firmly, making me swallow hard, and it was a motion he watched intently. It also prompted him to tighten his hold on me as if the sight had affected him.

"Answer me, girl!" he snapped, making me jerk back, even if it was only an inch as that was the most I was allowed to do so with his massive arms around me.

"I...I..."

"*You* are trouble, that is what you are," he said, emphasizing the word 'you', making me frown back up at him before I finally said,

"I didn't ask for any of this."

"And in that, you are not the only one... now come, it is time to find out just how much shit you got yourself into this time," he said, making my mouth drop open in shock, now asking myself exactly what that was supposed to mean!

Then before anything could come out of my lips and trust me when I say, there was a lot of thoughts going there, he let go of me. Let go of me and then gave me his back. Something I loathed as much as I didn't. Because, holy Christ, just seeing him now without his jacket on and just a black T-shirt, it had all those forming words jumbled into nothing important. It rendered me unable to form my thoughts into anything useful as I just stared at all the muscles straining the material. Those huge shoulders that connected to even bigger biceps. One arm covered in tattoos, which, like I said, I shamefully wished I could have been free to explore. Tattoos that would now most likely end up becoming a new focus in my dreams, now that I knew they were there. And yes, it also had to be said that I had a thing for guys with tattoos. But then ever since him, I also had a thing for bad boy bikers, despite never allowing myself to find one.

Not when I knew the trouble they could cause.

And he had called me trouble… Ha, that was laughable compared to him!

"You comin' or what?" he said in a gruff tone over his shoulder, and when I didn't reply quick enough, he rolled his eyes and reached back to grab me, taking me by the wrist again. However, as I started to follow him through the crowd, one that seemed to part for us which I knew was likely out of fear, was when something strange happened. That strong grip started to loosen before those thick strong fingers of his started to slip purposely from my wrist. I was just thankful that the sound of the crowd was loud enough to drown out my gasp of shock when his hand found its way to my own. This, before he entwined those strong fingers with my own.

He was holding my hand. Jared Cerberus was holding my hand! And it had to be noted that he was doing so in what I considered an intimate way. Making me now wonder if he thought the same and if so, had he done it for that purpose? In fact, when it came to Jared, I seemed to question everything thing he did. Every little reaction, every word and every movement had me wondering the true meaning behind it.

Yes… *I had it that bad.*

Of course, as I followed behind him like some little lost girl, I felt numb to all but him. Numb to my surroundings and the people in it that should have scared me. But then in all honesty, with Jared's hand entwined with mine, I had no fear for anything other the man in front of me. The man whose back I was nearly drooling over. Talk about a conflict of emotions! Jesus, but I was scared of nothing when with him, *but him!* A feeling that was both exhilarating as it was terrifying. Because walking with him was like waking up one day and finding out you were invincible. That you were untouchable to the entire world but of course, that wasn't entirely true as even superman had his Kryptonite.

Which made his next actions even harder to accept or understand. Something that started after we approached the raised VIP area. He didn't even need to look at the guards that were stood there like sentinels before they were quickly moving out of his way. Then once we were up the steps was when his demeaner changed. Because when he finally got to where he had intended, he suddenly gripped my hand tighter before using it to yank me forward, and therefore make me go stumbling shamefully into Amelia's arms.

"I found your troublesome human, now it's time you tell me what the fuck she is doing in my club *again!*" he snarled at Amelia, and I was quickly asking myself where this new anger had come from. I huffed out a breath as I pushed my curls out of my face, the ones that always seemed to spring from my hair tie no matter how tight I tried to make it. Although that's what trying a new style gets me, thinking I could get away with shorter parts around my face... never cut curly hair wet. And like always, I was focusing on the mundane in my mind to hide the hurt and shame I now felt.

Damn him!

I stepped back from Amelia, who gave me an apologetic look before scowling at Jared. A man she had told me was more like an uncle to her as he had known her since she was born. I also saw we were now at the back of the club, which was more spaced out than the main area that was only a small staircase away. Although up here had more luxury, with its round carved tables that matched with comfortable looking seats, mainly plush forest green leather armchairs. The large room was also framed by booths that looked like little sitting rooms with sofa's set in old brick archways, with vintage rugs lay on the pale oak flooring. And the biggest seating area of all was of course reserved for the King.

This was a large semicircle of dark green leather, that was in the style of a chesterfield sofa with its leather buttons pinned in a diamond formation. Thick, carved arms of dark cherry wood curled around like rams' horns, that mirrored the style of the feet it sat on. The back was a rounded shape where the same leather curved over the wooden frame.

In the middle, stood a round, dark wood coffee table that was glass over a snarling mass of carved creatures all battling one another. A few drinks lay untouched as if people had only just been served. As for these people, there were some who I gathered were Jared's men, but having never seen them before I didn't know for sure. The only one I did recognise was who I knew to be his brother, Orthrus. As for the one named Marcus, well I was happy to see that he was missing.

As for Amelia, until I had been thrown into her arms, she had been stood with one of the most gorgeous men I had ever seen! In fact, he was like the Yin in hotness to Jared's Yang, being that they were both stunningly handsome in their own completely different ways. Whereas Jared was all rough lines and raw masculine beauty, Amelia's man was all smooth, clean cut and dangerously handsome. Like some sleek jungle cat, ready to pounce in the dark without you even knowing what was coming. A predator you wouldn't have even known was hunting you before it was too late. Jared was more like a lion that would roar at you before tearing you to pieces.

The man was also tall and well built, despite most of these muscles being concealed by a black suit. He also had sandy coloured, blonde hair that was neatly styled back, and a smooth face showing that strong jaw line and those perfect cheekbones. His intense and beautiful eyes were a grey-blue colour that were framed by thick lashes, and they were currently staring at Jared in a way as if trying to silently convey something important.

He also seemed to have another man with him who was a huge black guy that stood a little behind as if at the ready to do battle. A guy it also had to be said most definitely won the gene pool game as he too was drool worthy and oh so handsome. Jesus but what was it with these Supernatural guys, did they all get picked because of how hot they were or was there like a club of not so hot ones that didn't make the cut? Were there any geeky ones that wore skinnier jeans than me and hid greasy hair under baseball caps?

"What she's doing in your club? Really, Jared?! You know why!" Amelia snapped with a fold of her arms, making Jared scoff as he walked towards the centre of the sofa that faced us. A space clearly waiting for him as the empty spot was framed by two beauties dressed provocatively. Each, that snuggled closer to either side of him the second he sat down, and I shamefully felt the pain slash across my heart like a knife. *But of course, he would have the most beautiful women in existence falling over him*, I thought bitterly. In that moment, I honestly wanted to the earth to swallow me up just so as I was no longer being forced to watched them. Watch them as they each held onto a bicep, as if making their claim. The blonde threw her head back and laughed when the brunette spoke, as if they were having a great time at my expense. Both were wearing little black dresses that clung to every curve, some of which you could tell were fake as no amount of scaffolding in a bra could achieve that height on naturally big breasts. Besides, where was the jiggle on those puppies when she laughed like that?

Dark, sultry makeup was paired with glossy red lips, and blusher so deep if they had suddenly got up and ran off, I would have sworn them to be racing stripes. But no, *I wasn't bitter or anything,* I thought… *bitterly.* But then I had never felt so subconscious in all my life, as I couldn't help but look down, pushing my stray curls behind my ear.

Fuck! But I hated this. I hated being here in this stupid fucking club and I hated being this girl! I hated that the moment I had stepped inside this place and seen him, that my entire being had changed! My strong and fierce personality had simply up and left me. Well fuck me but I wanted it back! I wanted to stop acting like some skirmish little teenager I had once been around him and get the fuck on with the part where I found a backbone!

I was a Park Ranger for Christ's sake. I carried a gun and dealt with everything from drugs being sold, to pouching on the land and that was just the human variety, not to mention the dangerous animals. I had taken self-defence and despite the pain it caused my body, I worked my ass off at the job I loved when so many people told me I couldn't do it. Even now everything hurt, but I was so used to the pain it was like a familiarity that would never go away. Because there was no cure for what I had. There was only finding a way to live with it. So, what did that mean? Well, it meant that I had come too far and survived too much shit to let this asshole get to me and dictate my personality!

Dictate the person I truly was.

Oh, hell no, it was time to fight attitude with attitude. It was time to be a…

Bad Ass Red.

THIRTY TWO

THE DEVIL'S BACKBONE

So, with this new bad ass-ness in mind, I raised my head and the moment I did, I found his gaze was riveted on me. A pair of silver eyes that showed a glimmer of surprise when they saw my own harden with a steely determination. This was before I told him,

"Trust me, I wouldn't fucking be here if I didn't need to be! Which by the way, Fae, thanks for helping me but really if this is your solution, then I think I would rather face this *shit alone*." I snapped this last part at Jared, referring to what he had called it. Amelia looked at me with open shock and the hot guy next to her looked highly amused. However, Jared's eyes narrowed in anger before he looked as if he was clenching his jaw, doing so in a way as if wanting to say more but holding himself back.

"Ow... jeez, you want it rough later, baby, you just need to say," one of the girls complained when I saw him squeezing her thigh, and he released his bruising grip on her a second later. I frown even harder, and we seemed to enter into a staring battle. Then, without even looking at her, he snapped,

"I ain't your fucking baby, now go get me a drink, woman!" I tried not to show my shock but if he had spoken to me like that, then I would have slapped him and told him where to go and what he could kiss on the way out. But as for the girl, she just sighed as if she was used to his foul moods and got up to do his bidding, nodding to the other girl and saying,

"Come on, Bunny, let's go before he starts growling." And after this, I didn't know what came over me but I couldn't help but mouth the name 'Bunny' at him with a roll of my eyes and for some reason, he didn't get angry like I thought. No, instead he looked amused. In fact, that bad boy grin tugged at his scar on his face as he raised a brow in challenge.

"Well, considering we are all here now then may I suggest we sit, as I take it we are all welcome at your table, Cerberus," the man next to Amelia said in that smooth authoritative voice of his, and I could totally see my cousin close to swooning because of it. And well, in all honesty, I was nearly with her on that one as whenever he spoke, God in Heaven he was one of the most gorgeous sounding men I had ever heard. Growly assholes not withstanding of course.

No wonder my cousin had fallen for him, in fact, I was sure every female he came into contact with would find themselves the same way!

"Well, you gave me little choice, Lucius, seeing as we find ourselves at my club instead of yours as was planned," Jared replied dryly, making the man smirk and again, it was dangerously stunning. But this was when I finally heard his name and I couldn't help but suck in a startled breath, knowing now that it was him.

"Oh my God, it's you!" I said before I could stop myself. This was when he turned to me and raised a brow in question.

"You're the Vampire King, the one Amelia has been obse…" Suddenly my lips were covered by Fae's hand before she started saying quickly,

"Lalalala, moving on." To which Lucius started smirking, looking highly amused as if she had been busted. Then he grabbed her by the front of the jeans and yanked her closer. He hooked a bent finger under her chin and raised her face, not taking his eyes from her as he told me,

"Thank you for that ammunition, Ella, I am looking forward to using it later." Then he lowered his lips to hers and as she growled playfully at him, he snapped his fangs at her twice before kissing her. A kiss that made me blush just being in the same room as them as it was far from a quick, affectionate peck. It looked about five seconds and two gropes away from becoming X-rated. Naturally, this also meant that I tried to look at my feet again, only giving in to my impulse for a mere second before my eyes found Jared's.

Eyes that were rooted to mine and lips that were smirking.

"Of course, that obsession went both ways, unbeknown to my girl here," Lucius said after he had finished kissing her, now running his thumb over her wet lips in a sweet gesture.

"Now back to this meeting being here and not at

Transfusion, it's a fact I would apologise for but as you very well know, I rarely waste my time with bullshit, so I will save us all the wasted lies. Shit happens, Jared, and we move on… now if you would prefer to take this meeting to my club, then I will happily oblige…" Lucius said with a roll of his hand, letting the question linger and making Jared growl out,

"Sit your asses down." At this Lucius grinned and held out a hand to lead Amelia to a seat first, saying,

"My Queen." This had my mouth dropping open in shock, and Amelia knew it would as she shot me a look of panic before hissing back at him,

"Gods, you just can't help yourself, can you?" At which he grabbed the back of her neck and yanked her hard to him, before snarling down at her,

"No, I fucking can't and won't." Then he kissed her again, and let's just say it was most definitely reserved for behind closed doors! Meanwhile, Jared looked totally unaffected just like the rest of his crew, being two other bikers along with Orthrus. As for me, well it was obvious I was the only one who looked uncomfortable with this, and Jared even leaned to one side so as he could look around the couple to find my awkwardness. Something he looked to be enjoying yet again. Christ, but did he have to openly mock me with just a look?!

Finally, Lucius had had his fill of my cousin, who most definitely had a lot of explaining to do since the last time we spoke. The blush on her cheeks was one he ran the back of his fingers down, before pretending to snap his fangs at her again, making her laugh.

"Fucking delicious," he groaned, making her laugh harder before she grabbed his hand and dragged him down on a sofa with her, telling him,

"Come on, handsome, let's stop making people want to throw up and be polite." At this Lucius scoffed and said,

"I'm a fucking Vampire, sweetheart, not a politician."

"Yeah, thank fuck for that," the gorgeous black guy with Lucius said, before taking his own seat.

"Your job is hard enough, Clay," Amelia said with a smirk, making him wink at her.

"I have told you before, Clay, that unless you have some twisted desire to adopt the look of a pirate, then I would keep from winking at my woman unless you want to lose that fucking eye," Lucius said with deadly calm whilst playing with Amelia's fingertips, looking down at them before popping one in his mouth and sucking on her finger.

"Lucius! Don't say that! Gods, you sound like a caveman again."

"And I will again remind you what I can do with my club, should you misbehave again."

"Okay, well, this has been just delightful," I commented, making Orthrus chuckle before Clay winked at me, making Jared snarl at him. Something I really didn't understand but then again, there was very little I was understanding. Especially the way Jared was still staring at me as if he wanted something… I don't know what but maybe it was to eat me and have done with it! Of course, I unfortunately didn't mean this in the way I would have wanted him to and boy, didn't I just hate myself for even thinking it.

"Sit the fuck down, Red," he said suddenly, but unluckily for me there was only one place spare and that was next to Jared himself, which was why he mockingly patted the space and said,

"I promise not to bite… *this time.*" This got him some of his own chuckles from Orthrus, making me frown.

"Don't be an asshole, Jared," Amelia snapped, and I loved her for it. He held up his arms as if he was a child telling her was doing nothing wrong. But it was Lucius who decided to do something about my uncomfortable situation, as he plucked Amelia right of out of her seat and put her in his lap. Then he nodded to the space she had been forced to vacate. Not that she looked as if she minded this, because could anyone say… smitten much? Jeez, they were like a couple of horny teenagers.

"Problem solved, Pet," he said to me, getting a nod of gratitude in return.

"Thank you," I added as I took the seat, making Amelia wink at me, this time with a knowing smirk when she noticed how Jared didn't look happy.

"Well, I have to say, Luc, you must be losing your touch if a human feels more comfortable sitting next to an infamous killer like yourself," Jared remarked, making Amelia look like she was about to snap something. However, Lucius was quick to react and had her mouth covered quickly before she could get out a word. Then he grinned and simply taunted the HellBeast by saying,

"Jealous, Cerberus?" At this Jared growled before Amelia elbowed Lucius in the stomach, making him drop his hand and make a humph sound as if she had really gone for it, and said,

"Seriously… don't you think we have more important

shit to deal with, like how my cousin was attacked, so yeah… tell me, Jared, *how did that happen exactly?*" She said in a way I didn't miss, as if she was accusing him of something. And once again, it made him scowl, only this time at Amelia. I wanted to ask what was going on here as I felt like I was missing something. Something huge and definitely something that no one wanted to say.

Naturally, this was when I hit my limit and well… I hit it pretty fucking hard!

"Look, I don't know what's going on and nor do I give a shit beyond the HellHounds that are in my woods. HellHounds that I need gone along with an asshole Deputy that seems to be something else."

"Was he the one who did that to you or was it…?" Amelia asked, making me answer before she finished.

"It was him… the Hounds didn't get the chance although it wasn't through lack of trying," I told her, making Jared tense and his fists clenched, something he didn't try and hide.

"They came for you?" Lucius asked and I shook my head, telling him honestly,

"I have no clue, but my guess is I was just in the wrong place at the wrong time when they were there."

"And why the fuck were you there?!" Jared snapped, making me flinch back before I let my anger morph into mockery.

"Err hello, it's my job. There were missing hikers and I..."

"You were fucking foolish is what!" Jared interrupted again with a growl of words, pissing me off even further.

"And what do you think a Park Ranger does exactly, print out missing pictures to stick in windows and on lamp posts and then sits on their ass at a desk all day, waiting for the phone to ring? Missing people don't exactly find themselves!" I snapped back, making him grit his teeth.

"You risked your life for these humans, that's fucking foolish," he barked back in return, and my mouth dropped before I retorted,

"Yes, well that's what us lowly humans do, I guess, we look out for one another... you know, humanity and all that," I said sarcastically, making Jared actually growl at this.

"Umm, I am starting to see now why it was so amusing to others when we first..." Lucius started to say, only this got Amelia slapping her hand over his lips and warning,

"Don't go there, Vampy." At this his eyes started to seep

into a crimson glow as if he was enjoying this playfulness between them and it was turning him on. I knew that when his hands started to snake up her body, making her mouth the words,

'I'm serious' … something he was ignoring.

"Look, I don't know how this works, but I just want the problem dealt with and then I will be on my merry way," I said, deciding to cut straight to it. But little did I know that this would be the cause of the next crazed reaction I received. Everyone in the room suddenly tensed as if waiting for a bomb to go off, and that bomb was rightly named Jared. Someone who physically tensed every muscle in his body before leaning forward until resting a forearm on his knee. Then he told me in a deadly tone,

"Not. Fucking. Happening. Red." Hearing this made me swallow hard before trying to make sense of his reaction.

"What?" I hissed back with my disbelief easy to see. Even Amelia looked panicked for a minute, shooting her eyes between us and our silent game of chicken.

"Okay, so here's the thing, honey, it is not safe for you to go back there," she said after taking a breath.

"So, make it safe," I stated firmly.

"Well, it's a little more complicated than..." my cousin said before she was quickly cut off.

"What do you think it is we do, girly, send in our version of the army?" Jared mocked, making me cross my arms over my chest and say,

"Oh, I get it, human problems aren't high on your list of priorities but hey, say if they were affecting ticket sales into your freak show of a club, then it wouldn't be a problem!" Now this made him growl low and tell me,

"Watch it, Red, you're on thin ice with that one, my girl," he told me, making me jerk back a little before telling him,

"I am not your..." Amelia interrupted me with a sigh, putting her hand to my hand, before saying,

"Please, guys, this isn't helpful."

"No, you're right, it's not, and neither is me being here either!" I snapped getting to my feet, making Amelia say,

"Please, Ella, just sit down."

"Yeah, sit your ass down, Red, no one's impressed." At this I was so angry that I clenched my fists and tensed my arms straight behind me as I leant towards him,

"Why you utter assho..." It was at this point that Amelia actually got up and stood in between us, before trying to pull me off to one side.

"Ella, please, just come here," she urged before I stuck my middle finger up at him around her body, not caring if it was childish. It was just that the guy suddenly brought the inner bitch out in me as he was the most infuriating man I had ever come across! However, I heard his brother chuckle before saying,

"Oh yeah, shit is about to get so much more interesting at Devil's." To which Jared shot him a filthy look before snapping,

"Shut the fuck up, Orth."

"This is pointless, Fae," I told her, making her release a sigh of frustration.

"Look, things are complicated and there is more to these attacks and HellHounds than you know," she told me, making me tear my angry glare from Jared.

"Like what?"

"Like stuff I am not allowed to tell you," she replied, making my eyes widen in shock.

"Are you serious!?" This was when she started to look guilty before looking back over her shoulder at Jared for a second, telling me,

"It's not my call and nor is it my place. And I know

that sucks and sounds like a total classified bullshit some asshole in a suit at the FBI would say…"

"Seriously, you and movies," I mumbled, making her smile.

"But it's the truth, Ella, and I know it's going to be annoying as hell… no pun intended, but all you have to know is that going back right now isn't an option." This time I was the one to sigh.

"Then what am I supposed to do, go back to Evergreen and wait for the all clear?" At this Amelia started to look awkward and say,

"Erm, that's not exactly what I had in mind." I closed my eyes and started to rub my forehead in frustration, which was something I did often and would no doubt do even more around this group.

"Yeah, so what is your plan then huh, change my name to Bubba and buy myself a shrimping boat?" She chuckled and said,

"Ha, good one."

"Amelia Faith!" I warned using her full name.

"Okay, so yeah, not exactly what I had in mind either," she said wincing, and I knew then after glancing back at Jared what she had planned. I knew it the second he grinned in that devious knowing way of his.

"Oh, hell no!" I shouted, making Amelia close her eyes for a second, before telling me in a pained tone,

"You have no choice, Ella." This was when I gritted my teeth, telling her straight up,

"I won't go back there." She gave me a remorseful look that told me I was wrong and then came the horrifying truth…

"He's the only one that can keep you safe, so you have to go back, Ella…" I shook my head, but it was no use as it didn't stop her from finishing that dreaded sentence,

"Back to…"

"The Devil's Ring."

THIRTY THREE

THE STRENGTH OF A VOW

"Oh, no… No, no, no, not happening!" I said, shaking my head whilst walking back toward the seating and telling everyone,

"This was obviously a mistake but thanks all the same. Lucius, I should threaten to cut your balls off should you hurt my cousin again, but well, you know you kind of got me beat on the fang thing, so just know, that it's nothing personal but I will be sharpening my stake anyway."

"Ella!" Amelia shouted but Lucius chuckled and bowed a head to me, telling me,

"A stake would do you little good, but I appreciate the

sentiment of protecting your cousin all the same."

"Oh, I like this chick, J," Orthrus commented, jerking a thumb at me making Jared smirk, commenting cryptically in German,

"Behauptetes Arschloch." (Means 'Claimed asshole.') Fae chuckled at this, telling me she knew exactly what he had said, so I would have to remember to ask her at some point but as for now, well there was only one place I intended to go and that was out the front door.

"Besides, if anyone is gonna take his balls it would be me but as it stands, I kind of like them where they are… *for now,*" my cousin teased, making Lucius grin at her as though she was a giant piece of blood candy!

"Much obliged, my beauty," he replied in his cool arrogant manner that I had to admit, most definitely worked for him.

"Yeah, well anyway, if someone can just show me the door," I said, making his brother stand before Jared snapped,

"Sit down, asswipe." This made Orthrus burst out laughing as if this was the most fun he'd had in years.

"Sorry, Chicken Little, boss man has spoken, looks like you're staying," his brother said with a shrug of his shoulders, making me grit my teeth.

"First off, it's Ella, not Red, not Pet, Doll face, Cookie, especially NOT Chicken anything, and for that matter, not anything with 'Little' in it! And secondly, I am leaving, and you can't stop me." At this Jared slapped his hands to his knees in a casual, 'I am done fucking around' manner and challenged,

"Oh, I think you will find I can, and I will at that, now sit your ass back down… *Little Red*," he said, purposely saying the nickname he had given me with a knowing tone, and one that made me want to scream and slap that arrogant grin off his face! But then again, I wasn't suicidal, so I just fisted my hands instead.

"Gods, this is a disaster," Amelia muttered, holding the bridge of her nose in frustration which reminded me of her father.

"But highly entertaining at the very least," Lucius commented with a grin playing on his handsome lips.

"Lucius!" she snapped, making him chuckle and tell her,

"Alright, Pet, let me handle this." Then his version of handling it was to motion for her to sit back on his lap before he motioned for me to retake my own seat.

Something I declined quickly,

"I think I will stand, thanks." Jared rolled his eyes and scoffed, muttering,

"Suborn human." I wisely chose to ignore this, prompting Lucius to take the lead once more, something I was getting the impression came naturally to him. Although, as a King himself, then this was obviously going to be true.

"What My Queen says is true, this goes far beyond a simple solution as there are those in our world that are making a play, we cannot yet fathom the reasons why, but what we do know is that they include you." Hearing this, I frowned in question but before I could speak, Lucius held up a hand to stop me and continued,

"Now this means that protecting you is a priority, one I take seriously considering who you are to my girl, and seeing as HellHounds come under the jurisdiction of our HellBeast King, it also means he is the best one of us in knowing how to protect you." At this my mouth dropped before it snapped shut just as quick when that curse died on my lips. The cocky bastard even raised a brow as if pushing for my reaction, making me want to remove one of my boots and throw it at his handsome rugged head!

"And what does that mean for me exactly?" I questioned, having a bad feeling that I already knew, yet still, I needed confirmation. I needed someone to say the words. The words I dreaded the most. In the end they came from the man himself,

"You will come back to the Devil's Ring with me and my men," Jared stated, making me shout,

"No way! I am not going back to that Hell Hole!" I snapped, and this time he released a frustrated sigh before he got to his feet, shaking his head at the floor whilst he did, before warning,

"You need to watch your mouth, little girl." I ignored the growl in his tone and snapped,

"Little girl?! I am nearly thirty, you pig-headed biker!"

"Then how about you try fucking acting like it!" Jared argued back, and I swear the infuriating man actually made me growl.

"Oh, that's cute, Red," he said, making me react without thinking, something I had a feeling I was going to do a lot around him. Which is why I picked up an empty bottle and literally threw it at him! Although, he turned to the side quickly enough to dodge it, making it smash behind him. That was when the whole room seemed to go silent along with everyone at our table. As for Jared, he calmly raised a hand to his face and wiped off some of the spray that had hit his cheek without looking at me, doing that whole shaking his head at the floor thing.

Meanwhile, I had covered my mouth with my hands in shock, despite the actions being my own. At this Orthrus chuckled again and said,

"Oh yeah, shit is about to get interesting." Jared snarled his way, making him laugh harder. Then he raised his head, so his dangerous glare looked as though it came from a predator about to strike.

"You are going to regret that, Red," he warned in a deep growl of words before he took a step towards me, when suddenly everyone was standing, with Lucius, Amelia and even more surprising his own brother, between us. But Jared's gaze was glued to mine until he noticed this strange factor. He swung his narrowed gaze at Orthrus.

"Really?" he asked, making his brother shrug his massive shoulders and say,

"She's cute." Which made his brother really snarl at him this time, but Orthrus continued to look amused.

"Cute or not, she needs to learn some fucking respect and realise who the fuck she is dealing with!" Jared stated in a firm tone, making me suck in a breath before anger gripped me once more.

"An asshole and a bully is what I'm dealing with!" I shouted around Amelia, who whipped around to face me and say,

"That's not helping, Ella." And of course, she was right.

"Yeah, well I am the asshole who is gonna save your ass, little girl, and all you gotta do to stay alive, is do as I fucking say!" he shouted back. This was when I grabbed Amelia by the arm and said,

"Please, there must be someone else."

"Ella, you have to understand…" she started to say, making me shake my head.

"No, you do, Fae, because if I go with him, I am gonna strangle him!" I said interrupting her.

"Yeah, you could fucking try," he laughed, folding his arms and damn him, but his muscles bulged in a way they just begged to be touched… were they really as solid as they looked?

"Now that I would pay to see!" his brother said, making Jared snap,

"Go get the fucking car, it's time to stop wasting my

time," Jared said, making Amelia panic.

"No, you promised! You gave me your vow, Jared!" This made me frown and Lucius placed a calming hand on her shoulder, giving her a little shake of his head. Then, with that soft look in his gaze, it told me that he cared even without words. Cared so deeply it was ingrained in his very soul. It made my heart ache to watch, wondering if I would ever be lucky enough to have a man look at me that way. However, the moment my gaze was unconsciously pulled back to Jared, one look at him scowling at me and it was enough to crack that fantasy that it would ever be him.

As for Lucius, that handsome gaze soon turned deadly as they shifted back to Jared and said,

"You owe her, do not forget that HellBeast, or has your memory faded only three months after we left the battlefield." I frowned in question, wondering what that meant and what battle they spoke of. Did things actually still happen like that for these guys…? Were there still wars fought in Hell like he suggested there was. And who did he owe?

Was it Amelia?

Jared stepped closer to Lucius and warned him,

"You go too far, Vampire, when you think to question

my vow. I will take the girl and protect her as I said I fucking would, but if she doesn't come willingly, then I will simply *fucking take her*… that is what I mean when I say I am done wasting time… now… *Back. The. Fuck. Up!*" Jared warned with that growl coating his words again and making his eyes glow with power. Then, just like that, I was once again near shaking I was that afraid of him. But Lucius simply smirked as he stepped aside, held an arm out to me, and then to my astonishment said,

"Then have at it, Cerberus." At this he nodded his head once before Jared grabbed his jacket off the back of the chair and put it on. Then the next steps he took were made with more purpose, and his intent soon became clear. That's when my fear of him hit new heights, making me back up and this time doing so quickly.

"No… no… wait you can't… you… Ahhh!" I ended up shouting this last part the second he shoved his large shoulder to my belly and my world was flipped upside down… literally!

"Ella!" my cousin shouted, making me reply with her own name coming from my panicked lips.

"Amelia!" But then I pushed myself up enough to see that Lucius had hold of her and was talking in her ear, trying to sooth her fears and keep her back. She looked close to tears and was forced to tear her eyes from the sight of me being carried out of there. This was when Lucius cupped her cheek and moved her face to look up at him.

He said something I couldn't hear, but the moment she agreed with a nod of her head I knew I was screwed. Even more so when Amelia shouted at Jared,

"You'd better take care of her!" However, I couldn't say I had much faith of that when his reply came as a rumbled,

"Oh, I will take care of her alright."

THIRTY FOUR

A BRUTE KING

I didn't know what that promised vow meant exactly, but at this point, with how I had acted, I wouldn't have been surprised if he didn't just snap my neck the first chance he got. Then to dump my body in some woodland area I was sure Germany had close by, telling my cousin the bad guys got me. He was definitely acting as though I was too much trouble for my own good and right now, with his strong hold keeping me locked over his shoulder, I had to agree with him.

What had I been thinking?!

Damn it, but the man just seemed to make me crazy!

But despite this fact, I still didn't know what I had been thinking standing up to him like that. Oh well, that wasn't entirely true as I had foolishly felt safe thanks to having my cousin there and her... well, whatever he was to her... Boyfriend, although King seemed more appropriate, seeing as he kept calling her his Queen. Either way, having those two on my side had made me brave... actually scrap that, it had made me stupid!

Because never did I expect to find myself in this position. Never did I think Amelia would have allowed Jared to simply pluck me from the floor and carry me out of there like some bloody caveman!

"Put me down!" I demanded, because I couldn't just let him think he could do this, even though, yeah, he pretty much could and evidently would.

"Easy, Red, you don't wanna piss me off with this tasty ass of yours so close to my teeth," he warned, making me suck in a deep breath before hissing,

"You wouldn't!" At this he turned his head into my ass, and I felt him open his mouth at the ready to take a bite, making me still and tense my whole body in fear. Then he actually nipped at me, making me yelp at this little bite of pain, one that shamefully went straight to the place I

wanted it to avoid. Damn him and his ability to affect my girly parts!

"You were saying?" he said like the arrogant asshole he clearly was!

"Umm, well wouldn't you know, she can be tamed after all," he mused to himself as he continued to take me out of the club like some piece of meat he'd bought at the market!

"Asshole," I muttered in response, making him chuckle this time and I hated the sexy sound. Of course, being slung over his shoulder like this didn't exactly offer me much idea of what was happening. Meaning, I had no choice but to try and find a way to push myself up, doing so by grabbing his belt. But then by doing this, I ended up brushing his skin with my fingers, and that same bolt of electricity shot through me at the contact. Naturally, it wasn't real or painful but more like a current of sensation telling me exactly who I was touching. Because it felt like nothing else in the world and despite how much I loathed the way he was treating me, a part of me that I didn't want to acknowledge or delve too deeply into… well, it felt… *right.*

It was crazy of course and like I said, nothing I wanted

to dig into too deeply right at that moment, especially when I was being man-handled by a brute King who didn't understand the word *NO*.

Finally, we seemed to make it outside and I could hear a car running, no doubt one that would have his brother behind the wheel. But then, as if feeling the need to say something more, I told him,

"You can't do this, put me down, you brute!" Then suddenly I was tugged forward and dragged down his body. This with his hands spanning my waist and making me gasp at his touch as it made the waistband of my sweater rise, so he too was now touching my skin. And I knew… I knew… that by the time he pulled me down his body, it was done with purpose. Even if his heated gaze didn't tell me this, the next words out of his mouth most certainly did, as he stepped into me, pushing my back to the side of the car. So, with me wedged between him and the metal at my back, I had no choice but admit defeat with my silence… and the bastard knew it.

"Ah, so this is what it takes," he murmured softly, with amusement lacing his tone. Then I felt a crooked finger curl under my chin as he raised my head to his, to find him looking down at me with that silver glint darkening

roguishly. As if the thoughts running through his mind spoke of all the wicked things he wanted to do to me, yet the question was, would he dare to take it that far? His gentle fingers stretched out and turned into that of a palm shackling half of my neck, placing his thumb on my chin.

I had to say, when he lowered his head to my neck after using his hold to turn my face to the side, I questioned everything… *mostly my damn sanity!* Would he bite me… would he kiss me or simply tease me with the possibility of both? And Christ alive, why did the thought of both have me near squirming in his hold?

But this, combined with his large body towering over me, and it wasn't exactly surprising I was finding it hard to breathe. No, it was more astonishing that I wasn't full on panting in my fear and sexual need merging as one. Fear of the sexual need I felt towards him. It was a shame I couldn't hide myself from it. A truth I couldn't ignore, no matter how much I wished to. I wanted this man like my next breath, and then in the next I would be using it to curse his very existence. A crazy mixed up side of me that I had quickly come to loathe as I knew it would burn me whole and leave me hollow.

It would leave me empty.

That was what made him so dangerous to me. I had to remember that. The power this man held over me was like a drug... *it wasn't real.* The feelings, the escapism, the euphoria... it was all a lie. A lie that felt good for a split second of wasted time. An unclean happiness that turned into a bitter self-pity and hatred for being so weak.

And that was exactly what I was being right in that moment. Weak. And the worst thing about it was that he knew it too.

"This is what it takes to tame the wildness in you... *my touch,*" he said, whispering these last two words against my skin, making me sigh in shock. I wanted to shout, to deny it and curse him back to Hell for doing this to me! For being the cause of my shame. For pointing out my feebleness and using it against me like a weapon!

"Screw..." I would have finished but suddenly his thumb was held tight across my lips as his own found themselves whispering next to my ear, grazing feather light against my lobe.

"Tut tut, My Wild One, don't go spoiling it now... *Not now I know your dirty little secret.*" At this I ripped my face away from his hand, making him chuckle before he told me,

"Fear not, Red, your secret is safe with me…" he said softly, and then kissed my cheek like a gentle lover's touch before a switch was flipped, and his tone turned hard when ordering me,

"…Now get in the fucking car like the good girl I know you can be." Then he stepped away from me, tightening his hold on my side and pulling me away from the door he had me held against. Then, with his other hand, he opened it and cornered me, crowding me backwards until I had no choice but to sit down. Especially when he pushed a hand to my belly, using his other hand to cover my head like cops did when putting prisoners in the back seat of a cop car. Was that what I was now…?

His prisoner?

"You… you can't do this…" I said in a bewildered tone that didn't sound half as accusing as it could have been. Then, with his hand to the roof of the car and his other gripping the top of the door, he leaned his whole body into me, and said in a smug tone,

"I think you will find… *this is me doing it, Red.*" Then he stepped back and slammed the door.

"Ah!" I shouted in frustration, and in response he smacked his hand on the roof twice as if telling the driver, he could go. Then he smirked at me when he saw the sound he had made had in turn made me jump. That's when I gave him the middle finger and I watched the beautiful way he threw his head back and laughed, before shaking his head as if this was the most fun he'd had in years.

Damn him and his hotness!

But then, as I turned around to look through the back window, it was when I noticed something quite important that gave me chills for a very different reason than his touch. The big black guy who was his brother came staggering out of the back of the club where Jared must have carried me from. A gathering of parked bikes also stood with some of their riders at the ready, which must have been more of Jared's men.

But my eyes continued to focus on Orthrus as he held a hand to his head, that was now pouring with blood as if he had been attacked. But Jared didn't look concerned about this, as his focus was on something else. Something he deemed more important than the sight of his brother bleeding. I knew that when I watched as he grabbed his brother by the jacket and yanked him closer, before pointing a hand at the car I was in. I could just barely see then as Orthrus shook his head before Jared turned and watched as

I drove away in a car that was obviously taking me from him... *and not by someone he thought was driving.*

Which meant only one thing.

I was being kidnapped.

This was when I sucked in a frightened breath as my eyes shot to the front driver seat to see the private barrier was up. So, I reached a shaky hand out to the button I knew would bring it down. Then I pressed it, holding my breath this time as it lowered, only to let it out again on a scream the moment I saw who was driving.

The face now looking back at me with an evil demonic grin belonged to none other than...

Deputy Dickerson.

STEPHANIE HUDSON

THIRTY FIVE

BIKERS, BREAKS AND BEASTS

"*Oh fuck!*" I whispered, making him wink at me before he slammed his foot on the gas and made us rocket forward, pushing me back in my seat with a yell.

Then we went speeding past a Hard Rock Cafe and turned hard right, making me fall sideways in my seat, barely missing cracking my head on the window of the passenger door. I pushed myself back up to see as we continued down a one-way street, he didn't slow down at the junction, but instead pulled out quickly and straight onto oncoming traffic. A blare of horns sounded just before a car crashed into a taxi that had been parked along the street. I turned around trying to take in the destruction he was causing but he was driving so fast, the moment I moved one way, the erratic motions of the car moved me the other.

"Jesus!" I shouted at the sight of people trying desperately to get out of our way, and I was just thankful we hadn't hurt anyone yet, or worse. We continued speeding down the street and he manoeuvred the car around the tight corner, doing so far too fast and making the wheels spin and the car drift before hitting the back end against the building. I cried out in surprise, again fearful for all the pedestrians that were in danger of his unpredictable driving.

However, he straightened the car out and drove down another street, through an arch overhead that thankfully wasn't busy. Yet, the moment he saw bikers coming from the other end, he hit the brakes, slamming to a stop before quickly reversing back to the arch that connected two buildings together. After this he slammed the car into gear and took an immediate right down a side street that brought us out to the main road… one that was unfortunately *very busy!*

Which meant I soon found myself screaming again as

he had to do a handbrake turn to move quick enough to miss the oncoming traffic, giving the other drivers time for them swerve to miss us. The sound of crunching metal and slamming and squealing of brakes made me turn in my seat to find them crashing into other vehicles, that thankfully weren't going as fast as we were. I could even see the airbags that were deployed, and I just hoped that no one was hurt.

"You're going to kill someone!" I shouted at the deputy, making him laugh in that sinister way. But it was a grin that soon fell from his lips the second we could both hear the roar of exhausts, as a convoy of bikes emerged from the same street we had just come from. That was when I noticed him gritting his teeth in the mirror as he looked behind to see what I could… *we had not lost them.*

"Fucking HellBeasts!" he snarled angrily before putting his foot down so that we would go even faster. However, the moment that he took his eyes off the road ahead was when he didn't notice one of the parked cars along the side of the main road was now pulling out, believing the road was clear enough to do so. Of course, we looked quite a distance away when he had started the manoeuvre, obviously not realising the speed that we were travelling.

"Look out!" I screamed, and just in time as Dickerson saw the car and swerved, making me slide in the seat again which meant he had no choice but to change directions completely. He spun the wheel quickly, making the car spin around, so we were now travelling in the opposite direction. This meant that the bikes that had been tailing us, flew past us before they too could start to change direction. He took another sharp right down a side street and under a glass walkway that bridged the gap between two buildings for people to travel between. This took us to a cobbled street and driving past a large yellow stone building that had fancy columns at the front. There was also a large open space in front of it that told me it was some kind of important building situated on the right-hand side. The signs were all in German, so I had no clue, only that it looked like an important landmark of Munich. I barely had time to question whether it was a museum or some other state building before the next thing happened.

It was at this point that the bikes had caught up to us and they quickly used this open space to try and overtake the car. This was when I got my first glimpse of the bikers being led by Jared, who was riding at the front, leading the way. None of them wore helmets and each were riding a customised cruiser, and at just a glance I could see Harleys, Triumphs and Indians to name a few. Flashes of matt black and chrome, blurred at speed, as they skilfully drove through the street, trying to surround us.

Yet, despite the bikes being more manoeuvrable, they were no match for a swerving car and barely had time to move before they were side swiped. One violent serve and I was forced to slap my hand to the window just as I saw Jared's tense gaze focus on me. But then, with a nod of his head, I knew he was trying to communicate with me that it was going to be okay, he was going to get me out of this. And with that determined, furious look in his eyes, well in that moment I trusted him to do just that.

As for Deputy Dick, he continued speeding down the road and past another stately building, this time situated on the left of us, and one that was a pale green colour. It also had steps leading up to the open space before its entrance, so I knew Jared and his crew wouldn't be able to use the space as they had before. Which meant I was left wondering if and when this car chase would end and if so, just how badly. Because I had a bad feeling that the man behind the wheel would have more chance at surviving a crash than I would, especially seeing as I knew now he wasn't exactly human and as for me, I was unfortunately of the very breakable variety.

But at the end of this road, it veered off to the right, which meant another hard corner he took too fast, throwing me around the back. At one point I thought it would tip us up on two wheels, however it simply made the back end slide out once more, and me along with it.

"AHHHH!" I shouted in pain as I slammed my shoulder to the side of the door after he took the corner too fast. He then started weaving in and out of cars, and I screamed when he barely missed one of them coming straight at us from the other side. My hand slapped the window, trying in vain to hold myself steady as I was jerked around in the back seat. Then my eyes widened with fear when I knew what was coming, as I could see up ahead, the end of the road that led into a busy main intersection. Because if he wasn't going to stop for oncoming traffic, then there was no way he was going to stop at a red light, one that faced us now.

"No, no, no, no... NO!" I shouted in vain as he ran straight through the lights, barely missing a bus and making me scream as we drifted to a sharp left and onto a dual carriageway. As much as I hated him, there was no denying that being in this car, it had to be said that the guy could drive. Now, all I had to hope for was that I would survive the ending.

I heard the crash of cars behind us, something that was becoming a regular sound. I turned around, gripping onto the back of the seat to hold myself steady and watch as a line of black bikes following one after the other came into view, now swerving in between the wreckage. Thank God, they continued to make chase! We continued at speed down the dual carriageway, making it easier to overtake thanks to the two lanes of traffic going in the same direction. And again, in the moments it looked like the bikes were gaining up to us, he pulled another stunt in hopes of shaking them. At the right moment, he spun the wheel, letting the car drift around in a 360 so he was quickly facing the other way. This was so he could then take a sharp left down a single lane he had seen when we drove past. This ended up clipping one of the bikes that had been following at the back of the convoy, making me cry out for its rider.

"Watch it!" Of course, he took no notice of me as he kept his eyes on the road ahead, or on the mirror to see where the bikes were. We zoomed past tall residential buildings framed either side of the narrow road we travelled, but again, it wasn't long until we heard the bikes behind us. He growled in frustration as it was clear that no matter what he did, he wasn't shaking them. But nothing would slow him down, not even the cars parked down both sides… or the second someone opened their door.

"Whoa, watch that… *door!*" I started off screaming this and muttered the last part after we smashed into it, taking it clean off the car. It went flying in the air before landing behind us on the road. I turned in my seat to see the bikers just miss it, having to swerve, and I had to say I was impressed with how quick their reactions were.

He then turned left, barely missing another car and passing a modern looking office building that was all glass and steel. After another hard right, I felt like a single bean in a tin can as I actually fell off my seat and scrambled to get back onto it. Of course, I had already tried to open the doors at some point but after I'd heard the locking sound at the start of this, I knew even if it had been unlocked, I would have died the second I tried to roll from the vehicle.

This was made even more likely with the amount of stuff I would have crashed into as we travelled the busy city streets. Lines of tall buildings were a mixture of new and old, and all flew past in a blur of motion, and yet still the roaring of bikes could be heard echoing behind us. But then a truck started backing out in the road and made me scream as he only had a single car's width to get through, making sparks fly along one window as he sideswiped all the parked cars.

"FUCK!" I screamed, wincing in on myself as if this would help in keeping me safe. Yeah right. Only a gun to the head pointed at the driver's head would help me right about now. I knew this when, at the next junction ahead, he flew out without stopping, making me scream yet again. This time with a plea of words, words that would go ignored.

"Let me out!"

A jerk to the left and then we soon found ourselves travelling down the side of a park of sorts, which was a single lane alongside a tramline with cars parked along the other side. As soon as the bikes emerged, I could see Jared still leading the way when he raised a hand and motioned for the riders to split into three groups. The riders on the left started to ride along with the centre of the tram line to our left, while the right mounted the pavement, so they were free to overtake. I knew then that they were trying to box us in and put an end to this high-speed chase.

"Fuck!" The cop said as we shot forward and with the park to one side and no side streets to give them the slip this time, he knew he was fucked. This was when Jared overtook us, making me watch him through the window. He nodded once before speeding past us. I had no idea what he was planning to do but whatever it was, he was doing so alone. I knew this because his men had all fallen back but still continued close enough that they would be at the ready if the Deputy tried to backtrack. Something that would have made it impossible, seeing we were heading down a one-way street.

"What the fuck?!" Dickerson said in reference to the sight of Jared parking his bike further up the road and now dismounting it before shrugging off his jacket. Then I found myself questioning if his sanity was intact as he stepped out into the middle of the road and just stood there waiting for us.

"Fucking crazy bastard!" Dickerson muttered, before slamming his foot on the gas so we shot forward at greater speed, and I didn't know if it could be classed as playing chicken when it was only one car and one man.

"What are you doing?" I muttered when Jared made

a motion with his hand as if willing the car to continue forward, and the grin he gave us was *pure evil*. My panic started to rise the closer we got, before suddenly I was screaming for an entirely different reason, and this time the fear I felt wasn't for me… *it was for Jared.*

"No, no… please stop, please don't do this!" I begged from the back seat, and in response Dickerson changed gear and said,

"This fucker is gonna die!"

This time I screamed his name,

"Jared, No!" This was a cry he heard as I could tell when something new flickered over his features. As if my reaction had meant something to him. But then it was soon lost to a Hellish rage that I could see building up inside of him. I knew this the moment his arms started to give way to his other form. This meant that the small glimpse I had been given back in his club had been nothing but a mere slither of the raw power he held. This became obvious when that Hellish side of him started to transform both arms, and this time his intent to do damage was as deadly as it had been the first time.

"NOOOO!" I screamed even louder, so loud that it hurt my own ears as my expression of horror pierced the air, making it seem as if time itself had slowed down.

However, the moment we were inches from hitting him, Jared jumped at just the right second, and landed on the hood of the car with a resounding thud hard enough that it cracked the windscreen. He crouched low like a wild animal, snarling at the driver with his eyes glowing like molten steel. His fangs grew down past his lips as his face started to change into that of the beast he was, making me press myself further into the seat in fear.

Stone. Cold. Fear.

In fact, I had never been so afraid, especially when he started tearing into the engine with his bare hands! The metal of the hood tore as if it had been made from foil, curling back on itself before he delved right in and started taking chunks of the engine away. The car groaned in protest before Dickerson had no choice but to slam on the brakes.

Brakes that no longer worked.

This meant he quickly lost control of the car, spinning the wheel too sharply and at too great a speed. Jared leapt from the hood just in time before the car started to tip. Then time really did slow down as the whole thing started to rise up before time caught up with itself and the horror of my situation made me scream. A sound that became lost to the sound of metal being crushed after the car flew through the air and landed the first time, before rolling on its side…

Over and over again.

In fact, it continued to flip, landing on all four sides, making me cry out from inside, where I was being thrown around.

But that was when I heard it.

"ELLA!" The sound of someone else in panic. The sound of someone else's name being shouted in terror! A single name that was cried out by someone who was now worried I wouldn't survive. And it was the sound of my name being roared out that I focused on.

And the last thought I had before my world spiralled out of control and ended in darkness was…

Jared knew my name.

THIRTY SIX

THE SCENT OF BLOOD

I don't know how long I had passed out for, knowing that I had cracked the side of my head pretty good and hard enough that my ear was ringing. Which was why it was taking me a while to hear sounds that weren't muffled. But I could see, and that was something, as I blinked back the fog of what just happened. The driver's seat was slightly twisted but this wasn't the biggest thing as it no longer had a body occupying it.

I don't know how far we had rolled but I did know that it had landed on its roof, one that was now filled with broken glass. My head faced the passenger window with my body on its side, as if the moment I had started being tossed around I had automatically held myself in a protective ball. God, but my bones fucking hurt, and I knew instantly that I had broken my arm. Unfortunately, something that wouldn't have taken much with my condition. And well, I didn't even want to think of the bruises, as the saying bruised like a peach was a reference I could take quite literally. It barely took anything at all, so a car crash was going to mess up my weakened body like a bitch!

Thankfully, nothing else seemed broken, just my left forearm and a spit lip making me taste blood.

"Fuck," I muttered, hearing it muffled due to the thundering in my ear. But then, what was that… crunching glass? Yes, it was most definitely footsteps getting closer and I found myself praying for it to be Jared. However, when a man's pair of shoes came into view, and they weren't the biker boots he had been wearing, I knew my troubles weren't over yet. He started to crouch lower and the second the cop came into view, I tried to scramble back, crying out in pain that it caused.

The cop gritted his teeth and reached inside to grab me, and was inches from me when suddenly a thundering flash of darkness took him completely from me. In fact, it took my mind a few seconds to understand what it had been, as a bike had run into him, skidding side on to take him completely off his feet. I knew this when I looked to the broken windscreen and saw when he landed about fifteen feet ahead of the car. Orthrus had been the one to take him out, as he pushed his bent leg up making his bike straight again, not once coming off it during the manuevour.

This time when I heard boots approach, with a far heavier footstep and a deeper crunch of glass, I knew it was Jared. He lowered to a knee so he could look at me, his features tight and barely holding back the rage I could see in his eyes. But at the least they softened slightly when he looked at me. Then I watched as his mouth moved and a deep rumble could be heard, although I was yet to hear it properly.

"LL…A…SWER EE!" I closed my eyes and shook my head before saying what I thought was the right words,

"My ears… it's… muddy," I told him, making him frown before he said again, this time slowly,

"You hurt?" Finally, after he repeated it a few times, with each one more frustrated than the last, there was no doubt what he asked as I could finally hear him more clearly.

"I am... alright," I said, closing my eyes and holding back the pain I felt with a silent wince. *I was used to the pain,* I told myself. Of course, he would find out soon enough that I wasn't in one piece, but right now he looked as if he had bigger problems on his hands. Especially when Dickerson started to transform, and doing it so quickly that all I saw was a shred of material like a second skin being shed in seconds.

Then came the Hellish howling that was unlike any wolf I had ever heard. But then again... *he wasn't a wolf.*

"Fucking HellHounds!" Jared snarled, looking his way before telling me in a stern tone,

"Don't move. I will be back for you." Then he stood and soon I found even more booted steps followed. I thought this was an excessive amount of force for just one being, but then I realized when I heard even more howls, *that Dickerson wasn't alone*. That was also when I realised what the howling had been for... he had been calling out for backup. Meaning that they were close enough that he had been trying to lead them into an ambush. That's why he wanted to head towards the wooded area of the park that was on our left.

I also knew that if Jared and his men failed, I would just

be a sitting duck in here. So, despite Jared's stern order, I knew that I had to move, making me thankful that it wasn't my leg this time. So, I gritted my teeth and cradled my arm tight to my chest in order to try not to jar it too much as I tried to climb out. I decided my best chance was to use the back rear window that had blown out completely. The frame had been crushed, but it was still the biggest space for me to get through. So, with another grit of my teeth, I started to shimmy out after first rolling from my side to my back. Then I used my legs to push myself headfirst out of the space, using my back muscles and crying out when I snagged my skin on something. No doubt a jagged bit of metal, it cut into one side and pulled on the other where my injury was. I knew then that it must have opened some of the stitches, as I felt the warmth of blood soak my skin.

Fuck, I was a mess!

"Too bad, Ella, you have to keep going," I told myself aloud, clenching my teeth harder to fight back the pain and using my adrenaline to keep me going. But that was when I heard it… the growls. Growls along with another sound,

Ding. Ding. Ding.

That was what I heard. Short, little dainty sounds that started to get heavier and quicker, until soon I realised it was rain. A downpour as the heavens opened, making the heavy rain echo on the metal of the broken car.

Rain and angry snarls. A response to the growls that were getting closer. It had been the same growls I had heard in Lasca Creek. They were back, and this time I wasn't sticking around waiting for someone to save me. Because I didn't know Jared and his men. I didn't know how strong they were against such creatures, as it was clear now there must have been a great difference between the two species. HellHounds and HellBeasts weren't the same, just like Orthrus had told me.

This was confirmed when I finally made it from the car and rolled to my front so I could push myself up with my good arm. Then, whilst catching my breath bent on my knees, I looked up to see the dark cloud above consume the sunlight, making it dark and grey in seconds. Then as water poured down around me, soaking me to my skin, I saw the HellHounds emerge from the tree line.

Unlike Jared's men, they were in the form of Hellish hounds, all furless skin that glistened wet, making it look as if they had been dipped in crude oil. Snarling and snapping jaws that look thirsty for blood and fresh meat. They prowled forward as if at the ready to pounce. They were huge, with their massive razor tipped claws digging into the wet earth as their large paws sank from the weight of their movements.

"Orthrus, go get that fucker, I want him taken alive… he's mine to punish," Jared ordered, making his brother roll his shoulders and grin before he started to stalk the deputy who had transformed into the biggest HellHound of them all. But he also looked injured as he was trying to drag himself back to his feet so he could run.

"As for these other fuckers, have at it, boys!" Jared said, making his six men start shedding their clothes as if getting ready to shift. But as for me, I didn't want to stick around for the fight or what would happen should either side lose, because I couldn't forget that Jared had been the one to put me in this car himself. Not that I blamed him for it being ambushed, but I couldn't deny that he was intent on taking me back to his fight club regardless. A place I very much didn't want to go. In fact, the only place I knew I would feel safe now, was a club of a very different kind…

Afterlife.

I needed to get to my aunt and uncle, knowing that they could protect me. I no longer cared if they discovered that I knew of their world. At least I could trust them to keep me safe in their home, one that was admittedly more like a bloody fortress. Yes, that's what I needed to do. And unfortunately, I knew I couldn't trust Amelia to get me there. Not when it was obvious her Vampire King had other ideas.

But then I knew that if I was really going to do this, I had to act quickly whilst Jared and his men were busy with the hounds. So, taking a brave and steady breath, I pushed to my feet and with only one way to go, I ran towards the wooded area. Because I knew I would have a better chance at losing them in there as it was thick with trees. I also knew it was a city park area so the chances at getting lost were slim to none.

After that, I would get myself to a hospital somehow and call my aunt, who thankfully, I still had the number for written down and folded in the pocket of my jeans.

Yes... *she would know what to do.*

But first things first... get the hell outta Jared's Dodge!

However, the mistake I made was looking back one last time, and what did I see but the eyes of a furious man.

A furious HellBeast King who had been disobeyed.

Cerberus had seen me.

THIRTY SEVEN

FLAMES OF HELL'S WRATH

The moment our eyes met, I saw that same molten silver glow, and this time his anger was directed at me, making me shiver in fear. I must have looked like a wet deer caught in the headlights as I felt a loose curl slick against my cheek and stay there. As for him, he looked like a dark avenging demon with his hair almost looking black, being wet, and his hands curled into claws, one of which he gestured at me. It was one of those silent demands that was done to urge me to stay. Then he shook his head slowly, and mouthed a single worded, warning at me,

"Don't."

Of course, it was one I didn't listen to as I had come this far, I knew I had to try. I had to try and get away. Away from this new nightmare! So, after lowering my head in shame for a second more, I did something I didn't think even he expected, as a shocked expression was my only reply when I mouth a single word back,

"Sorry."

Then I turned and ran, having already crossed the tram lines and stepped over the metal rail. The moment I started to run in between the trees, I was thankful for the canopy overhead and break from the pelting rain. And as I forced myself on, I clenched my teeth through the pain my motions caused my arm, and I ran as fast as my unbroken legs would take me, hoping my bones didn't fail me this time. I felt my wet hair slap against the exposed skin at my back, thanks to my sweater that was doing little to keep me safe from the elements.

However, being that it was a city park, unsurprisingly I soon came across a pathway, but forced myself to ignore the temptation of it and continued on through the trees, using them to hide me. But then the moment I heard the sounds of twigs cracking under weight behind me, I knew I might have made a mistake. Because what if not all the

HellHounds were fighting like I thought? What if one had spotted me like Jared had and decided to break away from the fight and make chase.

"Fuck!" I muttered after spinning on my foot and facing the other way, scanning the trees for movement. A movement I soon caught at the side of me.

"No!" I uttered on a frightened breath the second I saw it.

My biggest fear had come true.

One had found me!

I knew it the moment I saw those glowing yellow eyes pierce through the shadows, with that dark, sleek wet figure snaking through the trees. It moved with its spiked heckles raised, as it stalked towards me slowly, getting ready for me to run.

I realised then what I had to do, which was look around for anything I could. Because I couldn't ever hope to outrun one of these things, I knew that. No, the best I could do was hit it with something and hope to stun it enough to give me the chance to get away. So, with my right hand, I slowly lowered down and reached for the large branch I had spotted about a metre long. This was when I made my stand, knowing deep down this could be it. This could be the end, and all because I had chosen to make it on my own over trusting Jared.

Now, the question was, would it end up being a deadly mistake and one I wouldn't live through long enough to regret? I was about to find out as it continued to stalk me until it was close enough, then it pounced at me. Which was when I raised the branch up from down by my leg, hoping to take it off guard when swinging it with all my might across his head the second it leapt at me. The end of the branch burst into splinters around his jaw and neck, working enough that it knocked it off course, making it skid to its side.

"No!" I uttered in horror the moment it just got back to its feet, giving me no time to run like I had hoped. It just shook its body from the jarring hit before whipping its head around and snarling at me, snapping its now glowing jaws. And in that single moment, something came over me and my heart made its choice, as the scream was out of my mouth before I could stop myself,

"JARED!!!"

A split second after that, the creature leapt at me once more, and this time it knocked me onto my back, meaning I had no choice but to hold what was left of the branch up as a shield between my face and its biting jaw! Pieces of wood rained down on my face along with a spray of saliva between its thick, yellow teeth and long, deadly fangs. Two more bites and the wood would be gone, and the only thing left for it to bite into would be my face.

But then I heard the bellowing rage of what I knew must be a HellBeast. One that echoed all around us, making the HellHound still a moment before suddenly, it was gone! Then, just like that, in its place was Jared's bulking figure looming over me. I sucked in a startled breath, and gazed up at him in complete shock, as it looked as if he had sprinted all the way here full pelt through the trees to get to me. As for me, I finally gasped for my stolen breath now the weight of the HellHound was off my body, yet found it stolen just as quickly when taking in the magnificent sight of Jared.

His furious breath expelled from his rising chest in anger morphing the air around him into an icy chill. He looked like some kind of mythological God just dropped from the sky, and was now stood over me ready to cast judgement and enforce vengeance. Water dripped down his tensed muscles from the T-shirt that clung to each hard ridge of muscle like a second skin. Each groove and line of his pecs and rippling abs made my mouth dry, despite all I needed to do was lick the drips from my lips for moisture. His hair had fallen in front of his face, like mine, clinging in parts to his face, making the stark pale tone of his scarred skin a contrast. But it was those eyes that had me held prisoner. Those silver-grey eyes that burned into me, taking in every inch and broken piece of me, now analyzing what they discovered. I knew that the moment his jaw hardened, and his eyes narrowed the second he saw my arm held cradled to my chest.

"You lied," he said, making me suck in a quick breath. I didn't have time to reply, as the threat wasn't over. Not that I would have known what to say, but the sound of growling stole the moment should I have found something to fill the void. Because right now he had something else to deal with other than me and my stupid defiance that could have got me killed.

I knew this when he narrowed those stunning eyes of his, making me near flinch at the power of them.

"Time to give you something to really run from," he growled down at me, angry and hurt, before turning his predatory gaze from me to the hound that was now circling us, getting ready to strike. I couldn't understand

the conflicting thoughts running through my mind. I couldn't understand why I would suddenly feel guilt. A guilt that made me shake my head as if this would help rid me of the emotion. I wanted to hate him but right in that moment, I hated my reaction to him even more. I hated that I would feel guilt and torment, after seeing his obvious disappointment. As that was what I had seen in those eyes. The accusing frown, silently asking me why I would run from his protection, why would I lie about if I had injured myself.

Which meant that this time when I got to my feet, I didn't do so with the intention of running like he suggested. But then, that was the thing with intentions, sometimes they became broken promises even before they had chance to be heard. And now was one of those times, and I turned to discover the true nature of the monsters of this hidden world.

One Jared was a King of.

My shaky hand slapped over my mouth to lock in the scream. This was because Jared was now half changed into a beast on two legs, not fully shifted like I knew he was capable of. Amelia had once told me that he wasn't like the rest of his kind. That he had a strength that couldn't be matched or bested. That he possessed powers no other HellBeast did, and it was rumored to be due to his connection to the gates of Hell itself. A direct link to the beasts he ruled down there, at the ready to obey their King, despite his lack of being there.

That was what she had told me.

That apparently, he had a whole army down there just waiting for their King to return. And well, in all honesty, at the time it had sounded more like some child's fable told to scare kids into doing as they were told. If you don't listen to your parents, then the bogeyman will get you whilst you sleep. She even told me that the Pied Piper had once been real. But then that night Amelia had told a lot of stories and up until this moment, in all honesty, I had only ever believed half of them. Thinking this was a way for her to scare me into keeping silent or trying to warn me away from ever being tempted to enter his world again.

But now...

I believed.

I believed it all.

I believed every last fucking word of it! And why, because Jared was every bit of the HellBeast King that Amelia had made him to be... *That and more.* He was the embodiment of what nightmares were made of and he was the reason other demons feared him. I understood that now. I understood why, in that club, others had been utterly terrified of him, despite what powers they too held.

Jared Cerberus was the Devil's warden and Keeper of the Gates just as Amelia had said he was. I knew that now. I knew it in the way he now had the monstrous hound in his hold and was using his deadly clawed hand to open up his underbelly, slicing four lines down the centre so its innards spilled out, making it howl and cry out in pain. He was cutting it open alive, making the very earth beneath him crack and spill with flames sizzling at his ankles, as if feeding from the essence of Hell. They climbed their way higher and higher, yet they never damaged Jared's skin or even the clothes he wore. It was as if some magical forcefield I couldn't see surrounded him.

But as for the hound, those flames licked at its hind legs, sparking and torching the furless skin, making it bubble and blister. As for myself, I couldn't help but start to walk backwards, the look of pure terror no doubt plastered all over my features as the cold, hard fear was consuming me whole. This man, this beast, had been so gentle with me I could barely believe it! Those hands… those hands of Hell had touched me, been so careful with me.

Hands I was now petrified of.

His demonic gaze shot to mine and there was no silver left, as only pure Hell's fire consumed them. They were like gazing into the fiery pits of Hell and finding yourself lucky you survived the look. Eyes that were just as dangerous as the fire beneath where he stood, if not more so. Glowing eyes of lava, which also filled his veins now, transforming him into a terrifying monster of a man.

"No... God, no!" I couldn't help but mutter, and the second he heard it and saw the real depth of my fear, he suddenly blinked. After this I saw his lips start moving, as if whispering some demonic command, and I watched as the flames extinguished, leaving the ground charred and dead beneath him. I also saw the way the lava in his veins reduced down to heated skin, leaving only demonic clawed hands left. and even as frightening as this HellBeast side of him was, it was nowhere near as bad as it had been when he looked like a demon trying to tear open a gateway to Hell.

Then, as if realising the HellHound in his grasp was still alive, he unhooked his claws still lodged in its belly and used both hands to snap its neck instantly, dropping the dead carcass. After that we both seemed frozen, staring at each other with me too afraid to move and him… well, I didn't know why. Maybe he had seen my fear and simply didn't want to add to it.

I honestly didn't know.

But one thing I did know was that I needed to get out of here. I needed to run as fast and as far away from here as I could get. I couldn't trust him. I couldn't trust a King of Hell. How could I… how could I have been so reckless!? Fuck me, but the things I had said to him! The way I had pushed him, I had been so foolish! He could have killed me a hundred times over… I knew that now… I knew what he was.

He was a killer.

Which was why I backed away and surprisingly he let me, with an emotion clouding his features I couldn't read. One that confused me as it looked similar to… *regret?* But surely not. A creature like him didn't feel like that… did they?

Fuck!

But I knew nothing, and why would I? I had been too busy burying my fucking head in the sand all these years, pretending that Amelia's world never existed!

The moment I heard movement was when I freaked and started to run, despite knowing how easily he could catch me. I just needed to get away from him... from them all! I needed I needed... Jesus, I needed to fucking run!

"No, let her go. They are all dead and we have their pack leader. Besides, she won't get far... *they never do.*" I heard Jared say, making me flinch and hoping that didn't mean what I feared the most. That he would hunt me down like he had done with those HellHounds.

But then, why did his last statement linger on my mind and wouldn't leave me.

Making me now question...

Just how many girls like me had there been?

THIRTY EIGHT

FEAR IS BUT A KISS AWAY

This time when I ran, I knew I had no fear that there was anything left of the HellHounds. No, I only had one fear...

Him.

Would he come after me or let me go? Surely if all the HellHounds had been killed there would be no reason for him to keep his vow? That was if there even had been one to begin with. In all honesty, I had no idea what was going on, only this lingering feeling as though I was being lied to. Or worse, I was being kept in the dark like the outsider I was. Because I still didn't know what reason the HellHounds would have in following me here or why Deputy Dickerson had? What had he hoped to gain?

No, there was still far too many holes in my own story to feel safe yet. So, the plan remained the same. I was going to contact my aunty Kaz and explain everything in hopes they would offer me protection and with it, an even greater hope for an explanation. I simply wanted my life back. My nice normal, simple life where my only problems were trying to schedule my life around the medical restrictions set against me. Speaking of which, every time my tired limbs gave out, I would fall, crying out in pain as I did.

Fuck, but I hated feeling weak!

Which was why the tears that ran down my cheeks now were more out of frustration. The evidence that I couldn't cope with all that was happening. Of course, I would have been a fool and a liar to say that not a single one that fell wasn't also out of fear and a painful feeling of loss. Because he had shattered years of an illusion I had painted of him to be. A mirror that reflected the handsome, rough face that shattered the moment I got my first glimpse of the real him.

But I also knew he wasn't to blame in that, as I was the one who pathed the way for his rising pedestal. I was the one who welcomed him to stand up there for all these years, meaning I had cut myself off from emotionally allowing myself to get attached to a man. In fact, Orson had been the first I had allowed in between the cracks of my armour.

Tears now fell for the right reason as it hit me once again that I had lost a friend, and in truth, that too had been my fault. I had gone into those woods when he had warned me away and what had happened, my stubborn sense of duty had been what had got him killed!

"Fuck!" I swore the moment I stumbled again, hammering a fist into the wet ground in frustration, welcoming the new pain, taking my mind off my arm, at least for now.

"Not now, Ella… don't think of him now," I said to myself before getting back to my feet with renewed determination. Which meant I continued on, knowing I hadn't exactly made much ground and wondering where they all were now. *One man in particular.*

Were Jared and his men now making their way back to their bikes, leaving me to fend for myself as I deserved. As I wanted. Or was Jared out there somewhere, stalking me from behind, watching and waiting for the right move to strike? God, but it was like torture not knowing, but his words still played over and over in my mind.

'Time to give you something to really run from.'

Those word would be forever burned to my memory, that was for sure!

"At last," I uttered on a sigh the moment I saw a building situated between a break in the trees and what looked like a small parking lot around one side. In fact, it looked like some sort of country club, making me wonder if I had stumbled on some cricket grounds. Either way, I was frustrated to see that it looked all closed up but at the very least, I could use the overhang of the roof to get out of the rain for a minute while I thought of what my next move would be.

So, I walked around the building, putting my back to the wooded area and now facing out to a cricket ground like I had suspected. It was framed by trees on my side and opposite, with open fields to the right and left which I didn't dare try and cross. I would be too easy to spot out in the open like that. No, I needed to go back on myself to the front of the club house and try and see if I could find a road that led to the main road, so I could try and get help. Maybe someone would see my broken arm and take pity on me by calling an ambulance. Then from the hospital I could call my aunty Kaz.

I looked down at my broken arm and saw that it had already started swelling pretty bad. I just hoped it didn't need a plate like my leg had done, an operation was the very last thing I needed right now! I leant my head back against the wall, closed my eyes and took a deep breath before taking the next step in getting out of here. I knew I needed to keep moving but, God, I was so tired. I knew I had pushed myself beyond the limit my body was willing to go and all I wanted now was to rest. Was to slide down this wall and just close my eyes for longer than the few seconds my mind would allow.

But if I did that, then I knew I wouldn't get up again. So, despite knowing my adrenaline had all but run dry, I opened my eyes and walked around the corner. Then, despite knowing it was risky, I stepped out into the open again, only to have my fears confirmed when suddenly a hand shot out and clamped over my mouth from behind. Then I was pulled roughly back into a hard and unyielding body. One quick breath through my nostrils told me instantly it was him.

He had found me.

"I never lost you," he said in a thick growly tone as if reading my thoughts.

"Now, are you going to scream or play nice?" he asked, making me nod my head telling him he could let go. Something he did but only so he could slide that hand from my lips to my neck where he left it, feeling me swallow hard, pushing against his palm.

"Why do you tremble so?" he asked on a husky whisper which was when I realised, he was right, I was trembling. But this was when something started to happen. Like a long forgotten memory was now seeping its way in, making me ask myself if this had happened before?

"Is it because you fear me?" he asked next, making me inhale a quick and shuddered breath.

"Answer me, little girl, and tell me… *has my little red Kitten lost her claws?*" he asked, now purring the question in my ear, and this time I shamefully shuddered for a different reason.

"I am cold, now let go of me!" I snapped, wondering how insane I truly was, doing so even after all I had seen.

"Ah, there she is. Now if you are cold, why would I let you go when I could quite easily be the one to warm you up?" he asked in a mocking tone, and I bit my lip to hold back the next insult I wanted to throw at him. I huffed out a breath of frustration.

"You're trying so hard, aren't you?" he said on a chuckle, as if he knew I was. This now making me question silently if he could in fact read some of my thoughts.

"Go ahead, girl, because no matter what you say, I will not hurt you." I huffed at this.

"You don't believe me?" he asked, and when I didn't reply he shifted me, making me cry out in pain as he caught my arm.

"You were saying!" I snapped, feeling bad the second I did because I knew it was a bitchy thing to do, as it was clearly an accident.

"Fuck!" he hissed, the second he looked down at my arm, seeing now how bad it was.

"In the crash?" he questioned, making me sigh before nodding.

"You're in a lot of pain?" he assumed again, making me give him a 'well duh' look, one he smirked at.

"Not enough to lose the attitude, so I will take that as a good sign," he remarked, making me roll my eyes, and he added,

"It's also time to drop the bravado act, Red. Now why

did you run?" he asked, stepping back and giving me space before folding his arms over his chest. Something that made me swallow even harder, and this time I nearly bloody choked on it! Jesus Christ, what did this guy do in his spare time, strong man competitions?! His arms were huge, making me wonder if the material around them wouldn't just split if he sneezed.

"Why do you think?" I snapped.

"At a guess, because I scared the shit out of you," he commented with an honesty that surprised me, given how blunt it was. But because I was also ashamed to admit it, I lowered my face and looked down at the ground, making him release a sigh.

"I don't…" he paused, making me frown in question as he suddenly sounded so uncertain. Admittedly, I hadn't known him for long but even I knew that for a man like him, it was out of character.

"You don't what?" I asked quietly, almost desperate to know.

"I don't usually lose it like that," he confessed, shocking me enough that my eyes went wide.

"Fuck, don't look at me like that, Red," he said with a groan, and I frowned, shaking my head a little, telling him that I didn't understand. However, he never explained but instead nodded down at my arm and stated,

"It's broken."

"I know," I replied, giving too much away in my tone. Telling him I knew what broken bones felt like. Telling him this wasn't my first time, nor did I think it was likely to be the last. His look said all the things he received from that answer but I was thankful that for now at least, he didn't ask or comment. No, instead he shocked me even more, taking a step closer to me, minding my arm. Then he said softly,

"I am sorry that I frightened you." My eyes shot to his, and I was so close I could see those soft lines at the corners telling me he actually did have laughter in his life. I would have liked to have seen how that looked, despite being scared shitless of him, like he already knew I was.

"You can't run again," he stated, making me narrow my gaze and tell him,

"You can't possibly think that I am going to come back with you after seeing that, do you?" I said in an incredulous tone.

"You are coming back with me one way or another, Red, of that you can be certain. Now how that happens, is up to you," he affirmed sternly.

"Yeah, and how's that then?" I pushed, still asking my crazy mind why!

"You can play nice, be the good girl I know is hidden deep down there, beneath the layer of what that bullshit fear is making you say... the same one I handled that night or..."

"Or what!" I snapped, hating he was referring to how I used to be on that first night. This was when he grinned, and it was the same wicked evil one I had seen when he had been stood in the middle of the road daring the threat to try beat him. Then he leaned in closer to me and whispered,

"Or I can give you another reason to fear me, something I really don't want to be forced to do... *you get me, Red?*" I sucked in a deep breath and said,

"You... you said you wouldn't hurt me," now being the one to remind him of the past.

"And I never would, but fear and pain are two very different things, Kitten," he told me with a slight cock of his head.

"So, fear or compliance, those are my two options?" I asked in a tone that was easy to decipher, being that it was basically pissed off.

"Those are the only two options that will prevent you from getting killed, so yeah, those are your choices," he replied, making me try and step away from him, daring him to try. Which is precisely what he did as he snarled at me, creating such a frightening sound I flinched, yelping back into place.

"Don't fucking push me!" he warned, making me release a jerky breath before admitting,

"You… you do scare me. You always have." At this he gave me an intense look and then took my face in his large hands, making my heart seem to stop.

"Like I said, fear and pain aren't the same, and I will show you the proof of that."

"Shh… show me?" I asked in a shaky voice, caused by a different emotion than fear, but all to do with him now having his hands on me.

"Yes, I will show you." Then he took the last step needed to put him so close, there was no more questioning his intentions. And if there had been, then his last words said to me would eradicate the last of my fears as to what his intentions truly were.

"Would a HellBeast who meant you harm kiss you like it could be his last?" I opened my mouth as a small sound of surprise escaped and, in the end, this was all he needed as his lips descended over mine, whispering over them,

"About fucking time."

And then a HellBeast King kissed me.

THE HELLBEAST KING

ACKNOWLEDGEMENTS

Well first and foremost my love goes out to all the people who deserve the most thanks which is you the FANS!

Without you wonderful people in my life, I would most likely still be serving burgers and writing in my spare time like some dirty little secret, with no chance to share my stories with the world.

You enable me to continue living out my dreams every day and for that I will be eternally grateful to each and every one of you!

Your support is never ending. Your trust in me and the story is never failing. But more than that, your love for me and all who you consider your 'Afterlife family' is to be commended, treasured and admired. Thank you just doesn't seem enough, so one day I hope to meet you all and buy you all a drink! ;)

To my family…

To my crazy mother, who had believed in me since the beginning and doesn't think that something great should be hidden from the world. I would like to thank you for all the hard work you put into my books and the endless hours spent caring about my words and making sure it is the best it can be for everyone to enjoy. You, along with the Hudson Indie Ink team make Afterlife shine.

To my crazy father who is and always has been my hero in life. Your strength astonishes me, even to this day! The love and care you hold for your family is a gift you give to the Hudson name.

To my lovely sister,

If Peter Pan had a female version, it would be you and Wendy combined. You have always been my big, little sister and another person in my life that has always believed me capable of doing great things. You were the one who gave Afterlife its first identity and I am honored to say that you continue to do so even today. We always dreamed of being able to work together and I am thrilled that we made it happened when you agreed to work as a designer at Hudson Indie Ink.

And last but not least, to the man that I consider my soul mate. The man who taught me about real love and makes me not only want to be a better person but makes me feel I am too. The amount of support you have given me since we met has been incredible and the greatest feeling was finding out you wanted to spend the rest of your life with me when you asked me to marry you.

All my love to my dear husband and my own personal Draven... Mr Blake Hudson.

To My Team...

I am so fortunate enough to rightly state the claim that I have the best team in the world!

It is a rare thing indeed to say that not a single person that works for Hudson Indie Ink doesn't feel like family, but there you have it. We Are a Family.

Sarah your editing is a stroke of genius and you, like others in my team, work incredibly hard to make the Afterlife world what it was always meant to be. But your personality is an utter joy to experience and getting to be a part of your crazy feels like a gift.

Sloane, it is an honor to call you friend and have you not only working for Hudson Indie Ink but also to have such a talented Author represented by us. Your formatting is flawless and makes my books look more polished than ever before.

Xen, your artwork is always a masterpiece that blows me away and again, I am lucky to have you not only a valued member of my team but also as another talented

Author represented by Hudson Indie Ink.

Lisa, my social media butterfly and count down Queen! I was so happy when you accepted to work with us, as I knew you would fit in perfectly with our family! Please know you are a dear friend to me and are a such an asset to the team. Plus, your backward dancing is the stuff of legends!

Libby, as our newest member of the team but someone I consider one of my oldest and dearest friends, you came in like a whirlwind of ideas and totally blew me away with your level of energy! You fit in instantly and I honestly don't know what Hudson Indie Ink would do without you. What you have achieved in such a short time is utterly incredible and want you to know you are such an asset to the team!

And last but by certainly not least is the wonderful Claire, my right-hand woman! I honestly have nightmares about waking one day and finding you not working for Hudson Indie Ink. You are the backbone of the company and without you and all your dedicated, hard work, there would honestly be no Hudson Indie Ink!

You have stuck by me for years, starting as a fan and quickly becoming one of my best friends. You have supported me for years and without fail have had my back through thick and thin, the ups and the downs. I could quite honestly write a book on how much you do and how lost I would be without you in my life!

I love you honey x

Thanks to all of my team for the hard work and devotion to the saga and myself. And always going that extra mile, pushing Afterlife into the spotlight you think it deserves. Basically helping me achieve my secret goal of world domination one day…evil laugh time… Mwahaha! Joking of course ;)

Another personal thank you goes to my dear friend Caroline Fairbairn and her wonderful family that have embraced my brand of crazy into their lives and given it a hug when most needed.

For their friendship I will forever be eternally grateful.

As before, a big shout has to go to all my wonderful fans who make it their mission to spread the Afterlife word and always go the extra mile. Those that have remained my fans all these years and supported me, my Afterlife family, you also meant the world to me.

All my eternal love and gratitude,

Stephanie x

ABOUT THE AUTHOR

Stephanie Hudson has dreamed of being a writer ever since her obsession with reading books at an early age. What first became a quest to overcome the boundaries set against her in the form of dyslexia has turned into a life's dream. She first started writing in the form of poetry and soon found a taste for horror and romance. Afterlife is her first book in the series of twelve, with the story of Keira and Draven becoming ever more complicated in a world that sets them miles apart.

When not writing, Stephanie enjoys spending time with her loving family and friends, chatting for hours with her biggest fan, her sister Cathy who is utterly obsessed with one gorgeous Dominic Draven. And of course, spending as much time with her supportive partner and personal muse, Blake who is there for her no matter what.

Author's words.

My love and devotion is to all my wonderful fans that keep me going into the wee hours of the night but foremost to my wonderful daughter Ava...who yes, is named after a cool, kick-ass, Demonic bird and my sons, Jack, who is a little hero and Baby Halen, who yes, keeps me up at night but it's okay because he is named after a Guitar legend!

Keep updated with all new release news & more on my website www.afterlifesaga.com

Never miss out, sign up to the mailing list at the website.

Also, please feel free to join myself and other Dravenites on my Facebook group Afterlife Saga Official Fan

Interact with me and other fans. Can't wait to see you there!

ALSO BY STEPHANIE HUDSON

Afterlife Saga

Afterlife

The Two Kings

The Triple Goddess

The Quarter Moon

The Pentagram Child /Part 1

The Pentagram Child /Part 2

The Cult of the Hexad

Sacrifice of the Septimus /Part 1

Sacrifice of the Septimus /Part 2

Blood of the Infinity War

Happy Ever Afterlife /Part 1

Happy Ever Afterlife / Part 2

The Forbidden Chapters

*

Transfusion Saga

Transfusion

Venom of God

STEPHANIE HUDSON

Blood of Kings
Rise of Ashes
Map of Sorrows
Tree of Souls
Kingdoms of Hell
Eyes of Crimson
Roots of Rage
Heart of Darkness
Wraith of Fire
Queen of Sins

*

King of Kings
Dravens Afterlife
Dravens Electus

*

Kings of Afterlife
Vincent's Immortal Curse
The Hellbeast King

*

The Shadow Imp Series
Imp and the Beast
Beast and the Imp

*

The HellBeast King Series
The HellBeast King

*

Afterlife Academy: (Young Adult Series)
The Glass Dagger
The Hells Ring

*

Stephanie Hudson and Blake Hudson
The Devil in Me

OTHER AUTHORS AT HUDSON INDIE INK

Paranormal Romance/Urban Fantasy

Sloane Murphy

Xen Randell

C. L. Monaghan

Sorcha Dawn

Sci-fi/Fantasy

Devin Hanson

Crime/Action

Blake Hudson

Mike Gomes

Contemporary Romance

Gemma Weir

Elodie Colt

Ann B. Harrison

Lightning Source UK Ltd.
Milton Keynes UK
UKHW010648071221
395242UK00002B/392